Damien watched her through eyes of molten silver, the heat in his gaze singeing her as surely as any flame.

With her quaking limbs supported by the welcome solidity of the wall, Darcie tried to get her ragged breathing under control. What was wrong with her? She wanted to flee, while at the same time she wanted to grab his waistcoast, twist the fabric in her hands, and drag him full against her. She wanted—

"What is it you want, Darcie?" he asked.

"I want . . ." Her gaze flicked to his lips once more. Full sensual lips formed in a firm masculine line. Her mind registered only a vague notion of what it was that she wanted; yet her body seemed to know exactly what it yearned for.

Suddenly the answer came to her with the clarity of a revelation. The emptiness inside of her, the terrible, ever present loneliness seemed to dwindle in his presence. She longed to feel him reach out and pull her into himself, to have him heal the isolation, the desolation of her soul.

"Touch me." She whispered the thought aloud, only to wish she could call the words back. He was her employer. A man with infinite power over her life. Moreover, he had his own secrets, his own demons, tightly leashed.

Too late she realized what her whispered request had released. She had but a millisecond to assimilate the sudden flare of desire that hardened his features. His lips sought hers, melding their mouths in a heated conflagration. Shifting slightly, he brought his knee between her thighs. Darcie whimpered against his mouth, clutching at the loose fabric of his shirt, pulling him closer. . .

BOOK YOUR PLACE ON OUR WEBSITE AND MAKE THE READING CONNECTION!

We've created a customized website just for our very special readers, where you can get the inside scoop on everything that's going on with Zebra, Pinnacle and Kensington books.

When you come online, you'll have the exciting opportunity to:

- View covers of upcoming books
- Read sample chapters
- Learn about our future publishing schedule (listed by publication month *and author*)
- Find out when your favorite authors will be visiting a city near you
- Search for and order backlist books from our online catalog
- Check out author bios and background information
- Send e-mail to your favorite authors
- Meet the Kensington staff online
- Join us in weekly chats with authors, readers and other guests
- Get writing guidelines
- AND MUCH MORE!

**Visit our website at
http://www.kensingtonbooks.com**

DARK DESIRES

EVE SILVER

ZEBRA BOOKS
KENSINGTON PUBLISHING CORP.
www.kensingtonbooks.com

ZEBRA BOOKS are published by

Kensington Publishing Corp.
850 Third Avenue
New York, NY 10022

All Kensington titles, imprints, and distributed lines are available at special quantity discounts for bulk purchases for sales
promotion, premiums, fund-raising, educational, or institu-
tional use.

Special book excerpts or customized printings can also be
created to fit specific needs. For details, write or phone the
office of the Kensington Special Sales Manager: Attn. Special
Sales Department. Kensington Publishing Corp., 850 Third
Avenue, New York, NY 10022. Phone: 1-800-221-2647.

Zebra and the Z logo Reg. U.S. Pat. & TM Off.

ISBN 0-8217-7966-4

First Printing: November 2005
10 9 8 7 6 5 4 3 2 1

Printed in the United States of America

Acknowledgments

For Henning Doose, my forever love, who supported my dream even when it meant that he had to conquer the twin mountains of dirty laundry and unwashed dishes all alone.

And for Sheridan and Dylan Doose, my extraordinary sons, who believed in me with unswerving tenacity, granting me writing time by valiantly forcing themselves to play video games for just . . . a little . . . longer.

And for Nancy Frost and Brenda Hammond, my remarkable critique partners, whose hard work on my behalf is a most precious gift.

CHAPTER ONE

A thick gray wall of fog hovered over the damp stones of Hanbury Street, carrying the stink of old blood and rotting entrails. Darcie Finch shivered as chilled wisps curled like talons about her slim frame, and she hastened her steps, her feet sliding precariously on the wet cobblestones. Clutching her battered leather folio against her side, she tried in vain to close her senses to the stench.

The frightened lowing of cattle drifted on the rank air, carried from the nearby abattoir. Come morning, the stones on the next block would glisten wetly; not from mist and rain as they did tonight, but from a river of blood flowing over them. Despite her attempts to block the sound, the piteous noise intruded. Darcie dragged in a shaky breath, fighting the panic that threatened to claw free of her breast. Did she feel the same dull fear as those poor beasts being herded to their doom, the same sense of the inevitable horror to be meted out by unfeeling hands? She could not help but compare their fate to hers, to the sorry lot she had chosen. But therein lay the distinction. The animals had been condemned without benefit of trial, born to the inevitable fate that awaited them—the slaughterhouse one block over. Those poor dumb beasts had no choice.

Her breath left her in a hiss. As if she did.

Darcie gave herself a mental shake. There were always choices, and she had made hers. Better to accept responsibility than to brandish her fist at the fates, crying and wailing against the burdens that were hers to bear.

She moved her feet mechanically, her worn boots scraping along the cobbled road as she rubbed her fingertips across the raised, puckered scar that marred the skin of her left hand. *Destiny*. Steppy had talked of destiny as though it were an old friend, or perhaps a mortal enemy with an ancient grudge. He always said that destiny brought all men to the same fate, a shroud and a bed in the cold hard ground. She clutched her flat leather case tighter against her chest as another thought struck her. A person might be dug up from a fresh grave and find their final end on an anatomist's table. Whitechapel was a favorite haunt of the ressurectionists—unscrupulous men who plundered fresh graves and were whispered to hasten the dying on their way.

Shrugging off the morbid thought, Darcie willed her exhausted body onward. Tragic and pitiable was the life that lay ahead, but no worse than so many young girls had faced before her. She sighed softly. Once she had believed in dreams and fairy tales, had relied on a gossamer web woven of privilege and fantasy. Now, she believed only in the harsh reality of life, relied only on her own ingenuity.

Suddenly, Darcie froze, every fiber in her body alert. Icy tendrils twisted around her heart. Her gaze darted this way and that, searching the darkest corners of the narrow thoroughfare. The certainty that she was no longer alone slithered across her mind. She could feel something—no, *someone*— and sense an evil intent. Peering into the shadows that loomed dark and frightful along the deserted street, she tried to place the cause of her unease.

Nothing materialized from the mist, and she shook her head at her own foolishness, at the fear that was a remnant of a time when she had lived a better life, a time when she would never have even considered roaming the back alleys of the worst part of the city. Those days were dusty memories. For so long now she had lived on these streets, existing from moment to moment, from meal to meal.

Again Darcie rubbed the length of the raised scar that crossed her hand, a memento of a poor choice, a reminder of Steppy. For a moment she thought of him as he had been, before storms and foolish decisions had taken his merchant's fortune to the black bottom of a pitiless ocean. Her stepfather had once been a man of means and a man of morals.

Just a few more steps and she'd be at Spitalfields market. She knew the way, knew the safest route, and the most dangerous one as well. The scar began to throb and ache. It seemed to swell beneath her light touch as she trudged onward, her folio of drawings tucked under one arm, her mind rooted in the past. She ought to have run in the opposite direction that day, ought to have chosen the safe road. Ought to—well, it didn't matter now.

Her footsteps faltered as the hair at the nape of her neck prickled and rose. Her earlier feeling of unease grew stronger, more insistent as it clamored for her attention. There *was* someone on the street with her. Slowly she turned to face the way she had come. The mist was thick as pottage. She could see nothing. No one. But though she could not see him, she could sense him, and she'd learned by trial and error that some senses didn't lie. Intuition was often the only safeguard between life and the oblivion of death.

Added to her own instinct was the weight of rumors that hovered over the streets of Whitechapel. Rumors of murder, of vile and painful death. Darcie knew the value of gossip. There was the probability of a frightening kernel of truth hidden beneath the layers of speculation and exaggeration.

Pulling back into the shadowed niche of a doorway, she used the night and the fog to her advantage. The thought that she had imagined the whole of it, that the sound was only the footfall of some poor soul on his way home from a hard night's labor, was one she wanted to consider. Still, instinct argued against the possibility.

Hide in the shadows. Run, girl. Run! Steppy's voice calling her from beyond the grave.

Darcie wedged herself into the dimmest corner of the doorway, praying that the mad pounding of her heart was audible only to her own ears. Though she tried to stay calm, her attempts to dissuade herself from suspecting the worst were unsuccessful. She sensed that whoever, whatever, shared the street with her was on a quest, a search for the surest path to misery—her misery.

As if conjured from her most terrible imaginings, the shape of a man emerged from the mist. No sound heralded his arrival, just a ripple, a current that moved the air. Darcie dared not breathe, though an odor, foul and frightful, came uninvited into her nostrils. The smell of evil.

Huddling in the doorway, she could hear the sound of his breathing, low and rough. He was close enough now that she could lean out and touch his cape if she were of a mind to summon his notice. The garment was long, nearly to the ground, black in color, and of a fine material. She could see the smooth surface of his highly polished Hessians, splattered by the mud of the road. A man of money, she surmised. A man of money who had come to the East End, to Whitechapel, to prey on the poorest of the poor.

Seconds ticked by with agonizing slowness. Abruptly, he turned and began to walk away, the hollow sound of his footfall ringing on the stones. A sense of relief so acute as to be almost painful washed over her.

As the echo of the man's footsteps faded, Darcie slunk from the shadows, cautious, ever watchful. Scanning the street, she found no cause for alarm. It was deserted.

Her stomach gave an ugly rumble, an unpleasant testament to her desperate hunger. She ignored it, having no choice given that she possessed not a crumb of food. She continued on her way, meeting no one as she walked. The hour was close to dawn. The prostitutes and the men who searched them out had left the street for the night, and honest folk had yet to stir.

A rat scurried across her path. Watching it blend into the shadows, she remembered another life, when such a sight would have drawn her revulsion, even her fear, a time when she had lived in a small house in Shrewsbury, with Mama and Abigail and Steppy, and later with Steppy alone. Wispy memories teased her thoughts. Warm cocoa and soft hugs, the smell of Christmas morning, the childhood innocence that allowed her to feel safe. . . . Ruthlessly she shoved the thoughts of a better time to the back of her mind. No sense pining for the past when the present was what she must face. She was so close to the end of her desperate journey.

Tears filled her eyes, not of relief, but of despair. The end of her journey would bring only grief. The irony was a bitter tonic.

"So, you have come, Darcie Finch. I wondered how long it would take you."

A woman with garish face paint and cold eyes stood in the doorway of 10 Hadley Street, summoned there by the scantily clad girl who had answered Darcie's tentative knock. Her lips were pulled in a tight sneer and her brows rose mockingly as she looked down at Darcie, who stood wet and bedraggled on the single time-worn stone step that led to the open door. Darcie swallowed and hesitated, though the woman swept her hand across the portal in a clear invitation to enter.

"Are you in, or out? I haven't all night. Not unless you've got a stiff rod and a bagful of coin." She emitted a bark of harsh laughter at her own joke.

Darcie tried to answer, to tell the woman why she had come. Her throat moved and she meant to speak, but despite her intentions, no sound issued forth.

"Lost your wits, girl?" With an impatient click of her tongue she reached out, closing her fingers forcefully around Darcie's wrist.

A sharp tug, and Darcie stumbled into the house. Grabbing the edge of the marble entry table to steady herself, she stopped just short of landing in an ignominious heap at the other woman's feet.

The place smelled of smoke and strong perfume. And some other smell that was heavy and cloyingly sweet.

"Is he dead and buried, then?"

At the ruthless question, Darcie swallowed convulsively and nodded. *Dead, dead, dead.* Steppy was dead. Buried? She had no idea.

"You'll call me Mrs. Feather, like the other girls. No special treatment for you."

"Of course, Mrs. Feather." Darcie found her voice at last. She had heard of Mrs. Feather's House—there were few in Whitechapel who had not. But when she had realized that the address she sought, taken from the faded and ratty old letter that was her final link to the past, was actually Mrs. Feather's House, she had been shocked beyond words.

Darcie stared at the woman before her. Hard and bitter, she bore the marks of a sad and savage life. Could this cold creature really be Abigail? Pretty Abigail who used to sing Darcie to sleep and hold her in the night when the bad dreams came? A heaviness burdened Darcie's heart as she realized that this shell was all that remained of her sister.

Mrs. Feather caught Darcie's chin between her thumb and forefinger, regarding her shrewdly through eyes that glittered like chips of ice. She stared without speaking for a long moment.

Darcie returned the perusal with a side-long glance, noticing that Mrs. Feather looked old and worn, when in truth she was barely thirty. Her lips, painted red and full, were drawn tight. The bright color couldn't disguise the furrows that bracketed her mouth. The powder and rouge that colored her skin did little to hide the deep grooves that marked her brow, the brittle cast to her features, or the sallow complexion.

Saddened, Darcie lowered her gaze, unwilling to acknowledge this woman who was but a caricature of the sister she remembered. She immediately realized her mistake. In looking away she had changed nothing, for she was yet confronted by the reality of her sister's life. Her gown was tight and low, her full breasts pushed up to the point that they nearly spilled over the top of her bodice, and the scent of her perfume swirled around Darcie in a sickening cloud.

Suddenly, Mrs. Feather snatched at the battered folio that Darcie clutched under one arm. "What's this, then? You're not still scratching out pictures?"

Darcie's fingers curled protectively around the edges of the tattered leather case, resisting Mrs. Feather's attempts to take it from her.

Raising her eyes, she met the other woman's contemptuous glare. "Yes, I still sketch, though it has been some time since I could buy any supplies to draw with. These pictures are old. Treasures. Memories." Darcie couldn't suppress a sad smile. "I have one of you."

"Not one of me," Mrs. Feather said in a flat voice. "What you have is a picture of a girl who died a long time ago."

Darcie made no reply. There was nothing to say to that.

"How old are you now?" The question was sharp, impatient.

"Twenty, come June."

"Well, you look younger," Mrs. Feather said, her eyes narrowing as she peered at Darcie's face. "I remember you being younger." With an impatient click of her tongue, she turned Darcie toward the large gilt-framed mirror that hung on the wall. "Look at yourself and tell me if you think I have much to work with. Eyes as sorrowful as a whipped puppy. And that hair. I don't know what to make of it. And you're as skinny as a post. Men like a woman who's soft and curved."

Darcie stared at her reflection. She did look a sight. Her brown eyes were huge in her face, made all the more so by her hollow cheeks and pale skin. The ill weather had done a thorough job of drenching her, and the mahogany hair that had once been soft and pretty was plastered to her skull, hanging in uneven clumps over her shoulders. The severe, uninterrupted black of her apparel did little to enhance her appearance. In all, she looked like a walking corpse, though a corpse likely boasted more color in its cheeks.

"It doesn't matter how I look," she said softly. "I don't care. I only want—"

Suddenly, a man stepped into the entry hall, his passage followed by raucous laughter that belched from the front parlor as he departed. From the corner of her eye, Darcie caught the swirl of garishly colored gowns, the image of rouged lips and kohl-rimmed eyes. Women of the night, she thought as the door closed, cutting off the scene.

Her attention returned to the man as he moved behind Mrs. Feather, one hand curving around her waist and the other sliding over the bare skin of her shoulder until his fingers rested just inside her gown and lay casually on the plump fullness of her breast. Darcie swallowed, staring at this violation of her sister's person, unable to look away. *This* was how men would treat her.

He was of medium height, sharp-featured, and dark, the cut of his superfine coat accentuating his stocky build. Some might think him handsome, but there was a nasty aura about him that made Darcie's stomach roll with nerves. She took a step back, wishing she were anywhere but here.

Mrs. Feather cast Darcie a hard glance, then turned from her, her lips curving in a practiced smile as she moved.

"Lord Albright, how lovely to have you grace us with your presence this night. All is arranged exactly as you desire. The red room, as you requested."

"Is this the girl?" he asked, his voice cold. Darcie shifted her gaze to the floor. "Looks like Haymarket ware. She's not as pretty as I wanted, or as young.

And she looks completely lacking in spirit. You know I like a fight. A few yelps and screams at the very least."

"This girl, my lord? She's just a maid. I have a lovely treat waiting for you upstairs."

"Hnn," he grunted, pulling his hand from Mrs. Feather's breast. Abruptly, he stepped toward Darcie, brushing his fingertips over her bodice. With a cry she shrank from his touch, banging her arm sharply against the marble-topped table at her side. Lord Albright's eyes lit up with an ugly glow that made Darcie cringe from him in apprehension and disgust. Her cry of pain had brought him pleasure, she realized.

Mrs. Feather moved smoothly between them, linking one arm with practiced ease through Lord Albright's and reaching behind at the same time to deliver a sharp pinch to Darcie's forearm with the other.

"Come, my lord," she purred. "We wouldn't want the tempting dish I've arranged to get cold, would we?"

Lord Albright bared his sharp, pointed teeth. "I shall enjoy sinking my teeth into her, warm or cold."

Revulsion rose in Darcie's throat.

As she guided Lord Albright toward the staircase, Mrs. Feather glanced back over her shoulder.

"Stay there." She mouthed the words soundlessly at Darcie, her lips moving with exaggeration.

Sagging against the wall, Darcie tried to force her racing heart to slow. She felt sick. Lord, it wouldn't do for her to toss up here on the shiny polished floor of the front hall. No danger of that, really. There was nothing inside of her to throw up.

The dull ache in her abdomen turned momentarily sharp, doubling her over with the sheer intensity of the pain. She was reminded of exactly how desperate her straits were. The subtle torment was always there of late, gnawing relentlessly at her empty insides, reminding her that a full belly was a dream of the past. The minutes and hours would creep by, and just when she thought she could bear it, the agony of ever present hunger tore at her with a pain that gnashed its evil teeth, lacerating her stomach, taunting her with her own desperation.

The sound of boisterous laughter filtered from the front parlor. Raising her head, Darcie forced herself to look about, to take in the reality of the choice she had made. *Mrs. Feather's House.* The name was so innocuous, so unassuming, but Darcie was hard-pressed to imagine anything worse than this place. No mere house, it was a den of debauchery. Mrs. Feather catered to the best of society, providing them with the means to indulge in their darkest, vilest desires.

A high-pitched scream echoed from above, and then another, only to be silenced with abrupt finality. The hallway spun before Darcie's eyes. She couldn't remember when she'd eaten last. Last night. No, the night before that. She'd snatched a potato that fell from a bushel at Spitalfields and devoured it raw. Nowhere to sleep. Nothing to eat. For weeks she'd banged on every door, pleaded for gainful employment at any job. Laundry maid. Step girl. There was nothing to be had. She was faced with a terrible choice. Sell herself on the street—what had Lord Albright called her? Haymarket ware—the lowest girl who sold herself in a doorway, a back alley, the darkened corner of a pub. Or she could sell herself to her sister.

Or she could die.

She'd thought of the poorhouse, but she had no illusions there. It was simply a longer and slower death.

Darcie pressed her balled fist into her belly. Her gaze strayed past the black-and-gold-papered walls of the front hallway, to the staircase that led to the upper floor, then flicked rapidly to the doorway that led to the parlor that Lord Albright had exited earlier.

Slowly, she began to back away. Her hip bumped against something, and she glanced down to find the knob of the front door pressing against her. The smooth cold surface of it beckoned.

Her fist closed around the brass knob, and she whirled, twisting the handle and flinging the door open. The darkness and the fresh smell of rain greeted her. Coming here had been a dreadful mistake. She couldn't do this. Whatever had made her think she could?

She took a deep breath, preparing to flee, when a hand clamped over her arm, the fingers biting into the sore place where she had banged it earlier. With a tiny gasp Darcie turned and faced Mrs. Feather. Her heart plummeted. Too late to run.

"Here, take this." Mrs. Feather pressed something into Darcie's palm. "But don't come back. You have no place here, and there's no more for you where this came from."

Looking down in amazement, Darcie stared at her sister's gift. A shilling. A fortune to a girl who was starving.

Her gaze collided with the madam's, and for a single beautiful shimmering moment, she saw her sister, Abigail, looking at her from behind Mrs. Feather's hard, cold mask.

"Thank you," she whispered, closing her fingers around the money.

"Go," Mrs. Feather said brusquely. "Go to Curzon Street, to Doctor Damien Cole. Tell him I sent you and that I'll thank him to do this one favor for his old friend, Mrs. Feather."

"To Curzon Street," Darcie echoed, barely able to believe in her good fortune or her reprieve. Impulsively, she cast her arms about her sister. "Thank you . . . Abigail."

Mrs. Feather squeezed her tight then pushed her out into the street.

"Don't come back," she said, her voice strangely hoarse. "And mind, have a care of him, Dr. Cole. He is a hard man, a man to fear. Stay out of his way. Stay clear of his work. And keep your nose out of his secrets."

Darcie gave a quick nod then hurried away, the shilling clutched in one hand pressed against her heart, her leather case tucked beneath the other. She had escaped the horror that awaited her, had been granted a reprieve from the fate that was her sister's. Tears of relief stung her eyes. She would gladly scrub floors from dusk to dawn, scrub the steps, empty slops, anything, if she was but given the chance.

Armed with a name, Dr. Damien Cole, and the

reference of her sister, the notorious madam, Mrs. Feather, Darcie forged onward. Her sister's warning swirled through her thoughts. *A man to fear.*

The words became a litany, spinning over and over in her mind as she pressed on. Soon she was beyond exhaustion, her mind numb to all but the need to reach Mayfair.

So blunted were her senses that she did not hear the rolling turmoil of horses' hooves on the cobblestone street, did not see the dark bulk of the carriage as it bore down on her. At the last second a shout penetrated the fog that shrouded her awareness, and she turned to see four great beasts pawing the air above her head, their hooves slashing dangerously close to her face. She threw herself to the side, landing with jarring impact on her right shoulder. Stunned, she lay on the wet ground, staring at the horses as their driver brought them under control.

When they quieted, he climbed down from the seat and approached her where she lay.

"What's wrong with you, girl? Have you not eyes in your head? Or ears? Did you not hear me coming? If I'd been moving any faster—here. . . ." The man crouched at her side and offered his hand. His words were bitten off in harsh tones, but focusing on his eyes, Darcie found only concern mirrored there.

"Is she hurt?" A second voice, mellifluous in both texture and pitch, washed over Darcie's shattered nerves like a soothing balm.

"I don't think so, sir. Maybe shaken up a bit," the driver replied.

Turning her head, Darcie studied the second

man, his confident stride bringing him into her
line of vision. Her heart gave a hard, sharp kick
against her ribs as she took in his long black cloak
and polished boots, splattered with the mud of the
road.

The fears she had entertained earlier that night
on the mist-shrouded street echoed through her
mind. Was this the same man who had followed
her, the ominous presence that had caused her to
hide in the shadowed doorway?

Panicking, she scuttled backwards, the memory
of the threatening stranger on Hanbury Street
fresh in her thoughts. She stared at the man who
approached her now, his long cloak and boots too
similar for comfort. Her pulse raced as she struggled for reason. On Hanbury Street she had sensed
evil buffeting her in great crashing waves that
rolled violently from the stranger on the street, yet
she sensed no such threat now, sensed no evil emanating from the man approaching her.

Her gaze shifted to his face, and what she saw
made her eyes widen and her fear fade away, replaced by a surreal sense of resignation.

She had died, then. And here was the angel
who'd been sent to guide her.

Squinting in the watery gray light of dawn,
Darcie stared at the newcomer, her common sense
telling her that he was just a man, surely no celes-
tial being, despite her initial impression and despite the strange fascination that suffused her.

He moved closer, his stride graceful and sure,
until he loomed over her. With a negligent flick of
his wrist, he set the wings of his long coat aside and

hunkered down, close enough that Darcie could see the stormy gray of his eyes. The hint of a frown shadowed his brow as he studied her with a long slow perusal that took in all parts of her body.

"Are you hurt?" he asked.

She shook her head slowly, afraid to trust the sound of her voice. Her body seemed to tingle in each place his gaze rested.

"Have we a blanket, John?" He glanced at the coachman, and as he turned his head his burnished gold hair caressed his shoulder. Darcie had the strangest urge to touch it, to see if the honeyed strands were as thick and soft as they looked.

"I don't think so, sir."

"I do not require a blanket. I'm fine," Darcie managed, her heart drumming loudly in her ears.

"Are you?" The man turned a dispassionate gaze on her. Slowly, he raised one hand, reaching out to rest his fingers on the side of her throat. She jumped at the sensation of his warm hand against her chilled skin, at the feel of her pulse fluttering wildly against his touch.

"Y-yes," she replied.

His brows rose. "How fortunate," he finished dryly, and she felt bereft as he drew his hand away.

Rubbing her sore shoulder, Darcie lowered her eyes and pressed her lips together, uncertain of what to say. The stranger remained crouched at her side, his weight resting on the balls of his feet, arms folded casually across his bent knees. With a careless gesture, he motioned the coachman off.

"What day is it?" he asked, his gaze fixed on her. Darcie stared into his eyes, caught by the intensity of his expression. "T-t-tuesday," she stammered. "At least, it was Tuesday last night. So I suppose it is now Wednesday."

He nodded slowly, and the frown lines between his brows vanished.

"Well, you seem to be quite rational," he observed. "No dizziness?"

Darcie shook her head.

He almost smiled, the barest curve of his lips. "This position is extremely uncomfortable, and my leg is beginning to lose circulation. Would you mind terribly if we regained our footing?"

That said, he rose gracefully to his feet and offered his hand. Darcie stared at it for a moment, her thoughts fuzzy and vague. With a soft sound of impatience he twined his warm fingers through her icy ones and pulled her to her feet. She stood before him looking straight ahead at the elegantly simple buttons of his waistcoat. He was tall, she realized, more than a head taller than she was. Tipping her head back, she found him watching her. She had the strangest urge to smooth her bedraggled skirt and pat her hair into some semblance of order.

Suddenly, she realized that her hand remained linked with his, a warm bond in the chilly air of the breaking dawn. Embarrassed, she tugged, pulling her fingers from his grasp.

He glanced down, but made no comment on her precipitous action.

Darcie's movements were slow, careful, as she bent forward and retrieved her leather folio from the place it had landed when she fell. Her fingers moved over the battered surface, quick assessing little touches meant to determine the damage to her one worldly treasure. She released a tiny sigh of relief when she found the case undamaged.

She looked up once more. He was watching her, cool gray eyes glinting like polished metal, his features reflecting only polite interest.

"I shall not ask you what you are doing hurrying about on the outskirts of Whitechapel at this hour of the day. But I should like to offer the use of my carriage to take you to your destination."

"Oh," Darcie said, astonished by the offer. She closed her arms tighter around her folio, rocking it slightly like a baby. "Oh. I am looking for Curzon Street."

"A somewhat distant but worthy place." The man's brow furrowed questioningly. "Did you intend to walk there? Clear to the other side of town?"

At her single brief nod, his brows rose in surprise.

"Indeed. And whom do you seek on Curzon Street?"

Darcie glanced at the ground. How much to tell a stranger? And why was he even asking? She was clearly a woman beneath his touch.

As if reading her doubts and concerns, he spoke. "I ask only because I myself am from Curzon Street. It would be a matter of little difficulty to see you safely there." His glance flicked over her, impersonal, assessing. "I suspect you will not make it if left to your own devices."

The driver had returned to the coach. Darcie watched from the corner of her eye as he climbed up and took the reins. The horses shifted restlessly.

The man gestured at the fidgety beasts. "Come. My horses won't tolerate the delay."

Without waiting for her reply, he strode to the waiting carriage, and Darcie found herself trailing behind him. In her exhausted state it would be sheer stupidity to refuse the ride. Hiking up her skirt, she paused, startled, as he offered his hand to help her into the carriage as though she were the finest lady out for a morning ride. Such courtesy for a common girl whom he'd nearly run down in the roadway. She was amazed.

She had barely settled on the seat when he climbed in and lowered his body down beside her, his shoulder pressing against hers in the confined space. He smelled clean and fresh, and Darcie was ashamed of her own state of disrepair. She must smell like the docks, she thought. Each morning she performed her ablutions as best she could, searching out a rain barrel, or any clean water that was handy. In her small, black cloth bag she carried a sliver of scented soap, a luxury she had splurged on in a moment of supreme foolishness. The soap was nearly gone now, melted by her attempts at personal hygiene. The money would have been better spent on food.

Dragging in a shaky breath, Darcie looked down at her hands, clasping the tips of her left fingers with her right. She pressed her lips together and cast a sidelong glance in the man's direction. Likely he bathed every day, she thought enviously.

He had let his head fall back against the seat, baring the strong column of his throat. His golden hair fanned across the dark velvet upholstery. His eyes were closed and the curled sweep of his lashes formed dark crescent shadows against his golden skin. Everything about this man was beautiful. The sculpted angle of his cheek. The straight length of his nose, accented by the tiny bump at the bridge. Forcing her gaze away from him, Darcie turned to look out the side window, uncertain what to do, what to say.

The coach lurched and began to move, picking up speed as the seconds passed. Darcie stared out the window watching the buildings move by in a blur. Tears pooled in her eyes. She was exhausted, hungry, and disgusted by the horror she had nearly been driven to. But there was hope, she reminded herself, the thought igniting in her breast like a dormant flame. She had a name, Dr. Damien Cole, and a reference—so much more than she had started out with.

Suddenly, her sister's warning echoed hollowly in her mind. *He is a man to fear. Stay out of his way. Stay clear of his work. And keep your nose out of his secrets.*

Shifting on the soft seat, Darcie looked straight ahead into the confines of the coach. With a start, she realized that there was a third person in the vehicle. A man was sprawled on the velvet upholstery of the seat across from her, his clothing coarse, his boots scuffed and worn. In the burgeoning light of morning he seemed unnaturally pale. Watching him for some minutes, Darcie frowned. There was something strange about the man, something odd about his posture.

Darcie ducked her head and looked through

the rain-dampened tendrils of hair that had escaped her pins toward the man at her side. Her rescuer.

"Y-your friend is sleeping very deeply, sir." The words jumped from her lips before she could restrain herself.

He opened his eyes, but kept the base of his skull resting against the seat back. When he spoke, he did not look at her, merely stared at the roof of the coach.

"He is not my friend."

"Oh." Darcie looked again at the sleeping man across from her. He half sat, half lay across the cushions of the opposite bench. He had not moved, had not made a sound. "That man . . . Is he ill? Or drunk?"

Her companion made a harsh sound. Darcie thought it might have been a laugh. She turned to face him and found that he was regarding her intently, the strangest expression in his eyes.

"No, he is neither ill nor drunk." The words were low and soft. "He's well past the possibility of either."

Darcie felt her stomach clench, not with hunger, but with an irrefutable certainty. A chill crawled across her skin, raising goose flesh. She drew a deep, shuddering breath. Unable to tear her gaze from the stormy depths of her rescuer's eyes, she whispered the question to which she already knew the answer.

"Is he dead, then?"

His expression did not change, betraying neither emotion nor concern. Darcie watched his lips form the words, though the rushing in her ears nearly obscured the sound of his reply.

"Oh, yes. He is dead. Has been for at least a day."

And he smiled most amiably as he said it.

Darcie swallowed against a rising nausea as she stared at her companion in dismay. She shared the coach with two men, one dead, and the other quite possibly mad.

CHAPTER TWO

"Where did you say you wished to go?" The man at Darcie's side shifted slightly as he spoke, bringing his shoulder in closer contact with hers.

She could feel the heat of his body crossing the space between them. Swallowing, she wondered how to conduct a conversation with a stranger while she sat in the company of a corpse. "To Curzon Street, sir."

"Yes, so you stated earlier." There was a hint of wry amusement in his tone. "But where on Curzon Street?"

"Do you require a constable?" Her gaze slid to the body on the bench across from her, then away. "To report the man's death?"

"No, nothing a constable could do now that the fellow's expired." He shrugged, clearly dismissing the matter, leaving Darcie with a plethora of questions while he doggedly pursued the answer to but one. "Where on Curzon Street?"

"To the home of Dr. Damien Cole, sir. I'm to seek employment there."

He was silent for a moment, and when at last he spoke his tone hinted at both surprise and curiosity. "The home of Dr. Damien Cole," he mused. "And what sort of employment do you seek?"

"As a maid, sir."

"Hmm. Have you references?"

She could feel his eyes on her now, his attention focused. If she had references, she would hardly have been compelled to knock on Mrs. Feather's door, she thought acerbically.

"I have none written, sir. Lost, they are. And the family I worked for has gone to India, so there's no one to vouch for my character."

"Rather inconvenient," he said softly. His face was half turned toward her, highlighted by a thin stream of light that filtered through the window. His gray eyes glittered as they sought hers.

Darcie waited for him to say more, and when he didn't, she continued, "But I have the reference of my sister, who says she is an old friend of the doctor."

The man sat up and turned to face her fully. She had no choice but to return his gaze. He seemed to expect it. To do otherwise would be unforgivably rude, and in truth, she was glad to have a reason to look somewhere other than at the dead body across from her.

His perusal was intent, assessing. "Your sister is an old friend of the doctor?" He paused. "The doctor has few friends."

So he knew Dr. Cole then. She wasn't sure whether to feel relieved or dismayed.

He narrowed his eyes in thought. "Who is your sister?"

Darcie shook her head. What to say to this man? She could hardly tell him who her sister was.

"Please, sir, just leave me at the house of Dr. Cole, and I'll explain it all to him."

He stared at her for a long moment, then the corner of his full mouth tipped up, the movement there, then gone, a fleeting hint of amusement. For some reason, she had the thought that he was a man who did not smile often.

"How extraordinarily convenient for you," he said softly. "I am Dr. Damien Cole."

"Oh." Oh, dear. Her heart began to dance in an erratic rhythm as she realized that her erstwhile savior was her potential employer. A wry amusement overcame her. She should have learned by now not to be surprised by the strange twists and turns of life.

"Now, tell me. Who is this mystery woman who claims to be friend to me?"

"My sister said to ask you, sir, if you would please do this one favor for your old friend Mrs. Feather."

She could feel the sudden tension in his thigh where it pressed against hers. The carriage rolled onward and Dr. Cole sat rigid, the silence stretched taut in the small space.

So, he *was* acquainted with her sister. Darcie felt an inexplicable sadness in a corner of her heart when she thought of this man and the ways he might know Mrs. Feather. An image of Lord Albright flickered to life in her imagination, a recollection of the flare of malicious pleasure in his eyes when she'd gasped in pain. Such were the men who attended Mrs. Feather's House. Dr. Cole had been kind to her. Surely he could not frequent her sister's dark domain.

"When did you last eat, Miss Feather?"

Darcie jerked, startled by the sound of his voice. The content of his question confused her, as she couldn't imagine how he could possibly know—or why he should care—that she was so very hungry.

"Oh, no. Not Feather. I don't know why she chooses to use that name. Finch. Darcie Finch," she blurted.

"When did you last eat, Darcie?" The sound of her name spoken in his deep, warm voice made her shiver.

She pressed her lips together, using the time to ponder his motives. Seeing no harm in it, she replied honestly. "I'm not certain. Two nights ago. Maybe three."

"You will begin your duties tomorrow. Today you will rest. And eat."

"Then you'll take me on," she whispered, astounded by the good fortune that had come upon her this night.

"I find myself in urgent need of a maid-of-all-work," he replied, pausing for a mere second before continuing in a sardonic tone. "It seems my last one has disappeared rather suddenly."

Darcie wondered what he meant by that, but hadn't the nerve to question him. Likely the girl had run off. It was not uncommon.

"Fourteen pounds per year," he continued, "and an allowance for tea, sugar, and beer."

Darcie's head spun with the sum. She thought the position warranted less than ten pounds per

year. Dr. Cole was a generous man. She glanced at
him once more, not trusting that generosity. What
hold could her sister have over him that he took
her on so easily, without reference or even a cursory conversation as to her qualifications?

"I'll work hard, sir. Thank you, sir." She meant
those words with all her heart. He would not be
sorry that he had given her a chance.

Resting her elbows on the leather folio that now
lay across her lap, Darcie pressed her palms together, twining her fingers, trying to contain the
wave of joy that crashed over her. Then she thought
about his offer. An allowance for tea, sugar, and
beer. Regardless of her current status, she'd been
raised in a genteel household, raised with proper
values and morals. She could almost hear her
mother's voice telling her that avoiding the truth
was just the same as telling an untruth.

"I don't drink beer," she said with blunt honesty.

He raised a brow and inclined his head. "An allowance for tea, sugar, and beer," he repeated. "If
you have no wish to drink the beer, I shall see that
you are given its value in coin. Spend the extra
on"—his gaze flicked over her, grazing over the
worn and well-mended cloak—"on something
pretty. A ribbon, perhaps."

Darcie felt heat creep into her cheeks, though
she couldn't say if she was flushed with pleasure,
or mortification. Pleasure at the thought of buying
something as frivolous as a ribbon when she'd not
had enough to buy a crust of bread in a very long
time. Mortification that he'd mentioned her lack,
though he hadn't seemed unkind when he said it.

The exchange proved to hold the last of his in-

terest, and he turned his face from her to stare out
the side window. Her gaze returned in morbid fascination to the dead man slumped on the seat
across from her. Freshly dead, she thought, for no
smell permeated the carriage, and surely it must
had the man been deceased for any length of
time. Pressing her palm hard against the center of
her forehead, she wondered if it was her fatigue
that made the whole of it seem so frightening and
macabre, or if any sane person would question the
events of this night and the strangeness of her fellow passengers. Before she could fashion an answer, the coach swayed and rocked to a halt.

"Ah, here we are." Dr. Cole stepped from the
carriage and, to Darcie's amazement, turned to
help her down.

Gingerly placing her hand in his, she stepped
down from the coach, wary of his manners and his
intent. Once more the image of Lord Albright skittered across her mind. She recalled the revulsion
she had felt in his presence, the genuine fear that
had chilled her, and she could not help but compare him to Dr. Cole, with his impeccable etiquette,
cool demeanor, and lifeless companion. Better to
suffer the company of a man who was mad than
one who was purely evil she decided with a mental
shrug.

Her hand dropping from his, Darcie paused to
look up at the white facade of the house before
her. Large sash windows trimmed with black iron
railings overlooked the street. There was a tall
fence surrounding the property, the pointed tops
of the iron rails standing sentinel against any who
might dare to trespass. Two gates interrupted the

continuity, one leading to a servants' entrance that was at the bottom of a narrow stone stairwell, and the other opening to a short walkway leading to five stone steps that ascended to the wide-paneled front door. Darcie began to move forward, then stopped abruptly. That door was off limits to her. She ought to go down to the servants' entrance.

As if reading her thoughts, Dr. Cole shook his head. "Time enough to stand on circumstance tomorrow," he said. "For today, you may as well come in this way with me."

He moved his hand in a smooth, beckoning motion, indicating that she should accompany him.

Darcie looked once more towards the house. This place would be her home, the only home she had known in a very long time. Her gaze shifted back to Dr. Cole. He was an enigma, this man who would be her employer. His treatment of her thus far had been exemplary. In fact, he had been more than kind. And she so desperately needed this post. Just standing here taxed her pathetic reserves of strength.

Turning back toward the carriage, she stared at the door, closed now against the macabre contents of the vehicle. Still, she knew he was there, the dead man who had shared their ride. Dr. Cole had not been forthcoming as to the reason that a fresh corpse sat in his carriage. He had offered neither explanation nor reassurance, and in truth, he owed her neither.

He was as beautiful as an angel, Dr. Damien Cole, but she knew that appearances were not to be trusted. Like the frozen surface of a river, a pretty, sparkly outer face could hide a treacherous undercurrent. Moreover, her sister's warning tolled like a portent of doom in her thoughts. Mrs. Feather had called Dr. Cole a man to fear. Darcie drew in a slow breath. At the very least, he was a man to be wary of. After all, few people would travel through the city in the early morning hours with a dead man for company.

Swiftly, she assessed her choices. Return to the street, return to Mrs. Feather's, or follow Dr. Cole into his home. Squelching the tiny feeling of apprehension that blossomed in her breast, she glanced at him once more. He waited patiently, seemingly unperturbed by her indecision.

Desperation and longing warred in her breast. She needed this position so badly. That her prospective employer was mysterious and somewhat peculiar was truly none of her affair, nor was the fact that he fraternized with a cadaver. Could Dr. Cole be a resurrectionist? Or perhaps an anatomist? The latter was a possibility, for he *was* a doctor.

Licking her lips nervously, she thrust the sense of wariness and doubt away from conscious thought to the back of her mind, for if she was to work within this household, she could not let suspicion blossom and grow.

Her stomach rolled, twisting on its own empty core, and the world tilted eerily as a tide of weakness tugged at her. There really was no choice, she acknowledged. She must accept this position, for her other options were well and truly exhausted.

She glanced at Dr. Cole, who waited calmly by the gate, one foot resting negligently on the iron rail. Placing her right foot before her left, Darcie began the brief journey up the path to the front door, the dark-paneled portal swinging open as they approached.

The following morning, Darcie rose before dawn. Well fed and well rested, she felt better than she had in months. Dressing swiftly, she made her way down the back stairs from her attic chamber, past the upper floor of empty bedrooms and the next level that she had been told housed the doctor's suite and study. She hurried to the scullery, shown to her the previous day. There she filled a bucket and collected the items she would need to scrub the front steps.

Lugging the heavy bucket of soapy water outside, she paused for a moment, wiping her hand across her brow, already feeling the strain of her exertions. She called upon all her reserves of strength, intent on completing her task as quickly as possible so she might move on to the next task. Kneeling on the top step, she began to scrub, her hand working in a circular pattern as she washed away the dirt and grime.

Poole, the butler, had been very clear as to his expectations. Darcie shivered as she pictured his glacial gaze fixed on her, a look of utter disdain puckering his features as he explained her duties. She had been left with few illusions as to the fact that Poole disliked her in the extreme, though she had no idea why this should be so.

She began to scrub faster, harder, intent on proving him wrong, desperate to demonstrate her worth and value. This position as maid-of-all-work in Dr. Cole's household was her one shining chance. She could ill afford to make any mistakes.

Suddenly, the sound of footsteps rang along the deserted street. Darcie paused in her chore, turning to look up and down the cobbled road. Mist hugged the ground, wrapping it in cool gray silence. She could see nothing, no one. It was unnerving, being out here in the thin pre-dawn light, the street barren and empty, with only her imagination and the ever present fear she had learned in Whitechapel for company. Turning to her task once more, she began to scrub with renewed vigor.

The top step was done, and she moved to the second, then the third, until she had worked her way to the bottom. She no longer felt chilly; her exertions had warmed her, and tendrils of hair clung to her damp brow. Wiggling backwards, she began to scrub the short walkway, shifting herself back a few inches every few moments.

Darcie rested one hand on the ground and lifted her knee to crawl back yet another foot. Her buttock came in contact with something hard. The gate, she thought, turning her head to look over her shoulder, wondering how she had moved all the way to the fence in so short a time.

A high squeak of fear escaped her lips as her gaze fell on two booted feet, standing directly at her back. The boots were crusted with mud, as was the hem of the long black cloak that hovered and swayed just above the ground. Scrambling to her feet, she stood, chest heaving, gasping for breath.

Her gaze collided with that of Dr. Cole. He

watched her through eyes the color of smooth stones at the bottom of a stream.

"I-I-I'm s-s-sorry," she stammered, pressing the flat of her palm against her breastbone. "I didn't hear you approach. I thought I was alone."

"I saw you from the house."

"Oh," she said softly, her gaze shifting to the front door. He couldn't have come out that way, she thought. She had been washing the steps. He could not have passed without her seeing. Nor could he have come through the gate, for he would have had to pass her that way as well. She would have heard his steps, the creak of the hinges. Bewildered, she returned her attention to his person. He was looking down at the cobbled walkway.

Following his gaze, she too stared at the dirty gray water swirling on the stones, puddling at his feet.

"Oh, dear. Your boots . . ." Her voice trailed off as the sight of his boots, speckled with mud from the street, reminded her of the night she had hidden in a shadowed doorway on Hanbury Street, looking at eerily similar boots and the hem of a fine cloak. She shivered.

"You are cold." Dr. Cole reached out and closed his fingers over hers. His hand was warm, his grasp firm. "Your skin is like ice."

Unsure how to respond to his observation, Darcie snatched her hand away and dropped her gaze to the ground.

"Here," he said softly, his voice gentle. "Take this."

Glancing up, she saw that he held a blue shawl

draped over one arm. Hesitantly, Darcie stretched out her hand and touched the fine wool. Soft.

"It won't bite," Dr. Cole said, holding the garment out toward her.

"For me?" Darcie raised her eyes, unable to hide her confusion. Clearly the garment was not new. Still, it was fine, obviously expensive. She could not help but wonder what he was doing out here at this early hour, offering her a shawl. "You mean to give this fine shawl to me?"

"Precisely." He inclined his head slightly, and she thought she saw a tiny glimmer of amusement in his eyes.

"Why?" she asked, bewildered.

"Because you looked cold." He spoke slowly and clearly, as though explaining something to a child.

Heat flooded her cheeks. Likely he thought she was dimwitted.

"Thank you," she whispered at last, taking the shawl and spreading it over her shoulders. She noticed a small seam in one corner, a tear that had been repaired with precise, tiny stitches. "I shouldn't like to put anyone out. Won't the owner miss this shawl?"

She was startled at the change that her question wrought in Dr. Cole's expression. Gone was any hint of warmth, replaced by a chilly nothingness, a barren terrain of absent emotion. With lightning speed his mood had shifted from congenial to cold. It was disconcerting.

"The owner has no further use for it," he said woodenly, then turned and strode up the stairs and through the front door, leaving Darcie standing on the stoop wondering at the cause of his mercurial shift in mood.

Carefully folding the shawl, she hung it over the iron fence. She had no wish to have it slip from her shoulders while she worked and fall into the filthy water that swirled across the walk. With one last curious glance at the garment, she bent to her task once more, thinking that she would be greatly appreciative of it on chilly mornings.

Pausing, she looked up at the silent house. What an enigmatic man, she thought. So kind that he brought a servant a shawl because he thought she might be cold. So erratic that his mood changed with the rapidity of a heartbeat.

As she continued to scrub the grime from the walkway, Darcie lost herself in thoughts of Dr. Cole, recalling the glint of amusement in his eyes. The image blurred and shifted as she visualized his abrupt change of countenance, and she was reminded of her earlier speculation that perhaps Dr. Damien Cole was just a bit mad.

In the days that followed, Darcie spent her time cleaning, tidying, helping the laundry maid or Cook, making herself generally useful, and performing any chore that required her attention. Slowly, she hollowed a shallow niche for herself, but remained vigilant lest her fortunes change once more.

Dr. Cole kept very strange hours, which left the routine of the household staff subject to his whim. He worked all night, and then slept all day. Sometimes, he slept not at all. The cleaning of his chamber, his study, and others rooms of the house were fitted in at opportune times, so as not to disturb his work. Sometimes, Darcie went for days without seeing him, but when she did encounter him in a hallway, in the parlor, on the stairs, he invariably greeted her with quiet cordiality. She wondered that he noticed her at all, that he spoke to her as though she was a person rather than a fixture in his household.

The staff went about their business with unobtrusive efficiency, guided by the rigidly demanding Poole, but Darcie noticed that other than working around his unpredictable schedule, no one catered to the doctor in any special way. No trays were sent up when he missed a meal. No warm chocolate or coffee kept at the ready for his request.

Thinking back to smiling Mrs. Beales, the cook who had worked in the home of her childhood, Darcie remembered the tray of cold meat and cheese, the sweet tarts, the hot coffee, always at the ready should Steppy return from work late in the night. It seemed sad that Dr. Cole had no such consideration, no one at all to care about him.

One afternoon Darcie placed a freshly delivered fish in the wet larder and after working up her courage, she approached Cook with her thoughts.

"I noticed that Dr. Cole has eaten nothing today," she began.

Cook's hand, which was wielding a knife in a rapid chopping motion expertly cutting vegetables, paused midair at Darcie's observation. The portly woman turned and looked at her with a questioning expression. "Nothing new there, dear."

Darcie nodded. "Shall I take him a tray?"

Cook's brows shot upward in surprise. "Won't eat it," she muttered and returned her attention to chopping the carrots in front of her.

"Perhaps I could just take it up to him?" Darcie surprised herself by persevering.

Shaking her head, Cook set aside the knife for a moment and turned to meet Darcie's gaze. "Don't think I haven't tried. But no one's allowed out to the carriage house, and if I leave it at the foot of the stairs, the food's still there hours later. He'll eat when he's ready."

"He isn't in the carriage house," Darcie said softly, her heart pounding as she forced herself to stand her ground. "He's in his study. I saw him go up an hour past."

Setting her fists on her ample hips, Cook stared at Darcie for a long minute. Then she shrugged and took down a plate, heaping it with cheese, bread, and some fresh berries. "Go on and take it up, then. You'll see. He won't take a bite. Like as not, he's in the drink."

Darcie had placed the plate on a tray and turned to leave the kitchen, but Cook's words stopped her.

"In the drink?" she asked, looking at Cook over her shoulder.

The other woman nodded. "He'll go on for a good long while right as rain, then the melancholy'll come on him." She shrugged, took up her knife, and resumed the chore of preparing supper.

Clearly Cook had no intention of saying more.

Darcie ascended to the doctor's study, tray in hand, her thoughts troubled by Cook's revelations. She rapped lightly on the door.

"Come in."

Balancing the tray on one hip, she eased the door open and stepped into the room. The heavy drapery was closed against the afternoon sun, leaving the room in dim shadow.

Dr. Cole sat behind his desk, a book open before him. He blinked against the light that entered the room from the hallway.

"Why do you read in the dark?" Darcie asked, an echo of her own mother. She bit her lip as she wished she could call the words back. He was hardly a child, and she was in no position to be lecturing him.

He ignored her question, glancing instead at the tray she set on the desk before him.

"What is this?" he asked, his brows drawing together in bewilderment.

For some reason, his expression made Darcie want to smooth her hand across his brow.

Instead, she answered his question.

"This is food," she said. "Human beings require it to survive."

His head jerked up sharply and he gazed quizzically into her eyes. A rusty laugh escaped him.

"You are a brave little mouse."

Darcie shook her head, but said nothing. She was not brave at all; rather, she was foolish in the extreme to speak to him so, and she was at a loss to explain why she did. She should have simply set the tray down and scurried away.

Turning to do just that, she was surprised when his fingers closed lightly about her wrist.

"Stay." His voice was low and rough.

She glanced back at him, taking in the half-empty brandy snifter on the desk, her senses catching the aroma of alcohol that hung dark and rich in the air. Cook's mention of Dr. Cole's melancholy drifted across her thoughts and a warning sounded in the corner of her mind. A man and a brandy glass could be a dangerous combination. She knew that so very well. Her eyes met his and she found them clear, not bleary and red-flecked as Steppy's had been when he drank too much brandy.

In one hand he held a small gilt-framed miniature that she had dusted often. She knew it was a picture of a pretty, dark-haired girl in a softly ruffled dress. For a moment, she was tempted to ask him about her, about the girl who meant enough to him that he kept her picture close at hand.

Shaking her head, Darcie drew away, dropping her gaze to the floor. She sidled in the direction of the door, but the sound of his voice rolled over her before she could escape.

"Thank you," he said gruffly. "I'll leave the tray outside the door when I'm done."

Darcie nodded and stepped into the hallway, closing the heavy portal behind her with a soft click. As she descended the stairs on her way back to the kitchen, she could not help but wonder why that brief encounter with her employer had left her heart pounding and her thoughts in turmoil, why his quiet request that she stay had thrilled her to the depths of her soul.

CHAPTER THREE

Darcie moved the feather duster back and forth across the window ledge the following morning as she stared fixedly through the glass pane of the large window overlooking the cobbled drive that lay behind the house. She absently cleaned the same spot over and over, her attention focused on Dr. Cole where he lounged beside the carriage house on a small ornamental bench. Next to him, a large patch of petunias burst from the stone confines of a small flower bed like prisoners from a jail.

The sun glinted off his golden hair, and as she watched, he shifted his tall, lithe frame as if to redirect the midmorning glare away from his eyes. She wondered at the book that held his rapt attention. He'd been immersed in it for hours. Not for the first time she pondered his interests, his likes and dislikes, the things that might fascinate him and those he would disdain.

For a moment Darcie wished that she were the page that he gazed at so intently. She could picture his clear gray eyes, focused with unwavering intensity on the object of his interest. He had that way about him, a way of looking at a person and listening to her words as though every syllable was of great concern to him. She felt ambivalent when he looked at her thus, as he did even when he made a simple comment or request. His attention brought her joy. Yet, at the same time, she was terrified of his notice, accustomed as she was to hiding in the shadows.

Pressing her lips together, Darcie forced herself to turn away. She had lingered too long as it was. Poole, the butler, would surely rebuke her, just as he had scolded her for washing the dishes too slowly, wasting precious time. Then he took her to task for washing them too quickly, not paying enough attention to the chore. And all the while he watched her with those icy eyes, pale and chilly as a winter morn.

With deft movements, Darcie dusted the desktop. The gilt-framed miniature of the dark-haired young woman sat in one corner. Each day she dusted the small picture, wondering who the woman was, what place she held in Dr. Cole's life.

Turning away, Darcie began to arrange the books on the dark wood shelves that lined the doctor's study. They were in constant disarray. She straightened them daily, but it seemed Dr. Cole came at some point between cleanings and pulled the tomes haphazardly from the shelves, then left them where they fell. Carefully she lifted a journal and slid it back into place, noticing as she did so that it was a publication of the Royal Society of

London, dated 1665. *Micrographia, or some physio-logical descriptions of minute bodies made by magnifying glasses, with observations and inquiries thereupon.* Darcie shook her head. The doctor's books and journals had interesting names, but more often than not she had no idea what the titles actually meant.

"Hurry, Darcie! Poole's in a foul mood again."

Darcie jerked her hand back as if burned and whirled to find Mary Fitzgerald standing in the doorway, her unruly red hair escaping from her cap, her sparkling green eyes wide with concern.

"Oh! Mary!" Darcie exclaimed. "You gave me a fright."

Mary nodded her head in the direction of the doctor's shelves. "Those books are what give *me* a fright. You ever looked in them? Horrible things."

Running her index finger over the spine of the closest volume, Darcie frowned. William Harvey. 1628. *On the Motion of the Heart and Blood in Animals.* She read the unfamiliar title out loud.

"Oh! You can read! I just look at the pictures."

Darcie frowned. "What is it about the pictures that gives you a fright?"

Mary glanced around to make sure that there was no one else about. She quickly crossed the room and approached Darcie's side. "You really never looked at them? I'd 'ave thought that you'd 'ave poked your nose in one of them by now. You've been here a month. And I told you the doctor's a strange one."

"And I told you that it's plain as the nose on your face that he's a good man. He has a kind heart." Darcie decided not to mention that she had, in fact, opened one or two of the doctor's books and had found the writings therein both fascinating and confounding, perhaps even frightening.

"A good heart? You think so, do you? Just 'cause he took you in. Well, you work hard for your pay, Darcie Finch. Harder than the rest of us." Mary narrowed her eyes as she glared at Darcie, then leaned close and spoke just above a whisper. "I think he has no heart. I've seen people come and go at odd hours of the night when no honest person ought to be out. I think he's doing something . . . I don't know, something evil, I think."

Darcie recalled the corpse that had shared her coach the night she arrived. Pushing aside the thought, she rolled her eyes and scolded Mary. "Dr. Cole is not evil, Mary. You have such an imagination. People have no control over when they take sick. If they need a doctor at a late hour, then that is when they need him!"

"Sick? Ha!" Mary pushed her face close to Darcie's, her words low and hard. "I never said they were sick. I remember a time when I first started in the doctor's service, five years ago, or thereabouts. Dr. Cole had a good practice then. Lots of society matrons and their snooty daughters. Then he started to restrict his hours, to spend more time at his surgery in the East End, or in that place"—she jerked her head towards the back window where the shadow of the carriage house darkened the back of the large yard—"in his laboratory on the upper floor, and suddenly it seemed as though the people who passed his door were more likely dead than not. There's something wicked in there, mind my words, Darcie Finch. Something wicked."

As Mary stepped forward, Darcie moved aside, allowing the other maid easier access to the shelves.

"There was Janie, the maid who was here before you." Mary lowered her voice even further and sent a quick, furtive glance over her shoulder. "One day she was just up and gone, like she'd never been, and no one ever heard from her again." She paused dramatically, waiting for the meaning of her words to sink in.

Darcie held her silence, but a recollection tickled the edge of her thoughts. Yes, she remembered now. Dr. Cole had made reference to a missing maid on the night he had first hired her.

"And once," Mary continued, "I found his handkerchief tossed on the floor. It was soaked in blood, still bright and wet."

Darcie felt as though a cold wind whispered against the back of her neck. "He's a doctor, Mary. Doctors sometimes get blood on their handkerchiefs."

Shaking her head, Mary said nothing as she peered at the spines of the books that lined the shelves, then her eyes lit on the volume she desired, and she pulled it out.

"I recognize it 'cause it doesn't 'ave no fancy gold writing like the others," she said, gesturing at the book's plain binding.

It wasn't a printed book, Darcie saw, but rather a leather-bound sketchbook. Casting a quick glance over her shoulder, Mary flipped the cover open, turning the pages carefully until she found what she sought.

"Look at this," she said. "Right here."

Darcie looked, and her breath caught and hung

suspended in her throat. The page revealed a detailed sketch of a leg, though it was not the subject that was so disturbing, but rather the manner of detail that was depicted. The drawing showed the skin pulled back from the naked limb, and even the muscle in parts, so the underlying bone was revealed. Tracing the image with shaking fingers, Darcie noticed that the artist was one of mediocre skill. The foreshortening was wrong, she thought.

Footsteps echoed in the empty hallway. With a squeak of fright Mary dropped the book to the floor, shoving it with the toe of her boot until it was partially hidden beneath the desk. She whipped a cloth and small bottle of lemon juice mixed with salt from the voluminous pocket at the front of her apron. With shaking hands she began to polish the brass fittings on the doctor's desk.

"What are you doing in here?"

Both women turned at the sound of the harshly barked query. Poole stood in the doorway, his frigid glance targeting first Mary, then Darcie.

"We thought if we worked together we could get things done quicker," Mary said smoothly, keeping her eyes fixed on the gleaming brass fittings.

Poole's gaze skimmed over Mary, then settled on Darcie as he pinned her with a look of disgust. "More likely, you thought you could waste the doctor's paid time by chattering away like a pair of magpies."

"No, sir," Mary insisted, shaking her head from side to side to emphasize her point.

"Go now, Mary." It seemed that the butler bit the words out through gritted teeth. Darcie could imagine him spitting metal pieces from his mouth.

Mary gathered her cloth and slunk toward the door, turning sideways to slide past Poole, as he made no move to vacate the entryway. With a quick, pitying glance at Darcie, she fled. Poole watched her go, and something indecipherable flickered in his gaze.

"I—" Darcie cleared her throat nervously as Poole swung his head, freezing her with his wintry scrutiny. "I'm almost done here, sir." She allowed herself no hesitation as she rushed on. "I've noticed that no one goes out to clean the doctor's laboratory, sir. I could do that if you like."

"You are not to go near the doctor's laboratory." The words came out on a hiss. "You are to notice nothing. You are to do as I tell you. You are not to think. You are not to overstep your bounds. Have I made myself clear?"

Darcie nodded, feeling the force of the words buffet her as though she had been struck.

"You, Darcie Finch," Poole continued, speaking her name as though the taste of it was vile on his tongue. "There are many maids in this fine city, any of whom would far surpass you in both manner and mien, who would be glad for this position. Watch yourself, Finch, for I am watching you."

Running his finger over a tabletop that Darcie had dusted earlier, he rubbed the pads of his index finger and thumb together, a slow precise movement. His cold eyes scanned the room before he advanced on her, moving close enough that she could see the small dot of dried blood on his chin where he had nicked himself shaving. She couldn't seem to drag her gaze away from that tiny dark spot.

"Do not overstep," he said, then wheeled about and stalked from the room.

His parting words echoed menacingly in the ensuing silence. Darcie waited at least a minute after his departure, her heart pounding in her chest. Eventually the frantic rhythm began to slow, and she bent to scoop the fallen book from the floor beneath the desk.

Laying the book flat, she carefully smoothed the pages and with a practiced eye assessed the drawing of the leg that Mary had shown her earlier. Yes, if the outer edge was moved here and the bottom, there . . . Darcie ran her finger over the paper, imagining how she would draw the thing. It mattered not that the subject was unpleasant. She viewed it with an artist's eye, seeing beauty where others would not.

Unthinkingly, she reached for a quill and dipped it in the nearby inkwell. How long was it since she had enjoyed the luxury of drawing? Passion rose within her, an instinct she could no sooner deny than the natural urge to draw breath into her body. With a few simply placed lines she rendered her version of the shape of the limb right next to the original on the page. Several rapid strokes added light and shade. There, she thought with satisfaction. That looked better.

Suddenly, the enormity of her trespass hit her. She had taken up pen and ink and marked one of the doctor's books, perhaps his own sketchbook. What had possessed her? A shaking began at her core and spread like a palsy through her limbs. He would send her away, back to the street, to the hideous fate she had barely escaped. She could scarcely believe her own foolishness, the temerity of her actions.

Horrified by what she had done, Darcie snapped the sketchbook shut. Swallowing convulsively, she glanced from side to side before sliding the book back onto the shelf. She stared at the spine of the slim volume in morbid fascination, hoping that she had replaced it in the correct spot and that the sketch would fail to draw the doctor's notice.

Forcing herself to turn away, she resumed her chores, though her fingers felt numb, barely able to hold tight to the feather duster. With just a bit of luck on her side, Dr. Cole would not search out that particular book for a good long while, and when he did, perhaps her luck would hold, and he would choose a drawing other than the one of the human leg to examine.

Moving to the door, she cast one last despairing glance over her shoulder as she exited the room.

That night, Darcie lay stiff and tense upon her bed, bone weary from an endless day's work. Despite her fatigue, her nerves were wound so tight that sleep eluded her. Mary's faint snores reverberated through the room, punctuated by the rustling of the covers as she shifted position in her sleep. Darcie tried to ignore the sounds, but her efforts met with little success.

The two women shared a small room beneath the eaves, and Darcie was grateful that the chamber held a separate bed for each of them. She knew that many girls in service shared one narrow pallet with two or even three other women. That could be a blessing in the cold winter months when the girls would share their body heat to keep warm. But Dr. Cole was a generous employer. He provided ample coal for the iron grate and Darcie and Mary had no need to combine the warmth of their bodies.

"Pssst. Darcie? Are you asleep?" Mary's quiet whisper edged aside her memories.

"No, but I thought you were sleeping. I hope I didn't wake you."

"What are you thinking about?"

"I was just remembering the day I first came here. How Dr. Cole asked you to bring me a tray."

"I never minded," Mary insisted.

"I know. But I think Poole did. He was angry that I came in by the front door. And then, when Dr. Cole bid you to serve me . . . I think Poole's hated me ever since," Darcie confided.

"His face turned a bright shade of red, and I thought he'd explode for certain." Mary gave a soft huff of laughter. "That Poole, he's a regular charmer."

Picturing Poole's ever censorious gaze, Darcie thought that he was anything but a charmer.

"I was amazed when I saw this room for the first time," she said softly. "It had been so long since I slept in anything more comfortable than a damp doorway. And here I was to have my own warm bed."

"I know just what you mean. I've been in service for ten years, two places before this one, and I'll say this for Dr. Cole, he treats us well."

Darcie ran her hand over the coverlet. The room was furnished with two single beds, each adorned with a pretty green-and-white quilt. The linens were as fresh and clean as any person could desire. And beside the grate, there was a full bin of coal.

"The doctor's a generous one when it comes to the coal. There's another thing I'll say for the doctor, he keeps us warm. . . ." Mary's voice carried low and slurred from across the room, her words trailing together as her exhaustion limited her ability to converse.

"Sleep, Mary," Darcie whispered, feeling bad that her earlier tossing and turning had woken the other woman and wishing that she, too, could shake off this restlessness and sleep.

She moved her feet restively beneath the sheets and tried to lecture herself to sleep, concentrating on the lessons in deportment her mother had recited to her during her childhood. At the time she had resented the endless reminders of proper decorum. Now, she would give almost anything just to hear her mother's voice once more.

Darcie couldn't stop the wave of sadness and longing that rolled over her. Her father had died when she was a toddler, and her mother had remarried within two years to a rich merchant who adored her. Though he had been the only father she had ever known, Darcie had called her step-father Steppy. Her mother had wanted to keep some memory of her first husband alive in her little girl's mind, so she had suggested the distinction.

Oh, how Darcie missed her mother's voice. Her smell. Her touch. She had been a gentle woman, soft-spoken and kind, with a ready smile and a generous spirit. For years all Darcie had known was a mother's love, a stepfather's doting regard—but that was before Steppy lost his fortune, before Abigail went away, before Mama coughed her life into a handkerchief mottled and stained with red, red blood.

A handkerchief stained with blood. Mary's words, spoken in the doctor's study earlier that day, rose to the forefront of Darcie's mind, and with them came the memory of Dr. Cole's sketchbook and her own foolish misconduct. She slammed her lids shut, but nothing could erase the image. *Stained with blood. Red, red blood. Mama coughing her life away.*

Darcie shifted on the bed, her thoughts darting this way and that, her edginess unremitting. Then, from nowhere came a terrible question. *Had there been blood, pools of blood, when Dr. Cole sawed the leg from the body for dissection?*

At a frantic pace, her thoughts skittered back to the sketchbook in Dr. Cole's study. She had reasoned herself full circle, back to the disembodied limb. Her belly rolled with nerves.

How could she have done what she did?

She had taken up pen and ink and drawn in one of the doctor's books, drafting her idea of a human leg, skinned and denuded. The subject matter itself caused her great anguish as she pondered it in retrospect. Dr. Cole must be an anatomist, a man who studied the mysteries of the human body, she decided. That would explain the frightful sketches.

Darcie digested the concept, wondering where his subjects came from, and then abruptly decided that it was better not to let curiosity carry her mind to a place she truly had no wish to visit. In White-chapel there were terrible rumors about where anatomists got their bodies. People whispered of fresh graves emptied and coins exchanged, and they whispered of murder most foul. Medical schools provided a huge demand for subjects, and un-scrupulous men were more than ready to supply that need.

With a sigh, she cast aside the near-stifling warmth of her covers and pushed herself to a sit-ting position. She reached for her shawl to wrap about her shoulders, touching the soft wool rever-ently, thinking how much she valued its warmth.

Dr. Cole was an enigma. Silent and forbidding one moment, kind and generous the next. He'd given her the shawl that first morning, and later, a simple change of clothes.

"I can hardly have you darting about looking as though you've been claimed from the rag bin," he had stated matter-of-factly, as though his actions were completely usual for any employer. But Darcie had known better, and the jaundiced look that Poole had cast her had confirmed her suspicion that Dr. Cole was being amazingly kind.

Darcie glanced toward Mary's sleeping form, wishing that she, too, could find the blessed obliv-ion of a restful slumber. But the memory of her trespass into the doctor's sketchbook ate at her like a cancer. The possible consequences of her ac-tions were terrible to consider.

A half-formed plan hovered at the edge of her thoughts, then shimmered and coalesced into a

solid strategy. She would tear the page from the
book and burn it, burn the drawing that was evidence of her transgression.

Taking up the stub of candle from the scarred
three-legged stool that served as a bedside table,
Darcie cautiously made her way down the narrow
back stairs to the main landing. As she reached the
long corridor at the foot of the stairs, she caught
sight of a strange apparition hovering in the hallway. She clamped her teeth down with painful force,
biting back a squeak of fear. The thing hovered,
white and eerie, with long dark tendrils snaking
over the paleness of its disincarnate form.

Her heart tripped over itself and a shiver of apprehension slithered coldly along her spine as she
stared in horror at the disincarnate specter that
hovered before her.

A soft exclamation escaped her lips as she realized that the ghostly pale face and trailing white
night dress were her own, the apparition a reflection of herself in the large ornately carved wood-
framed mirror at the end of the hall. She swallowed
her fear and slowly wet her lips before pressing
them together and continuing on her way, silently
acknowledging that she was overwrought, her nerves
stretched taut, her mind prone to ridiculous fancy.

Pushing open the door to the doctor's study,
she held the candle high and scanned the room,
though she couldn't say exactly what she hoped to
find. The shelves were perfectly arranged, the desktop as neat and tidy as she had left it earlier that
day. Silently she moved to stand before the shelf
where the sketchbook rested between two other

leather-bound volumes. It was there. Undisturbed. She slumped in relief, her head falling forward until it rested against the edge of the shelf. Closing her eyes, Darcie drew in a slow breath.

Suddenly, she froze. A sound, muffled and harsh, caught her attention, grating along her nerves. Someone was dragging something heavy across the cobblestones of the back drive.

Drawn by the noise, she moved swiftly toward the window, accidentally catching her hip on the edge of Dr. Cole's desk as she passed. With a small cry, she stumbled, righting herself just before she crashed to the ground. The candleholder fell from her fingers, the flame snuffed against the floor.

Alone in the dark, Darcie tried to reason herself out of her growing panic. It was only a noise, she reassured herself silently. She was tired and over-wrought. That was all. Still, no matter how resolutely she chided herself, she could not quell the rising alarm that snaked through her.

Unable to explain the disturbing agitation that curdled in her belly, she willed her limbs to carry her to the window, inexplicably determined to discover the source of the rough, grating sound. She pressed her body against the wall beside the window frame, pushing aside the heavy drapery and staring out into the night.

The moon was full, a great white orb hanging in the star-speckled sky, its glow illuminating the figures of two men who shoved at a large trunk, pushing it across the yard in the direction of the carriage house that served as the doctor's laboratory. The sound drifted upward, muted by the glass panes of the window, but audible nonetheless. They were dressed roughly, their garb little more than rags. Even from this distance she could detect the hardness of their expressions, their furtive movements as they scanned the vicinity for onlookers. She noticed that they carried no lantern.

The men stopped part way toward their apparent destination, and the shorter, more heavyset one flopped down on the lid of the trunk. Though she could not see his face clearly, something about the cast of his features gave Darcie pause. That, combined with the fact that the men were dragging a battered chest across the drive in the dead of night sent a prickle of unease up her spine. What sort of delivery would necessitate a clandestine visit shrouded in darkness?

Resurrectionists. The word popped unbidden to her mind. Men who took fresh bodies from fresh graves and delivered them to the anatomist's laboratory. Rumor said such men often didn't bother to wait for the grave, but helped victims on their way to eternity in return for the anatomist's coin. Her gaze slid to the carriage house, where a light shone in the second floor window, and then back to the two strangers.

After a moment, the seated man rose and the two resumed their exertions. As the taller of the two knocked at the door to the carriage house, a dark silhouette moved across the second floor window. A long moment passed, then the main door was opened, and with a grunt and a heave the men pushed the trunk past the doorway.

Darcie remained where she was, her hand

curled around the edge of the drapery. The velvet was thick and soft beneath her fingers, and she clung to it as though it would steady her while the world seemed to careen and list unsteadily beneath her. A trick of her imagination, she knew.

Straining her ears, she fancied she could hear the muffled sounds of a commotion as the men struggled to hoist the heavy chest to the second floor.

She waited for some time. Ten minutes, perhaps twenty. At length, they left the doctor's laboratory, hefting the trunk between them, each taking one of the handles. Their easy stride gave evidence to the lightness of their load. Whatever had been in that trunk was no longer a burden to those men, Darcie thought.

Suddenly they froze and glanced uneasily about, searching the shadows. Darcie shrank instinctively from the window, though they did not look her way. Then, apparently satisfied that they could move on unchallenged, the men resumed their pace. The taller one made some comment to his companion, receiving a mocking reply. The sound of their voices drifted upward on the night air, muffled by the window glass. Even after they moved from her line of vision she could hear the muted tone of their words trailing behind them like a tail.

They were just men, she told herself resolutely, but her reassurances did little to calm the sinister feeling that gripped her. There had been something unpleasant—no, more than unpleasant—something dangerous about those men. Unbidden, the image of the amputated limb that was sketched in the doctor's book, bare and stripped to the bone, sprang to her mind, and she wondered how heavy a person's leg was. Closing her eyes, Darcie visualized the weight of the chest, carried between two grown men. Not heavy enough, she decided.

But an entire man, dead and stuffed in a chest. . . . Her eyes popped open at the thought.

Suddenly, the light in the carriage house window died. Darcie huddled in the velvet drapery that hung about her shoulders like a cloak. Dr. Cole stepped from the doorway of the carriage house, his tall form unmistakable even from this distance. He paused to lock the door behind him. She could see the broad expanse of his shoulders, the muscles moving beneath the cloth of his well-tailored coat as he turned the key in the lock. Completing his task, he turned and froze. His head jerked up, and he stood motionless, listening, scenting the night air. The soft glow of the moon reflected from his hair, his skin, casting him in a preternatural light.

He took a single step forward, and then slowly spun a full circle, taking in his surroundings, searching the shadows.

Darcie's heart began to pound, a fast, steady rhythm that sent the blood rushing in her ears. Dr. Cole was looking for something. For someone. Perhaps for the men who had left with the now-empty chest.

With a subtle shift of his body, Dr. Cole moved to face the house. Slowly, he tilted his head back and fixed his gaze on the window of his study. She fancied she could see his eyes, feel his gaze boring deep into her soul. With a gasp, she pulled away from the glass panes, pressing her back against the wall and staring at the dark outline of the furnishings that graced his study.

Her! He was searching for her! And he had found her, she thought.

No, more than that. He had *known* she was there, sensed her presence with some unholy perception. The certainty of it terrified her.

Nonsense! Nonsense! she reasoned. It was impossible for him to see her in the dark and from that distance. And even more impossible for him to have some strange cognition of her presence. . . .

Still, her heart beat so hard and fast that she thought it would burst from her chest to lie pulsing and bloody on the floor.

Because she was afraid he would see her.

Afraid he will see you? Her thoughts taunted her. *Is that not what you truly wish? For him to see you, to know you, to draw you close in his embrace? Oh, God!*

Darcie closed her teeth around the bent knuckle of her index finger. It was only because of his kindness that she harbored such inappropriate imaginings, she insisted inwardly. But the truth of it could not be denied. She was drawn to more than that. To the physicality of him. It was a carnal attraction, and she would do well to bury it deep, to deny the urge that had kindled in her breast.

Still she could not stop herself from leaning forward, from searching for Dr. Cole in the moondrenched night. With a gasp, she realized that he stood still as marble, staring up at the study window. Then before her mystified gaze, he seemed to draw back without actually moving, blending with the shadows of the night, until he was gone, having vanished in the darkness.

Pausing only to snatch her snuffed candle from the place it had fallen on the floor, Darcie fled the room, forgetting to rip the page from the sketchbook, forgetting the task that had drawn her to the doctor's study in the first place. She ran all the way to her attic room, not stopping until she huddled beneath her covers and drew them up over her head, blocking out the night.

CHAPTER FOUR

"Darcie, wake up! Oh, do wake up!"

Groggily, Darcie opened her eyes to find Mary leaning close, shaking her shoulder roughly.

"Come on, now. Hurry!" Mary shoved a pile of clothing at her and yanked the covers from the bed. "Dress quickly. Poole's in a terrible state, just terrible. We've all been called from our beds. 'At once,' he said. We're to assemble at once."

Darcie rolled to her side then pushed herself to a sitting position. The room was dim, a single taper sending flickering shadows cavorting across the wall. It was yet night, she realized as the last tendrils of Morpheus's embrace bid her adieu.

"What time is it?" she asked, sleep making her voice rough.

"Long before dawn," Mary muttered, rolling her eyes. She took a brush to Darcie's hair, dragging it through the long tresses with hasty, ungentle strokes.

Darcie closed her hand around Mary's and pried

the brush from her grasp. She dressed quickly, pausing only to clean her teeth with the mint powder that had been among the first purchases she had made with her newly earned wages.

No sooner had she splashed cold water on her face than Mary grabbed her wrist and began to pull her toward the stairs.

"Come on, then. Hurry!"

With rapid steps they scurried down, descending to the entry hall where the other servants waited in uncomfortable silence, their clothing hastily donned and slightly askew, attesting to a hurried arrival. Mary slid into place in the line, and Darcie followed.

She could hear the murmur of masculine voices drifting through the open door of the front parlor. Dr. Cole stepped from the room into the hallway. His glance scraped over the row of servants. In his right hand, Dr. Cole held the book, the one she had drawn in. Darcie dropped her gaze to the floor, her mouth growing dry, panic clawing at her entrails.

Peeking through her lashes, Darcie watched as Poole slid smoothly behind Dr. Cole, a wary expression creasing his features. Her focus switched to the doctor. He looked pensive, remote.

"Something strange has come to my attention," Dr. Cole began, the palm of his left hand skimming lightly over the cover of the book he held in his right. "When last I looked at this book of sketches, there was but one drawing on page sixty-three. Tonight, I found not one, but two drawings."

His announcement was met by stilted silence.

Darcie pressed her lips together, trying to still her burgeoning panic as she stared at the tiled floor. The first fingers of dawn trickled through the small window at the front of the hallway and crawled slowly across the floor. Tension hung thick and heavy in the air, stifling in its intensity. No sound issued from the other servants, no clearing of throats, no shuffling of feet. So great was the absence of audible interruption that Darcie imagined she could hear the sound of the light creeping across the tiles.

"Has anyone here any knowledge of how a second sketch might have miraculously appeared on the page?" Dr. Cole's voice was smooth and low. There was no censure in his tone, no threat. In fact, Darcie thought she heard a hint of rigidly contained excitement.

None of the other servants stirred.

Shifting her gaze, Darcie looked at Dr. Cole, and found him regarding her with a calm, questioning expression. Earlier that night, as she had watched him from the study window, she could have sworn that he was swallowed by the shadows, as if woven of darkness. Now the gentle glow of dawn touched him, bathing him in a shimmering halo of gold and light.

Darcie noticed that he wore the same clothes she had seen him in the previous evening. There were faint shadows beneath his eyes and his hair was rumpled and mussed as though he had drawn his fingers through it repeatedly during the endless night. From the look of him, she doubted he had slept at all. The thought gave her a strange pang of sadness, though why she should mourn his lost rest when her entire life balanced in his hands was a question she had not the time to ponder.

Acutely aware that her transgression was the source of everyone's trepidation and concern, the reason they had all been dragged from their beds, she knew that there were no choices available to her. The others could not be made to suffer for her lapse.

Swallowing painfully against the constriction of her throat, Darcie took a single step forward, out of her place in line. She raised her chin, glancing first at Poole whose features were arranged in an expressionless mask, and then quickly to the side, at Mary, who gave her one single pitying look before returning her attention to the marble-tiled floor. At last, she forced herself to meet the silvery gaze of Damien Cole.

She silently reassured herself that he was good, he was kind. He had offered her a chance. Then she recalled the dead man in the carriage, the one that had accompanied them when Dr. Cole had brought her here that first morning. The bubble of hope that had bolstered her spirits burst abruptly. Of course he was a good, kind man. A good, kind man who drove about town in the wee hours before dawn with only a corpse for company. He had never explained the corpse's presence, and she, frightened of losing her one shining chance, had never dared to ask, thrusting aside all qualms and questions. Perhaps she hadn't wanted to know the answers.

He was a man who hired a destitute girl whom he'd nearly run down in the street.

A man who kept sketches of mutilated human limbs; a man who met unsavory characters in the dead of night.

But there was no real question as to Dr. Cole's character, no argument as to his probity. *He* was not on trial. She was. Regardless of any explanation she might offer, there was no excusing her actions. She had trespassed where she had no right to, stupidly, thoughtlessly . . . reflexively. And now her reprieve was surely over. Dr. Cole would cast her back out on the street. If he did not use her as a subject for his anatomical study, instead.

"I did the sketch, sir." Darcie spoke clearly, though her voice trembled, echoing in the silence.

There was a chorus of sound, a collective intake of breath, the involuntary response of the other servants to her startling statement. Darcie stared straight ahead, at the faint smudge on the far wall, concentrating on that faded mark, willing her trembling legs not to collapse out from under her. Though she could feel Dr. Cole's eyes upon her, she could not bring herself to meet his gaze, watching him instead from the corner of her eye.

"Ah." After a breath of silence he said, "Come with me." He turned and began to walk toward the stairs.

Darcie blinked in surprise at the speed, the ruthless celerity of the sentence meted out to her. Just that, *come with me*, and her life here was over.

Poole stepped forward, looking down at her as though she were a particularly repugnant species of insect, one he'd like to crush under the heel of his boot.

"Go on with you," he said.

She glanced at the line of servants: Cook, who'd been kind to her—slipping her an extra biscuit or cake while muttering about girls who could blow away in a breeze. John, the coachman, who said little, but whose eyes spoke more clearly than any long-winded speech. Mary, her roommate, her friend. Tears blurred her vision as she hurried after Dr. Cole, who'd already begun to ascend the stairs.

Confused, Darcie stopped abruptly, hesitating at the bottom step. She expected to be tossed on the street, without ceremony or fanfare, not escorted up the main staircase. Perhaps he meant for her to leave of her own accord. She looked about uncertainly.

Dr. Cole stopped on the third step and glanced over his shoulder.

"Well, come along," he said.

"Please, sir," Darcie began softly, drawing on a reserve of bravery that she had not known she possessed. She only knew with a dogged certainty that she could not leave this house without her drawings. "I have only one possession, one thing I brought to this house. My folio of drawings. May I get it?"

Dr. Cole frowned, then turned and quickly descended the steps until he stood on level ground with her. Pressing her lips together, her belly writhing like a pit of serpents, Darcie lifted her eyes up to meet his questioning glance.

He didn't appear angry, she noted with surprise, only puzzled. "You wish to retrieve your folio of drawings? To what purpose?"

"To take with me when I go."

"Where are you going?" There was genuine confusion in his tone, along with a subtle thread of impatience.

Darcie watched him warily. Was he truly insane? she wondered, not for the first time.

"Where should I go but out on the street?" she replied, forcing herself to maintain eye contact, rather than obey the nearly overwhelming urge to drop her head and peek at him through sidelong glances as was her wont.

"What do you need from the street?" His annoyance was more apparent now. He made a slight impatient gesture with his hand. "It can wait. I have need of you now. Come along."

He began to ascend the stairs once more, then stopped abruptly. Turning, he spoke to Poole.

"Poole, I trust I can leave it to you to find a replacement maid-of-all-work. Darcie no longer serves in that capacity."

Drawing himself up, Poole smirked with oily superiority. "Of course, sir."

Darcie glanced at the other servants. None met her gaze, but she could feel their compassion rolling from them in waves. Suddenly, Mary looked at her and sent her a wavering smile meant to reassure.

"One can hardly have Finch continue in her present position after what you have discovered, sir." Poole spoke the words softly, but with pointed venom that ate through Darcie's defenses.

Please don't let me cry, she thought. *I'll have an eternity for tears later.*

"No, she cannot continue in her present position," Dr. Cole agreed, shaking his head slowly. "There must be dozens of girls eager to earn an honest wage. I'm sure you'll have no trouble finding another to take her place." He slanted an enigmatic glance at Poole. "We seem to lose our maids at an alarming rate. Try to find one that will last more than a few weeks."

"I'll see to it immediately, sir."

"Good." Turning to Darcie, Dr. Cole made a beckoning gesture. "Come with me. Now that I have seen the evidence . . ."

The word made Darcie cringe inwardly, her heart heavy as she waited for him to cast her out.

". . . I can hardly keep you on as a maid-of-all-work," Dr. Cole pronounced. "It would be a terrible waste of your talent. Talent that I have need of, given that my own skill as an artist is abysmal."

She heard the unified gasps of the other servants even as the meaning of Dr. Cole's statement sank into her benumbed mind. As she turned her head, her glance collided with the butler's. His face was impassive, but high color marked his cheeks.

Darcie whirled back towards the doctor, and her arm inadvertently knocked at a vase of spring flowers set on the table by the stairs. Horrified, she found herself caught in the endless mortification of the moment. Just a second too slow, her hands grasped empty air as the porcelain vase crashed to the floor, splintering into a multitude of razor-sharp fragments.

Her stomach pitched and dropped, followed by a hideous wave of nausea that clawed its way into her chest. She heard Dr. Cole take a step forward and her head snapped up, one arm rising reflexively to shield her face, half expecting him to land a backhanded blow. Even a man who seemed kind could be driven to fits of temper. But there was no blow. The doctor stood over her, his expression calm and mildly expectant.

"I'm sorry," she whispered desperately, crouching beside the ruined porcelain, grasping the pieces frantically, with only a fraction of the attention the task required.

"Leave it," he commanded, even as a sharp sliver sliced into the tender fleshy mound at the base of her thumb.

Blood welled from the wound, dripping to the floor and swirling in a wild pattern through the puddle of water that pooled on the marble tile. She stared in horrified fascination, mesmerized by the eddy of dark red that crept in an ever widening pattern, becoming paler and paler as it mixed with the water covering the floor.

Soundlessly, he came to her. She sucked in a startled breath as Dr. Cole's firm grasp circled her wrist and he drew her damaged hand upward, pressing a white handkerchief against the wound. Staring at the doctor's long lean fingers holding the cloth firmly to her hand, Darcie frowned at the blood welling from the cut, staining the pristine fabric with a dark blotch. Unbidden, Mary's words about the bloody handkerchief she had found in his study and the macabre suspicions she harbored seeped into Darcie's thoughts.

Resolutely, she pushed them aside. Her situation was tenuous enough without adding Mary's suppositions and fears to her load.

"Here. Press firmly against the cut." Pulling her gently to her feet, Dr. Cole suited action to words, drawing Darcie's free hand from her side and positioning her fingers so she could do as he instructed. With one hand cupping her elbow, he guided her toward the stairs. Stunned, unable to assimilate the events of the morning, she allowed him to lead her, a sleepwalker directed by his touch.

On an afterthought, Dr. Cole paused, speaking over his shoulder without turning. "Poole, see to the mess," he said brusquely. "And see that we are not disturbed."

Darcie sat alone in Dr. Cole's study, her thoughts in turmoil, edgy uncertainty confounding her. He had excused himself to fetch bandages from his surgery on the main floor of the house, leaving Darcie to her own devices. Sinking into a leather chair in front of the doctor's desk, Darcie found her eyes drawn to the gilt-framed miniature that sat in a place of honor, the girl's face reflected in the polished wood. She wondered again who the woman was—obviously someone greatly beloved by Damien Cole. At the thought, a strange spasm in the region of her heart pricked her and brought the unwelcome sting of tears to her eyes. She pressed her fingers against the cloth she held to her wound, blinking against the droplets that clung to her lashes. Clearly she was overwrought. What other explanation could there be for her lamentation over nothing more than a portrait?

Her attention shifted away from the picture, back to the sketchbook that had brought her to this pass. It lay on the desk, the pages open to the very drawing she had tampered with. The soft snick of the door closing alerted her to Dr. Cole's return.

He moved to her side, his warm hands gentle as he dressed the cut on her hand, wrapping it in fresh gauze and tying off the bandage with a small, neat knot. "Not as deep as I first thought," he observed. "The bleeding has already stopped."

His grasp was firm, gentle, and she realized that her hand still rested in his. "Thank you," she said and made to rise, but he rested one hand on her shoulder, holding her in place.

"You are welcome." Reaching across the desk, he drew the sketchbook closer, turning it so they both had a clear view of Darcie's drawing.

"Can you do this again?" He pulled a chair next to hers, and sat in it, leaning close to examine the drawing before them.

Nodding in answer to his question, Darcie closed her eyes, inhaling the clean male scent of him. He smelled like . . . like summer! What an odd notion. Still, the comparison was apt. She could feel the warmth of his leg where it pressed against hers, feel the heat of him through the cloth of his trousers, through the layers of her petticoat and skirt. Swallowing, she shivered, though the room was warm.

He had rescued her. Again.

The thought made her oddly uncomfortable. She glanced at her bandaged hand. He had tended her wound. Darcie touched the base of her thumb, wondering why she felt both elated and appalled to have Damien Cole as her own personal savior.

"Is the pain very bad?" he asked, his breath fanning her cheek, rousing the strangest sensations in her breast.

"No." *Yes*, she longed to say. Yes, she felt pain. The pain of lost dreams. The pain of knowing that once, as a wealthy merchant's daughter, she might have sat next to this man at a soiree or country ball, flirted with him, danced with him. Now, she was reliant on his largesse, his tolerance in allowing her a place to stay, a means of support. Whereas once she might have dreamed of having him as her beau, now she was reduced to praying that he did not toss her out on the street. The enormity and poignancy of her loss nearly overwhelmed her. She pushed the feeling aside, disgusted by her own melancholy.

The fright of only moments ago, when she had imagined herself homeless and on the street, trapped once more in the horrible cycle of poverty from which she had escaped, was as fresh a wound as the one to her hand. Yet her thoughts fixed on Dr. Cole, on the dream, the fabrication, of what might have once come to pass. In some dark, hidden recess of her mind, she acknowledged that part of her fear had been based on the realization that once removed from this house, she would likely never see Damien Cole again. And that possibility did cause her pain.

"I noticed your scar." He touched the tip of his index finger to the puckered raised mark on her hand, rubbing it lightly as she was often wont to do. His finger traced the well-worn path. She drew a shuddering breath.

"It looks deep," he continued. "I'm surprised you suffered no permanent loss of function."

Shooting him a nervous glance, Darcie pulled her hand from his, burying it in her lap. Those memories were too private, too terrible to share.

She could feel him watching her. Measuring. Waiting.

"Secrets, Darcie?" he prodded gently.

Licking her lips, she stared, unseeing, at her clasped hands. Silence was her only defense against the concern in his tone, against the horror that lurked in her memories.

He drew back, as though acknowledging her need for distance, and turned his attention to the sketch on the desk, taking no obvious offense to her less-than-enthusiastic response to his subtle query. She supposed he was caught up in his own thoughts, his own vision, willing to let her secrets stay buried, amenable to turning their combined efforts to the task he wished her to undertake. Or was he simply a man who respected privacy?

Dr. Cole stroked his fingers over the sketch she had made.

"You see, I have no talent with charcoal, ink, or paint," he began. "My art lies in the ability to slice the specimen in such a way that in drawing it, the artist could truly represent the muscle, the sinew, the bone. Here." His finger moved across the book to the opposite page, to the ink sketch of a human foot. "It looks nothing like the foot I set out to draw. But you could be my hands. You could draw all that I wish to study. Make detailed diagrams of my dissections."

"I'm not certain that I can, sir," Darcie protested, her voice a mere notch above a whisper.

"Why ever not? You drew the leg. There's little difference between a leg or an arm or a foot, save the specifics. If you can draw one, I suspect you could draw any of them."

Shaking her head, Darcie tried to articulate her thoughts. The idea of standing next to him while he systematically dissected a body, expecting all the while that she would document the result of his actions, was an expectation she felt little able to live up to. She had heard that in Edinburgh, as well as London, some anatomists sold tickets to the spectacle of their dissections, as though it were a form of entertainment. The idea disgusted her. Frowning, Darcie struggled to find a way to clarify her concerns. In the end, she could not find the words to explain.

Dr. Cole rose and crossed to the window. Resting his shoulder against the frame, he pulled back the edge of the curtain and stared out toward the carriage house. At length, he spoke, uncannily voicing her thoughts aloud as though he sensed and understood her fears.

"You get used to it, Darcie. The bodies are a means to an end. They are the treasure chest just waiting to be unlocked. The knowledge buried inside is tremendous. . . ." He turned to face her. "They hold the key to life and death."

At his mention of a treasure chest, she thought of the two men from the previous night, dragging the trunk across the back drive to the carriage house laboratory. She shivered, forcing herself to push the thought aside and concentrate on the conversation at hand.

"Is that what you want, sir? To understand life?"

He did not answer right away, and in the silence she perceived his answer even before he spoke. She sensed the dark undercurrent of his thoughts, and the enormity of his meaning made her feel a new terror. Not the dread of being thrown on the street, or the fear of being cold and hungry and alone. She felt the trepidation of losing herself in Damien Cole's quest.

"Life, Darcie?" he asked softly, his voice threading silkily over her senses. "I have little interest in the secrets of life. I leave that to rash young scholars and fools."

Darcie's breath hung frozen in her throat. She knew what he would say next. She knew.

"I want to know death. For in knowing the enemy, I may find a way to cheat it."

Simple words, spoken in the same tone that he might say he wished for sunshine, or balmy weather. A cold flame flickered in the center of her heart. Yet, despite the deep foreboding that permeated her mind, she would not deny him.

He had offered her a life. She would help him seek the secrets of death. A reasonable exchange.

Looking up she met his eyes, searched the bleak landscape of his controlled gaze, and suddenly she knew that the barricades erected around his emotions were cast in iron, hewn of stone. She knew with certainty that the days and nights he spent barricaded in the carriage house, doing whatever terrible things he did behind the drawn shades and locked door, were the product of a battered and lost soul.

The weeks passed, and the days began to meld together until she forgot whether it was Monday or Thursday, Friday or Sunday. Dr. Cole was not a harsh taskmaster, nor did he demand of Darcie that which he was not willing to do himself—though he harbored such enthusiasm for his topic that he often forgot to sleep or eat. Hence, Darcie, who was by necessity following his schedule, found herself eating dinner at midnight or sleeping until noon.

They worked together, side by side, his thigh pressed tight against hers, the callused tips of his fingers brushing her hand, his chiseled lips inches from her own. And all the while he was respectful and kind, seemingly unaware of the desperate twinge of adoration that flickered, then roared within her aching heart. At least, it seemed that he was unaware of her the majority of the time, yet there were those occasions when she caught him watching her with an intensity that was both frightening and alluring, his eyes gliding over her like liquid silver, leaving her feeling shaken and breathless.

For endless hours, Darcie drew and redrew better versions of the sketches that filled endless books, pictures that Dr. Cole had drawn, but which had failed to capture his vision of anatomy. More than once he derided his lack of artistic skill. More than once he praised hers, sending a warm glow cascading through her veins.

In time, Darcie became inured to the images on the pages. No longer did they represent pieces of a broken body. She began to see Dr. Cole's perspective, to share his conception of their beauty. Yet, every so often, she would remind herself that there was a great deal of difference between making sketches of Dr. Cole's drawings and actually coming in contact with human remains. She was undecided as to whether or not she would be able in reality to draw an original specimen.

Having worked particularly late the previous night, Darcie came to the study one morning, yawning, covering her mouth with her palm.

"Good morning, Dr. Cole," she said, pausing in the doorway, watching as he finished an informal breakfast of bread and cheese.

He looked up. "Damien."

Darcie blinked at his abrupt tone. "Excuse me, sir?"

"No more 'sir' and 'Dr. Cole.' My name is Damien. Given that we spend hours together each day, and given that I have been calling you 'Darcie' for weeks, I believe that the use of my name would be more appropriate."

Drawing a deep breath, she hovered in the doorway, uncertain of how to proceed. In her mind, she had called him by his name more than once. In whispers, in the dead of night, she had spoken those treasured syllables, caressing the sound like a precious thing. *Damien.* But, to say it out loud and in his presence . . . that was another matter entirely.

Ignoring her incertitude, or perhaps not recognizing it at all, the doctor rose, folding a cloth serviette around a roll and some cheese.

"You can eat on the way." He gestured for her to precede him out the door.

Darcie hesitated, pressing her lips together.

"On the way, sir?"

He fixed her with a stern look.

"Damien," he prodded. "Say my name, Darcie. I promise it will pain you less than you imagine."

The side of his mouth curved slightly, accentuating the dimple in his cheek. Darcie felt that strange sensation, the tightening in her chest that she felt so often when he was near. Oh, she loved the sight of that too infrequent smile.

"On the way to where . . . Damien?"

He stared at her for a protracted moment, his eyes darkening. Darcie shivered, darting her tongue across her lower lip, feeling uncertain and fluttery.

"There. You said my name. You see? It was not so difficult." His voice rolled over her, low and rough, and she felt as though each syllable touched her.

Drawing a shuddering breath, she watched him, caught in the snare of his magnetic gaze. He cast a glance at her lips, and unwittingly she followed his lead, her own eyes drawn to his mouth, to the hard, firm line of it. What would he taste like? The thought whispered in her mind, snaking insidiously through her body, making it thrum with a strange longing.

With a small gasp, she stepped back, and her movement seemed to pull Dr. Cole from whatever contemplation had occupied him. She felt an odd sense of loss as he turned away.

Handing her the cloth-wrapped bundle of food, he put his palm against the small of her back. Darcie felt the warmth of his hand through the fabric of her dress. At his silent urging, she preceded him into the hallway and down the stairs, aware that he had not answered her question, and that she was as yet unenlightened as to their destination.

They rode in the same carriage that she had arrived in those many nights past. The side shades were pulled up, letting the light of day stream through the windows. And they were alone on this ride. To Darcie's boundless relief, no dead man shared the conveyance with them.

"Where are we going, sir?"

In response to Darcie's query, Dr. Cole merely turned his head and stared at her intently. Seconds passed, and still he did not respond.

Darcie licked her lips nervously. "Where are we going, *Damien?*"

He smiled, and she thought the sun had surely grown brighter.

"We go to Whitechapel." He gestured to a flat case on the floor. "I have brought supplies, and I would like you to sketch the human form."

Whitechapel. The East End. A part of her had hoped that she would never return there. The remainder of his explanation registered—the plan to sketch the human form—and Darcie swallowed at the thought of being so close to a dead body. The time of reckoning had come and she wasn't at all certain that her nerves would prove worthy of the challenge, but she intended to try her best. In fact, a small part of her was profoundly interested, curious about the reality of human anatomy. During the past weeks, she had done more than just copy pictures. She had begun to learn what those pictures represented, to memorize the strange and fascinating words that anatomists used to describe the body.

Each muscle had its own name. *Peroneus tertius. Scalenus anticus. Opponens pollicis.* She had mixed emotions about her new and unusual position as assistant to an anatomist, entranced by the subject even as she was repelled by the thought of watching the dissection of human remains.

"I hope I shall be up to the task," Darcie murmured.

"Why would you not be?" Damien frowned. "Ah, because the woman will be unclothed, you mean? Well, you are a woman yourself. There will be no surprises."

Darcie stared downwards as the fingers of her right hand closed around those of her left, clasping and unclasping with nervous energy. So the body was that of a woman. . . . Old? Young? Diseased? Or dead by some terrible accident? She conjured all manner of dreadful thoughts.

"Darcie," Damien said softly, "I would prefer that you look at me while we speak. I find it disconcerting to engage in conversation with the top of your head."

Startled, she glanced up, meeting his gaze.

"I'm sorry," she whispered. "One's life tends to shape one's habits."

"And what has happened in your life that makes you cling to shadows and view the world through indirect glances?"

Unconsciously she rubbed the tips of her fingers over her scar, silently marveling that he had noticed, so much about her. Her heart sped up—*kathump, kathump*—the rhythm loud and frantic in her ears. She didn't want to talk about Steppy, about what had become of her life after her stepfather's ships went down, one after the other, taking her hopes, her dreams, a piece of her soul to the depths of the ocean. Once she had been a girl, warm and loved, with a future, or so she had thought. That was a memory from a long-ago time, before her mother died, before her stepfather's fortune sank to the bottom of the unforgiving Atlantic. For a time, she had held fast to her dreams, and then she had woken and faced the reality of her nightmare.

"Nothing happened." She chewed her lower lip.

Damien's eyes glittered as he watched her. "We all have our secrets," he mused softly. "Who am I to demand the confessions of your soul?"

His words sent a strange vibration through Darcie. *Who was he to demand her confessions?* "I have no confessions to make."

He said nothing to that and looked up, his gaze focused out the window. "We have arrived."

Opening the door, he stepped from the carriage and then turned to help her down. Not for the first time, Darcie marveled at the courtly manners he showed her, as if she were more than a maid, elevated to the level of assistant in his employ. He showed her courtesies fit for a lady of standing, the lady she might have been, once.

She stepped from the carriage into the narrow street. The rank smell of poverty struck her. They had arrived, indeed. Whitechapel. She had lived here, on these streets, and survived by some miracle. Unpleasant memories flooded her, leaving her gasping for breath.

Damien reached past her and retrieved the case of artist's materials from the floor of the coach, along with his black leather physician's bag. His actions returned her to the present, beating back the disagreeable recollections that tugged at her.

"Return for us at three o'clock, John," he said to the coachman. Taking her arm, he led Darcie around the back of the carriage and through a narrow alleyway.

They walked for a bit before Damien drew her to a doorway. Suddenly, Darcie balked, her feet freezing in place, her entire body straining away as she recognized the house he had brought her to. Her pulse began to race as she turned her head to look at him. Damien returned her gaze, confusion evident in his expression. Then slowly, like the sun rising over a hill, understanding dawned.

"I hadn't thought . . ." he began. "That is, I *had* thought that with Mrs. Feather being your sister, you would not be adverse to working here at her house, but if you find the concept so offensive, we could fetch her and take her elsewhere."

Darcie shook her head rapidly back and forth, her heart wrenching in her breast as she stared at the door they had arrived at, a door she had thought never to return to. Mrs. Feather's House.

Oh, please, not Abigail. Let the dead woman they had come here to draw not be Abigail.

She could feel Damien's hand cup her elbow, steadying her.

"Is she—" She swallowed against the knot of dread that clogged her throat. "Is the dead woman Mrs. Feather?"

CHAPTER FIVE

"Tell me," Darcie repeated. "Is the dead woman Mrs. Feather?"

Damien stared at her oddly, as though she were speaking in a language unfamiliar to him. Then his brows rose in surprise and the corner of his mouth lifted slightly.

"There is no dead woman, Darcie. Only a live one. I want you to draw a live woman. Her leg, to start with. She has a fetid carbuncle that I've come to drain and I want you to document it, a record of sorts. In payment for my medical services, she's agreed to let you sketch her form."

"Sketch her form?" Darcie echoed uncertainly. "Unclothed?"

"Yes." He made an unconscious gesture with his hand. "I hardly require a drawing of a clothed woman."

"Oh," she said, vaguely disconcerted by the thought of being in a room with Damien and a naked woman.

"Darcie, have you seen the works of the many artists who have documented medicine throughout history? Da Vinci. Rembrandt. Hans Holbein. Though art and healing appear two disparate fields, they are in fact in perfect complement with each other." He gave a self-deprecating shrug. "Unfortunately, I was born with talent for only one. You will be my hands, documenting the lesion both before and after treatment."

Darcie looked away, her gaze roaming the dirty street; a lumpy form huddled in the shadows at the end of the roadway—a man or woman with no place to call home, sleeping in the paltry protection of a doorway. Her gut twisted. She had slept there not so very long ago. "You are kind to come all this way to treat her. I doubt that there are many physicians who would venture here. A West End surgery is the goal of most."

"Kind? An odd choice of words." Damien shrugged lightly at her observation. "I'd wager that some would venture here readily enough at night."

She made no reply. Likely, his statement was neither more, nor less, than fact. Had *he* come here at night, to her sister's den of debauchery? she wondered forlornly.

"I vowed that I would never return here." So she had promised her sister that night so many weeks ago.

At her softly uttered statement, Damien raised a brow and something hard flickered in his eyes. "So, once, did I," he stated enigmatically, leaving her wondering when, and why, he had made such a vow. "People have a habit of changing their minds."

Lifting his hand, he rapped sharply on the door. A woman answered, her eyes rimmed with smudged kohl, her fine hair falling in tumbled disarray, the pale skin of her body barely covered by the hastily donned dressing gown. She was a small woman, with delicate features and a sweet smile.

Darcie felt bile rise in her throat. A girl. She was barely more than a girl. Working here in this terrible place.

"Dr. Cole," the girl greeted him respectfully, tugging on her dressing gown and covering herself as best she could. "Everyone's still asleep, but we can work in my room if we're quiet."

"That will be fine, Sally," he said, motioning Darcie to precede him through the doorway as the girl stepped back to allow their entry. "This is Darcie Finch. She's come to draw you."

Sally frowned, then her soft brown eyes widened in shock after a brief moment of contemplation. She looked Darcie up and down, examining her as though she were something very interesting indeed.

"Darcie Finch!" she exclaimed. "But you were here before. I remember, 'cause it was the night Lord Albright—" The girl broke off abruptly, sending a quick glance in Damien's direction. "Well it was the night that one of our regular gentry was last here. We had a spot of trouble with him, and he hasn't been back since. I'm the one who answered the door that night, the one who fetched Mrs. Feather. Do you recall? You were so skinny and wet, looking like some half-dead thing the night dragged in. You don't look anything like that now! Why, you're fair pretty!"

Darcie opened her mouth to speak, but could think of no reply. She had known that her form had filled out a bit since she had entered Dr. Cole's employ—regular meals could do that for a body. And she knew, too, that her cheeks boasted a bit of color . . . but it had been a very long time since she had thought of herself as pretty. Pretty had mattered in the life she had lived long ago. It hardly mattered now.

Embarrassed, she glanced at Damien and found him watching her, his eyes focused on her with the same intense regard that she had seen more than once of late. Something in the way he looked at her made her think that he agreed with Sally's comment, and that he, too, thought she was "fair pretty." The realization brought a hot blush to her cheeks. Pressing her lips tightly together, she looked away, focusing her attention on the floor. Her heart thumped steadily in her breast, each beat pounding in her ears.

"Well, don't stand there all day," Sally said, pulling the door wide and stepping back so they could enter.

Silently she led them up the narrow staircase to her room on the upper floor. "All the girls are asleep," she whispered, softly closing the door to her bedroom.

Darcie scanned her surroundings as unobtrusively as possible. The room was small, dominated by an enormous bed draped with heavy cream-colored velvet curtains. The walls were painted a garish shade of dark red, making the bed seem all the more conspicuous with its pale linens and curtains.

"Sally, we'll need some fresh water." Damien

spoke quietly as he put the case of artist's materials at the foot of the bed and his black leather surgeon's bag beside it. "And soap, Sally. I'll need some soap."

As the girl ducked out to do his bidding, Darcie moved to the foot of the bed and retrieved paper and charcoal from the case. Perching on the small chair angled in the corner, she began to sketch with practiced ease. A hand emerged on the paper, and beneath it, a tabletop boasting an orderly arrangement of knives, scissors, and tongs, a pile of clean white linen strips, and a small brown bottle.

In short order, Sally returned with a pitcher of water and some soap. Damien washed his hands slowly and carefully.

"I shall tell you one secret of death, Darcie," he said as he rinsed his hands. "Dirt on my hands or my tools can cause disease in the wound, for the dirt harbors the nature of contagion."

Darcie frowned. How odd. She remembered the physicians who had attended her mother. None had ever washed their hands before examining her.

Dr. Cole turned to Sally where she reclined against the multitude of pillows. He pulled aside her dressing gown and Darcie stared at the large red wound that marked the girl's thigh. It looked so painful.

"I'm sorry for it, Sally my girl, but this will hurt more than a bit," Damien said as he gently probed the open and oozing sore.

"It'll hurt more if you don't fix it and the poison seeps into my blood," Sally piped up good naturedly, but her voice was strained, and Darcie watched as the color slowly leached from her cheeks. "I'd rather have it hurt now, than end up needing the leg sawed off."

Turning to a fresh page, Darcie began a new sketch.

"See here, Darcie." Damien pointed to the large pustule and the angry red streaks that radiated from it. "The disease has spread to the subcutaneous tissue. Draw it carefully, for when next I examine Sally's leg, your sketch will serve as a comparison."

Darcie had no idea what he meant by subcutaneous tissue, but she could see that the skin of Sally's thigh was red and swollen and looked terribly painful.

"Sally, I'm going to incise it now and drain it. It'll hurt like the blazes," Damien warned.

Sally nodded, fisting her hands in the covers at her sides.

Quickly finishing the drawing of the pustule, Darcie waited as Damien lanced the lesion, then with rapid strokes, she sketched what she saw.

"All done now." He wrapped his used tools in a square of linen.

"Wasn't so bad." Sally grimaced.

Damien opened his black leather bag and removed a jar full of what appeared to be grayish green slime. With gentle hands he washed the area he had just lanced, then opened the jar.

"Are those leeches?" Sally asked shrilly, forgetting to whisper as she stared at the jar in disgust.

"No." Damien shook his head and laid a reassuring hand on Sally's arm. "I told you before, Sally. I don't use leeches, and I don't bleed my patients."

Darcie's head jerked up in surprise. Not bleed his patients? She had never heard of such a thing. Her mother had been bled until Darcie thought that all her blood had pooled in the dishes at her bedside and that none remained to course through her veins. "Why ever not?" she blurted.

Damien glanced at her. "I cannot see the benefit in drawing the life blood from one who is ill."

"But does the bloodletting not draw the evil humors from the body?" she asked, frowning.

"Evil humors," Damien repeated her words. "I have yet to see an evil humor, to touch one, to feel one. No, Darcie. My opinion of the nature of disease and contagion goes against popular theory." He looked back at Sally, who watched them wide-eyed, apparently confused by the exchange. "We can revisit this issue later. For now, let us proceed."

Removing some of the green slime from the jar, he placed it on Sally's wound. She watched him warily, but made no protest.

Though she sat nearly three feet from the bed, Darcie could smell the fetid odor of the concoction. It smelled like something rotten. "What *is* it?" she whispered.

"Bread rot. An old Irish woman imparted the secret to me. Some called her a witch." Damien paused, his gaze fixed on the far wall, clearly lost in a distant memory. Then he shook his head and continued. "I called her a healer. A wise woman. A friend. She knew much about the care of the sick, and she graciously shared some of her knowledge with me before she died. One of the things she gave me was this jar, as well as instructions to feed it periodically."

"Feed it?" Sally squawked, recoiling from Damien's touch.

Saying nothing, Darcie grimaced, her own disgust mirroring the emotion evident in Sally's expression.

Damien quirked a brow. "Just some crusts of bread," he said dryly. "Not blood or body parts."

Sally grimaced, clearly unimpressed by Damien's wit. But Darcie couldn't help the tiny smile that tugged at the corner of her mouth. He saw it and winked at her. Winked at her! Darcie pressed her lips together and lowered her head, pretending interest in her drawing. But that wink had sent a song soaring through her heart, for it implied an intimacy, a kinship that was warm and welcome.

"Speaking of body parts," Sally said, her voice dropping to the softest whisper. "There's been another killing."

Darcie looked up, her attention caught. Her heart gave a hard kick and her mouth felt suddenly dry. Another killing. She noticed that though Damien's hands stilled for a fraction of a second, he made no other outward indication that he had heard Sally's words. She hoped that she had not given away her own distress.

"There was old Marg a couple of months ago. Cut up something awful, they said," Sally continued. "Then the old man, but I think he might not have been killed by the same person." She emphasized her conjecture with a nod. "Cause all the others have been women, and he was the only man. Besides, nothing was taken."

"Taken?" Darcie croaked.

Sally nodded. "Each one had a piece missing.

Except the old man. The first girl was slit open stem to stern, and her female insides were gone, if you know what I mean."

Darcie felt the raw acid of horror claw up her throat. She had heard of the Whitechapel murders. Who could live on these streets and not hear of the killings? But she had never heard about body parts being taken, and the thought of it made her ill.

"They say he must be a doctor," Sally continued. "All his cuts are clean and sure, like he knows what he's doing."

For some inexplicable reason, Darcie thought of the two men and the heavy chest—the delivery she had witnessed when she had first arrived at the house on Curzon Street. Her gaze shot to the doctor's broad back. Looking up, he turned and caught her staring at him. His eyes were bleak and cold, his expression chilly as ice-kissed granite.

He knows, she thought. He knows something about those women. As quickly as the idea skittered across her mind, she thrust it aside, giving herself a mental shake. Oh, God! The terrible irony of it. She had no right to wonder what he knew, when she herself knew more than she should. The old man, the dead old man . . . Steppy.

"All done." Damien finished winding the bandage around Sally's thigh. Excusing herself to go to the water closet, Sally rose unsteadily and limped from the bedroom, leaving them alone.

Raising her head, Darcie watched as Damien poured fresh water over his hands, then slowly worked the soap between his long lean fingers. An inexplicable warmth washed over her, suffusing her limbs, and even the breath of air she drew into her lungs. Unable to look away, she stared at Damien's hands, his strong, masculine hands, as he poured more water to rinse away the soap. She wondered what it would feel like to have those hands on *her* thigh, touching *her* skin. She could almost feel the glide of them, wet and slick with soap, moving over her in a silky caress.

Startled by the bizarre turn of her thoughts, Darcie jerked her head back, blinking rapidly as she tried to push away the image of Damien Cole's hands on her body.

There was something terribly wrong with her. How could she listen to the terrible description of the Whitechapel murders in one instant and then lust for Damien's touch the next? For that was what it was. Lust. A desire to feel his hands on her, his lips on her, his body pressed to hers.

What depravity had overtaken her, that she would imagine this man taking liberties with her person? That she would find the image appealing? Darcie sank her teeth into her lower lip, frightened by the nature of her thoughts, alarmed that she would have such thoughts here, in this den of iniquity, where Sally had so recently sprawled nearly naked on the bed.

Ah, but perhaps that was her answer. Here in this place where life had soured and death waited somewhere in the alleyways outside the door . . . rules were different here.

Suddenly, Damien turned and met her gaze, as though he had sensed the inexplicably charged current that passed between them. With slow, precise movements he rubbed his hands on a clean towel, drying them. Tension pulled at the sensual line of his mouth.

Darcie swallowed, her gaze caught by his.

His eyes darkened, and he took a single step forward. *He was going to kiss her.* The thought pounded through her brain, tantalizing her.

"Y-you were kind to c-care for her," she stammered, desperate to break the frightening spell that wove about her senses like smoke curling from a flame.

"Was I?" His voice was rich and low. He tossed the towel on the table, his eyes never leaving hers.

Darcie held her breath, suspended in an agony of uncertainty. Unfamiliar emotions clawed at her. She opened her mouth to speak, to cry out in protest, or perhaps it was to beckon him nearer. She felt ashamed by her overwhelming attraction to him, appalled that she could feel such need here, in this place. Stunned by the intensity and rapidity of her reaction, she tried to sort out the disparity of these feelings against the backdrop of Mrs. Feather's House. Darcie cried out softly. It was a sound of confused despair.

She heard the soft click of the door as Sally returned. Abruptly, Damien turned away, his expression rapidly shifting. Gone was the heated regard, replaced by an expression of studied civility.

Darcie breathed a shallow sigh at the interruption. *If this was relief,* she wondered as she watched Damien clean and pack away his surgical tools, *why then did it feel so much like disappointment?*

* * *

"Mary, tell me about the maid who left." Darcie sat cross-legged on her bed running a brush through her dark hair. The day had been a long one, and the muscles of her lower back felt tired from the hours she had spent hunched over her sketch pad, drawing and redrawing her illustrations.

"Janie?" Mary asked, her voice hushed. "She just up and disappeared."

"Where did she go?" Darcie began to plait her hair into a single thick braid.

Mary shook her head and lowered her voice even further, as though afraid that the walls might have ears. "None of us knows. She was a nice girl. Her parents died of the pox, and her brother's wife wanted no part of her care. So she went into service. This house was her first place." She looked nervously towards the closed bedroom door. "And maybe her last."

Darcie raised her brows but made no comment on Mary's suspicions. In the weeks she had been at Curzon Street, she had come to know the other woman well enough to acknowledge her penchant for the melodramatic. "Were you friends?"

"We were friends. Like I said, she was a nice girl. Never talked much about her past, except to say that her brother's wife didn't 'ave much use for her. Still, I'd 'ave thought she'd at least take the time to say good-bye to me." Mary pursed her lips. "Unless she never had the chance."

She rose and crossed to the fire, using the poker to stir the glowing embers. A thoughtful frown creasing her brow, she turned back to face Darcie.

"You know, it was the day that she left that I

found the bloody handkerchief I told you about. The doctor, he left before dawn that morning. I know because I heard a strange noise and went to the window to see what it was about." Mary jutted her chin towards the small window above Darcie's bed.

As if in response to Mary's comments, the glass pane rattled and shook, buffeted by the wind. The two women exchanged a look as a jagged bolt of lightning sliced the darkness of the night sky.

"Storm's coming," Mary whispered, her face a pale oval in the dimness of the room.

"I have no fear of storms," Darcie said, thinking about the storms she had weathered, huddled in a doorway or a corner of an alley in Whitechapel. To face a bit of rain and thunder from the warmth of this chamber could hardly be viewed as a hardship. Returning to their earlier topic, she encouraged Mary to continue her story. "What did you see when you went to the window?"

"The noise drew me," Mary responded. "Janie wasn't in her bed. I kneeled there and looked out. It was dark, the first light just creeping into the sky." She paused, a faraway look in her eyes.

Darcie waited patiently for Mary to gather her thoughts.

"It was strange," Mary mused softly, resting her forefinger against her chin as she spoke. "Two men were dragging a chest across the cobbles."

Her interest snared by Mary's description, Darcie sat up straighter. "Two men?"

"Mmmm. A tall, skinny one and a short fat one. I couldn't see their faces."

Nibbling on her lower lip, Darcie clasped her

hands together in her lap. "They were carrying a chest?"

"No." Mary shook her head. "Not carrying. I think it was heavy. Looked to be, anyway, 'cause they were pushing at it and pulling on it, dragging it from the carriage house—"

"*From* the carriage house?" Darcie interrupted. When she had seen them, they'd been dragging the chest *to* the carriage house.

Mary continued. "I watched them till they were out of sight. Then I saw the doctor come out of the carriage house. I sneaked down the stairs and watched him go into his study."

Darcie waited for Mary to finish the story, but her friend just sat on her bed, staring into space, her fingers splayed across her throat. There was something in her expression that made Darcie shiver.

"What happened then?"

Mary started at the sound of Darcie's voice. "He was there only a short time, Dr. Cole was, then he came out again, and I followed him down to the entry hall. Poole was nowhere in sight. The doctor let himself out, and I ran to watch him through the small front window that looks out onto the road. You know the one."

Darcie nodded.

"The doctor himself climbed up to the box and drove the carriage, no John Coachman in sight. It was that morning that I found the bloody hand-kerchief, tossed on the study floor beneath the desk," she whispered, her voice tight. "And Janie never came back to bed. Not that night or any other. I never saw her again."

"You can't think Janie was in the trunk?" Darcie exclaimed, running her palms up and down along her upper arms, vainly trying to vanquish the horrible chill that shot through her. "That Dr. Cole drove her away in the carriage?"

"I don't think anything." Mary hugged herself and looked away. "All I know is he was gone for a day and a night."

"But you do think something!" Darcie exclaimed as any number of scenarios and denials clambered through her brain. "You cannot mean to imply that Dr. Cole perpetrated some evil upon the girl?"

"I've nothing more to say." The window rattled wildly in its casing, caught in the fury of the burgeoning storm, and Mary's gaze darted frantically to and fro.

"Mary, please—"

Waving one hand back and forth, Mary shook her head, her eyes wide, the pupils dark, and Darcie read the panic in her gaze. With a sigh, she let the matter drop, unwilling to press her friend's fragile nerves any further. Clearly, she would get no more answers tonight.

In silence, the women slid beneath their coverlets. Darcie hoped that sleep would overtake her in short order, though all that Mary had told her jumbled her thoughts. Still, the day had been long and tiring, and her lids felt heavy, her eyes gritty. Rolling to her side, she closed her eyes and willed her breath to come slow and even, her mind to seek a calm place. But the lovely oblivion of sleep eluded her and she was left tossing restlessly about. Sleeplessness had become a regular routine, she thought ruefully.

With a sigh, Darcie threw back the sheets and swung her legs over the side of the narrow bed. Taking up her shawl, she wrapped it around her shoulders as she rose and tiptoed to Mary's bedside. The other woman was fast asleep, curled on her side, her hands tucked under her cheek. Treading silently, Darcie slipped from the room.

Eschewing the need for a candle, she proceeded down the stairs, feeling her way in the darkness, quiet as a wraith. A book, she thought. Surely Damien would have a book that she could read, something that would calm her, help her sleep. Perhaps a volume of poetry. He had told her that she might borrow anything that caught her fancy. With that in mind, she made her way in the direction of his study.

As Darcie rested her hand on the door handle, a soft tapping sound drifted upward from the lower floor, followed by the creaking of the stairs. Someone was coming. She slipped swiftly into the doctor's study, leaving the door open a crack, unwilling to come face to face with Poole at this late hour. Through the narrow opening she watched as a quiet shadow moved along the hallway.

Not Poole, she thought, for as the man passed the study doorway, she saw the golden strands of his hair. Damien. Her heart thudded as she watched him move past.

He carried no candle, making his way sure-footed in the darkness, until he reached the end of the hallway. He paused, and then entered his bedroom.

Pushing the study door fully open, Darcie slipped from the room and moved soundlessly along the hall until she reached the end. She flattened herself against the wall. He had left the portal slightly ajar and a thin finger of light cut the darkness, spreading across the soft carpet that covered the floor of the hallway. Looking down, Darcie realized that the carpet was a dark, rich red. She had never before noticed that it resembled the color of dried blood. A shiver coursed through her body, and she wondered at the source of her unease. She had walked this hallway dozens of times. There was nothing sinister here. Yet, despite the fact that she repeated the thought to herself over and over again, she could not quite convince herself of its veracity.

She meant to walk past Damien's doorway, ascend to her chamber, but as she hovered on the threshold, a movement from within caught her attention. Sidling closer, she found she could look into Damien's bedroom without being observed. He stood with his back to her, staring into the fireplace, his shirt pulled from the waistband of his breeches and hanging loose from his broad shoulders to his hips.

Suddenly, he turned. Darcie bit her lip hard to keep from making a sound. Damien stood, his head cocked slightly to one side, his eyes fixed on the door.

Oh, please don't see me, she thought with mortification. To be caught spying on him would be the worst humiliation. On the tail of that thought came the realization that during her brief glimpse of Damien something had been wrong somehow. There was something out of place. . . .

Daring much, she leaned forward a bit more, breathing a faint sigh of relief when she saw that he was no longer looking her way. Her eyes traveled the length of him, pausing as she registered the source of her puzzlement. Damien's white lawn shirt hung open, revealing the skin of his chest, his abdomen. The front of the once-pristine garment was spattered with dark blotches, irreparably stained. He looked as though someone had thrown a bottle of ink at him, the marks spreading across the white cloth. Except the stains were not the color of ink. They were the color of the hall carpet. The color of blood.

Darcie slammed her eyes shut against the sight of it, trying to block out the imaginings conjured by the sight of his bloodstained shirt. There was a reasonable explanation for this. He was a doctor. But even as she insisted to herself that the blood had come from a patient, or that the dark stains truly had some other, non-sinister source, she could not completely thrust aside the feeling of foreboding that rose within her.

As she stood shivering in the chilly hallway, her eyes closed, her ears tuned to the slightest sound, she could hear the frightful howling of the wind as it whipped against the windowpanes, rattling and shaking them with the greatest force. The storm had grown stronger, more restless, she realized. A great rumbling of thunder shook the heavens, the windows, perhaps even the walls, and the frenzied illumination of bolts of lightning sent flickering shapes and shadows across the floor.

Slowly, Darcie opened her eyes, peering hesitantly into the chamber once more. Damien had not moved. He stood, angled toward the doorway, and she watched, mesmerized, as he slowly, sinuously, drew the shirt from one shoulder and then the other. With a careless motion, he tossed it into the fire. She saw his actions, but though she realized that burning one's shirt was an exceedingly odd thing to do, her thoughts were distracted by the sheer splendor of him.

The glowing embers of the fire cast him in light and shadow. He stood, wearing only his breeches, and even those he had loosened so they rested low on his hips. Darcie stared in fascination at the hard planes of his naked chest, the supple ridges of his abdomen. Her mouth felt dry, and she licked her lips. Suddenly, she had the terrible, tantalizing thought that she'd like to lick him. To run her tongue over his flat male nipples, to follow the thin line of hair that ran down his belly to the open waistband of his breeches.

Wrenching her gaze away, she sank her teeth into her bottom lip, mortified by the brazen wantonness of her thoughts. But even as she admonished herself silently, she couldn't quell the urge to look at him again, to sate her desire for the sight of his glorious body, truly more beautiful than any sculpture formed by the greatest master.

When she looked into the room once more, she found that he had moved to the washstand. Lifting a folded linen cloth, he poured water from the pitcher to the basin. In silent fascination, Darcie watched as he dipped the cloth and ran it around the back of his neck then across the top of his chest. Beads of water glistened on his golden skin.

Again, he dipped the cloth in the basin. She could see his reflection in the large oval mirror that hung above the washstand. He ran the wet cloth down, over the ridges of his abdomen to the waistband of his trousers. Darcie swallowed, her blood pounding thickly in her veins.

Damien raised his head and looked into the mirror. Darcie's gaze met his in the silvered glass. Her mouth rounded in a silent cry, she stumbled back, unable to tear her eyes away.

He knew she was there. He couldn't help but know.

No, no, it was mere coincidence that he had glanced up, their eyes meeting in the mirror. She was well-hidden by the shadows. Wasn't she?

Horrified by what she had done—hovering in the hallway spying on her employer—and terrified of the possibility that she had been found out, Darcie turned and bolted back to her chamber, where she crawled beneath the sheets, tears of humiliation pricking the backs of her eyelids. She seemed to be making a terrible habit of this, she thought. Spying on Damien Cole, watching him from the shadows with the bewildered longing of a schoolgirl in the throes of her first infatuation. Imagining scenarios that she had no business considering. For shame.

Yet, despite her mortification, she could not deny that a part of her wanted to return to his chamber, to pull his mouth to hers and assuage the gnawing hunger that tugged at her breasts, her belly, the juncture of her thighs. She lacked experience, but life on the streets of Whitechapel had lent her knowledge of the reality of the joining between a man and a woman.

With a sob, she burrowed deeper beneath the covers, beating back the desperate need that she had allowed to surface. At length, she drifted into restless slumber, and dreamed that she lay with Damien in a field of flowers, wrapped in his ardent embrace. In her sleep she cried out as the bright blooms shimmered and smudged—their petals dripping from their stems—and the field turned to a sea of blood.

CHAPTER SIX

The next morning Darcie ate breakfast below stairs, though she had to force herself to choke down each bite, the oppressive atmosphere among the servants who gathered at the table reflective of her own glum mood. She tried to tell herself it was the weather, but her imagination whispered that they knew, each and every one of them, that she had slunk to Dr. Cole's room, watched him at his ablutions. Of course, the idea was ridiculous, but she could not seem to quell her guilty conscience.

Mary sat at Darcie's side, huddled into herself, her food ignored, grown cold on her plate. The little scullery maid, Tandis, was abnormally quiet, her sunny disposition eclipsed by the morning's gloom. Only Poole seemed immune to the sensation. He reigned at the head of the table like a king, carrying forkfuls of food to his mouth with obvious relish and impeccable manners. He applied his absurdly high standards even to himself.

Suddenly he turned his cold eyes on Mary,

studying her for a long, protracted second before focusing on his meal once more. Darcie felt a flicker of surprise as she thought she saw a softening of his expression as he stared at Mary. But, no. Poole was horribly hard on everyone. She must have imagined the momentary thawing of his icy demeanor.

Darcie looked away, turning her attention back to her own plate, mechanically moving eggs and bacon to her lips, her actions fueled by the memory of days of endless hunger when she had barely survived on the streets of Whitechapel. Never would she treat food with the innocent indifference she had shown during the plenty of her childhood. At last, the interminable meal was over, and she hurried to Damien's study.

She was apprehensive about seeing him after last night, but there was also a part of her that was hoping to lose herself in her work, and if she was honest, in the joy of his presence.

He was not there.

Pressing her fingers to the glass, she looked out into the gray morning. She wished that for once the sun would peek from behind the clouds to cast the world in bright light rather than sullen gloom. Her own face was reflected back at her, the glass turned into a mirror by the gray backdrop of cloudy sky. She looked wan, forlorn.

With a sigh, she turned away from the window and moved to the doctor's desk. He had made no mention of being away this morning, given no indication that this day would differ from the many they had shared recently. Tipping her head to the side, she shifted a pile of papers. There was no evidence of a note for her, nor an indication of any work that the doctor might wish to see completed. Darcie sank into the leather chair in front of the desk.

"Good morning."

She jumped at the softly spoken words. Leaping to her feet, she turned to find Damien, standing in the doorway. There were purple shadows beneath his eyes. Again he had not slept. She wanted to go to him, to run soothing fingers along his brow.

Striding forward, he moved to stand directly before her. Slowly, he reached out and crooked his index finger beneath her chin. His touch sent a frisson of electricity through her body.

He tipped her face upwards and stared down at her, his eyes searching hers. He knew she had watched him, secretly, longingly. She was convinced of it. Slowly, her gaze slid from his as riotous feelings and competing urges battled within her breast. At once, she longed to press herself against him, to feel the strength of his arms close about her, while at the same time she trembled with the desire to withdraw from his touch, to protect herself from the frighteningly magnetic pull he exerted on her.

"You look tired," he said, his finger still resting lightly on the underside of her chin. "Have I been working you too hard, then?"

His softly spoken observation was nearly her undoing, his consideration drawing her closer, tugging at her emotions. The room seemed to spin. Her breath came in harsh little gasps and her heart raced frantically as her gaze strayed to the sculpted line of his lips. She wondered what they would feel like if she touched them. Hard? Smooth? Soft?

One side of his mouth curved, revealing the dimple in his cheek. Lured by his beauty, Darcie balked. She ought to distance herself from him and the strange and frightening feelings he sent cascading through her like a fire in her blood. But the need to retreat was overwhelmed by a much stronger urge to lean closer, to breathe in the clean, fresh smell of him, to reach up and run the tip of her finger along the fullness of his lower lip, and set free the fire in her veins until it roared, an inferno out of control.

Oh, God! What was happening to her?

Darcie's gaze flew to his. He was watching her with an intensity that was simultaneously alarming and appealing. His eyes darkened, the centers dilating until they were deep, endless pools surrounded by a rim of molten silver.

"What is it about you that draws me?" he asked hoarsely, moving closer until just a whisper of air separated them.

His hand strayed from her chin to run softly along the line of her jaw, to slowly trace the column of her neck. His touch was featherlight, the callused tips of his fingers scraping gently against her tender skin.

Licking her lips, she exhaled a soft whoosh of air as his fingers slipped just beneath the collar of her high-necked gown and came to rest on her collarbone.

"What is it about you?" he whispered again.

Staring up at him, she felt the weight of his touch on her skin. She had no answer for his question, though she knew well what it was about him that drew her. The agony of her attraction was a painful need, tearing at her, flaying her sensibilities with sharp-edged talons. Damien Cole drew her, like a fly to flypaper, but once caught, would she be snared forever in his spell? Had she not learned her hard-won lessons? He was so beautiful, like an angel fallen from heaven. Her common sense warned that he was dangerous to her, and she knew she ought to heed her own warnings lest she find herself well and truly lost.

Her employment, her comfort, her safety all rested in his strong hands, just as Steppy had once held the reins of her life. She would do well to remember what she had learned from Steppy's betrayal, and from the wasted life a man had led her sister to.

Suddenly, the hand he rested on her neck felt heavy and strange, and a cold whisper chilled her heated emotions, snaking through her mind, drawing to the fore images of Damien's blood-drenched shirt. The thought jarred her from her stupor, and she jerked away with a small cry.

She looked up to find him watching her, his expression grown cold and remote. Abruptly he turned away, making a great show of arranging an already immaculate pile of documents on his desk into imaginary order.

His hand brushed the small miniature in the gilt frame. Darcie had seen it dozens of times, dusted it dozens of times, devoted a thousand minutes to contemplation of why the picture held a place of honor on Damien's desk. The pretty, dark-haired girl posed delicately for the artist, but the painter had only moderate skill, and though his brush had caught her beauty, he had painted her

as stiff and unyielding as a board, with little vibrancy
or emotion.

Damien picked up the miniature, stared at it.
Darcie thought she could feel the seconds crawl-
ing along her skin, so slowly did time seem to pass.

"I did not mean to cause you distress. A man
who forces his attentions on a woman is no man at
all." His hoarse voice broke the silence.

"You did not!" The words leaped from her
throat.

He turned his head, glancing at her as he raised
a questioning brow. "You hardly seemed to welcome my touch. Did I misread?"

Darcie stretched out her hand, palm up, in a
gesture of supplication. "I only meant . . . your attentions . . . you hardly . . ." Dragging a breath past
the constriction in her throat, she went on in a
rush. "You forced nothing on me. Did me no harm."

Even as she said the word, thoughts of the
bloodied shirt, and her suspicions as to its source,
coiled through her consciousness. He had done
her no harm, but had he harmed another? No,
she could not believe ill of Damien. She would
not. "Please, let us simply proceed with our schedule for the day." Her voice was small, tinged with
desperation. It was so hard for her to trust anyone,
and she so wished that she could trust him, her
glorious golden angel.

Turning the miniature in his hand, Damien returned his gaze to it once more, then slowly replaced it on the desktop.

"Who was she?" Unable to stop the question,
Darcie laid her hand lightly on his forearm. She

desperately wanted to know, while at the same time she abhorred the thought of having him confess his affection for another aloud.

"She was part of my foolish youth. She represents all I once was, but am no longer," he said solemnly.

"You loved her."

He nodded once, a curt movement of his head. "I did."

"Where is she now? Why is she not here with you?"

Damien shot her a measuring glance. "Has the mouse grown fangs?" he asked.

Darcie felt a blush heat her cheeks, and she ducked her head, unable to hold his gaze, yet unwilling to let the matter go. She wanted to know. She needed to know. A part of her wished that she *were* that girl, that she held a piece of Damien's heart.

"Did she marry another?" The question came out in a whisper, spoken to the floor.

There was a slight rustling sound, and then Damien's boots, polished with a glossy finish, moved into her line of vision. She stared at the tips of his toes, unable to meet his gaze.

"She never married. She was not asked. A terrible thing, is it not, when a woman is passed over, left unclaimed like unwanted baggage." His words were hard. Cold. But Darcie heard the underlying anguish and her heart constricted in her breast.

He loved her still, she thought, the unnamed woman in the picture. Somehow, though she knew neither his story nor his history, she suspected that he would love that dark-haired girl until the day he died. And the realization was poignantly wrenching.

Darcie glanced at the miniature, wondering why, if Damien loved that girl, he had not asked her to marry him. *Passed over. Left unclaimed.* Like Abigail. Yet another betrayal, this one of a young girl in a picture, a girl she did not know.

"Come," Damien said, abruptly changing the subject. "I have something to show you. It is the reason I was late this morning."

Always the gentleman, he waited for Darcie to precede him out the door. Together they descended the stairs. He led her to the back door, the one that opened onto the cobbled back drive.

Exiting the house, they walked side by side to the carriage house. Darcie held her breath as he unlocked the door to his laboratory. At last, he would bring her to his lair.

Damien paused, resting his hands on her shoulders, turning her to face him. "I warn you, Darcie. What you see in this place may give you pause. But you are my hands, the extension of myself. I need to know that you can do what must be done."

Licking her lips, Darcie nodded. She would do what he willed. His words hovered around her heart like a bee near a flower. He had called her an extension of himself, though she doubted he had meant the words in any personal sense. She was an artist and he was not. She must not read anything special into his comment, Darcie reminded herself harshly.

He studied her face for a moment, then turned and led the way up the narrow wooden staircase to the upper floor of the carriage house. As they ascended, Darcie wrinkled her nose in distaste. There was a smell, like medicinal powders and alcohol and soap all mixed in one. But there was something more. Metallic and strong, the scent filled her nostrils.

"I have drawing implements here." Damien led her to a small, scarred wooden table that was pushed against the far wall, the one farthest from the main house.

The shades on the windows were drawn, and the room was dim and dull. Darcie stepped forward and stared down at the tabletop as Damien lit the candles of a large candelabrum set close at hand.

"Why don't we open the shades? Natural light is often best." Darcie reached for the shade as the harsh metallic smell of the room filled her lungs, and she thought that she would like to open the window as well. Her heart rate increased as she felt a sudden wave of inexplicable anxiety wash over her. She wanted to see the light of day. Suddenly, it seemed unbearably necessary for her to see the light of day.

Catching her hand, Damien pulled her away from the window. "No, don't open it. I want no prying eyes."

She tugged lightly on her hand, freeing it from his grasp, and allowed it to drop to her side.

"No prying eyes," she repeated softly.

"Here. Look." Damien stepped to the center of the room where a second table stood. This table was high and rectangular in shape. There were no chairs pulled next to it. Darcie thought it a strange piece of furniture, for it was long and narrow with a raised rim around the outer edge, and a hole at one end. Glancing down, she saw that there was a bucket placed on the floor beneath the hole, and it seemed that the smell she had detected earlier was wafting from that bucket, filling the air, making her feel faintly sick to her stomach.

Damien grasped the edge of a dark cloth that covered a small mound at one end of the table. Without further preamble, he tugged the cloth free of the mound and revealed a cone-shaped lump approximately the size of Darcie's fist.

Frowning, she stepped closer, uncertain of exactly what he was showing her. Then the smell hit her, like aged meat, tinged with the sickly sweet scent of blood.

With a gasp, she pressed the back of her hand to her mouth and stepped away. "What is it?"

"A heart. Draw it whole, then I shall dissect it, and we can see the inside, the valves, the septae, the chordae tendineae." He sounded quite pleased.

"A heart," she repeated woodenly, appalled at the thought. Then her common sense took hold. A heart, perhaps from a pig or a cow. Likely the cook was even now wondering what had become of the makings of a meal. Swallowing, she steeled herself and asked, "From the kitchen?"

He looked at her oddly. She had seen that expression before. It was the look he wore when she asked something he could not grasp, something he found inexplicably strange.

"From the kitchen?" he repeated questioningly, as though he was trying to place her question in some sort of intelligible context.

"From the butcher, then," Darcie muttered hopefully.

"No, not the butcher. I believe he is quite hale and hearty. Though he most certainly would not be if this was his heart," Damien replied.

"Ohhh," Darcie breathed the sound. "Then whose . . ."

"Does it matter?" He shrugged. Moving across the room, he dragged a chair closer. "Here. Sit."

"But the heart is h-h-human?"

"Yes, of course." He picked up a pair of tweezers and pulled at the surface of the heart, separating a layer of thin glistening tissue from what lay beneath. "See this layer? In fact it is not one, but three layers. The heart is protected by a three-layered sac. The pericardium." Glancing at Darcie, Damien gestured towards the pen and ink on the far table. "Come now. Make a quick sketch and then I will strip it away so you can draw the heart wall beneath. There is an area of necrosis at the tip of the left ventricle that I find particularly interesting. Then I shall hook it up to that apparatus"—he pointed to a series of hooks and wires that draped over the far end of the table—"and you can watch it beat."

"B-beat? But it's dead!" she squeaked, taking a small step sideways, and then another, her eyes never leaving the sight of the heart that sat, glistening wetly. "I thought—that is, I mean . . ."—she swallowed, then blurted—"it looks wet!"

"Well, it's fresh," Damien stated matter-of-factly.

"Fresh." She choked on the word. A fresh heart recently torn from a living, breathing being. No, she reminded herself. From a body; from one no longer of this world. Swallowing convulsively, Darcie fisted her hands in the material of her skirt, struggling to steady her nerves.

The room spun before her eyes. A crimson haze, as red as the stains she had seen on Damien's shirt the previous night colored her vision. The breakfast she had so stoically shoveled in was suddenly trying desperately to claw its way back out.

With a moan, she whirled and fled the doctor's laboratory, nearly stumbling as she clattered down the narrow wooden staircase in her haste to escape the terrible sight of the disembodied heart lying vulnerable, stripped bare on the cold hard table.

Leaning her forehead against the cool wall of the carriage house, Darcie dragged deep desperate breaths into her lungs, letting the fresh air wash away the stench of death and decay that soured her nostrils and filled her mouth with a bitter, metallic tang. She had made a fool of herself, she thought, fleeing the laboratory that way. Now that she was away from that room, standing in the midday sun that had finally peeked out from between the clouds, she felt silly. It should have come as no surprise that he wanted her to draw an actual specimen. She had known he was an anatomist, had been well aware that he carefully cut human bodies to pieces in order to study them. But faced with the reality of a heart, pulled from what had once been a live human being, she had crumbled.

Her heaving stomach had quieted some. She was no longer in danger of losing her breakfast. Well, at least that was something.

"Darcie."

She felt Damien's hand on her back even as he spoke her name.

"Not well-done of me, I'm afraid," he said ruefully. "Are you quite all right?"

"I'm fine." She sniffed. There had been no censure in his tone, only quiet concern. "I was overwhelmed for a moment." Turning to face him, she bolstered her courage and said, "I'm ready now if you wish to continue."

Staring down at her, his gray eyes slightly narrowed, he took a long moment to study her face. "You are white as a corpse."

She winced at his analogy. "Yes, I expect that I am. But it will pass. Come. We have a job to do." And with that she lifted her skirts and determinedly attempted to stride past him towards the laboratory stairs.

Damien raised his arm and pressed the flat of his palm against the wall of the carriage house, blocking her path, halting her in her tracks. She looked at the solid barrier of his arm, then turned her head towards her right shoulder and looked directly at him. The concern she read in his eyes stunned her.

"I'm fine," she said again. "Really. Fine."

"Fine is a terrible word," he replied carefully, his tone measured. "It can mean so many things, while meaning nothing at all."

Staring at the firm line of his lips, Darcie nodded. Oddly, she knew exactly what he meant. "Well, then I am wonderful, astounding . . . remarkable." Her voice rose to a higher pitch as she said the last word.

His eyes darkened as he took a step closer. She

let her head fall back and met his gaze. The warmth
of his body spanned the minimal distance between
them, sending tendrils of heat undulating through
her limbs.

"Remarkable. Yes, that describes you exactly."

Darcie opened her mouth to reply, but shut it
again without uttering a sound as his words penetrated her mind, and she realized exactly what he
had said. He found her remarkable.

She found him irresistible. She found him exciting, dangerous, and terrifyingly beautiful.

"Darcie." His voice was like melted chocolate
pouring over her. Rich and warm, flavored with
the promise of untold delight.

He took a single step towards her, bringing their
bodies flush against each other, leaving Darcie no
doubt that they had long passed the boundary of
acceptable interaction. With each shallow panting
breath, her chest brushed lightly against his, and
the tips of her breasts began to burn and ache,
sending heated sensations rioting through her belly
to the juncture of her thighs. She had a frantic
urge to press herself against him, to wriggle back
and forth.

A pleading sound escaped her lips. Floundering
in a tumult of novel perceptions and riotous emotions that was both thrilling and shocking, Darcie
latched onto a single thought. Retreat. The muscles of her legs quivered and shook, as though they
could no longer hold her weight. She reached
back, resting her palm on the solidity of the carriage house wall. With a sigh, she collapsed against
it, seeking support for her trembling limbs.

Damien watched her through eyes of molten silver, the heat in his gaze singeing her as surely as any flame.

With her quaking limbs supported by the welcome solidity of the wall, Darcie tried to get her ragged breathing under control. Oh, what was wrong with her? She wanted to flee, while at the same time she wanted to grab his waistcoat, twist the fabric in her hands and drag him full against her. She wanted—

"What is it you want, Darcie?" he asked, the words a direct reflection of her secret thoughts.

"I want . . ." Her gaze flicked to his lips once more. Full sensual lips formed in a firm masculine line. Her mind registered only a vague notion of what it was that she wanted; yet her body seemed to know exactly what it yearned for.

He closed the distance between them once more, standing close enough that she could see the fine lines that fanned from the corners of his eyes and count each individual lash. But he did not touch her.

Suddenly the answer came to her with the clarity of a revelation. The emptiness inside of her, the terrible, ever present loneliness seemed to dwindle in his presence. She longed to feel him reach out and pull her into himself, to have him heal the isolation, the desolation of her soul.

"Touch me." She whispered the thought aloud, only to wish she could call the words back. He was her employer. A man with infinite power over her life. Moreover, he had his own secrets, his own demons, tightly leashed.

He was a dangerous enigma. And she could never trust him.

She heard the harsh whoosh of his breath as it left his lips. Too late she realized what her whispered request had released. She had but a millisecond to assimilate the sudden flare of desire that hardened his features, and then he was there, crowded along her, his muscled body resting full against her breasts, her belly, her thighs, pressing her into the hard wall at her back.

His lips sought hers, and their mouths melded in a heated conflagration. The feel of his mouth on hers, the luscious caress of his lips, his tongue, robbed her of all vestiges of equilibrium. A sensation of liquid heat blazed at her core, threatening to consume her. Shifting slightly, he brought his knee between her thighs. Darcie whimpered against his mouth, clutching at the loose fabric of his shirt, pulling him closer still.

The pressure of his knee both soothed and fanned the fire. She moved awkwardly against him in a futile attempt to ease the terrible pressure that built inside of her.

Damien's fingers tangled in her hair, and he shifted above her, angling his head, taking her mouth now in hungry kisses, his tongue probing, withdrawing. Her only conscious thought was that she could taste him. At last. And he tasted better than fine wine or chocolate.

Their limbs tangled in her skirts. Darcie wished that she could be rid of the encumbering clothing. She could feel the solid thickness of his arousal rubbing against her. Of its own volition, her hand slid down over the side of his waist to the bone of his hip, then lower. She wanted to explore the length and width of him, to see him with her fingers, investigate him with her touch. The memory of how he had looked, shirtless, his breeches riding low on his hips, tantalized her.

Suddenly, she felt his fingers close around her wrist, stopping her exploration before it had truly begun. With a low chuckle that stroked her already sensitized nerves, he dragged her hand away from what it sought and arranged her arm so that it curved around his waist.

"I hadn't intended this," he muttered, resting his chin on the crown of her head, dragging in a ragged breath as he finished the sentence. "There is something about you, some intangible quality, that makes me forget who and what I am. You have a healing quality, Darcie. You calm even the darkest soul."

Darcie said nothing. She had no answer for his musings, no secret understanding of the blazing attraction that sizzled between them. He, too, made her forget, made her cast aside the memories of what had been done to her, made her dream the dreams of any young girl.

She was mortified. Painfully embarrassed. Secretly thrilled.

Uncertain of herself, she stared past him at the windowed back wall of the house on the opposite side of the drive, struggling for control. Suddenly, there was a movement in one of the upper windows, a flutter that she caught from the corner of her eye. There it was again. The curtain twitched.

They had been seen, she thought. By Mary? Oh, dear. Not by Poole. It would be terrible to have been seen by Poole.

"Damien." She tasted his name on her lips.

As if recalled to himself, he jerked away at the sound of his name, his hands hanging by his sides in a way that Darcie could only describe as forlorn. What an odd thought, she mused quizzically. Why would he be forlorn?

He looked at her as if seeing her for the first time.

"I'm sorry," he said stiffly. "It seems I have overstepped once more." So cold. So distant. So controlled. His protective armor was a wall of cool cordiality.

Darcie glanced up at the window where she had seen movement earlier. Now all was still.

Damien raised one hand, reaching out to run his finger along the curve of her cheek. Abruptly, he turned from her and led the way back to the laboratory. Only once did he pause on the stair to glance back at her, his expression unreadable, reflecting neither the heat of passion nor the warmth of affection.

"A wolf in sheep's clothing," he mused softly before continuing his ascent.

She had no idea what he meant. Did he mean to imply that she was the wolf hiding in the guise of a sheep? Or was he the wolf, waiting to pounce and devour her? The taste of him still on her lips, she found the thought of being devoured by him strangely alluring.

Climbing the narrow staircase behind him, Darcie stared up at Damien's broad back. She was bereft over the loss of the strange affinity that had overcome them, confused by his abrupt withdrawal. And in some distant recess of her mind she heard an imaginary whisper that warned of danger.

Hide in the shadows. Run, girl. Run. She could hear him. Steppy. Smell the scent of spilled liquor and rancid sweat. The glint of the knife. The pain of betrayal. Danger. Danger. The eternal, terrible memory of a man who became something other than what he had always seemed, other than what he should have been. And then the memory of Damien, the first time she had taken him a tray. She could see the half-empty glass, smell the rich scent of the brandy.

Darcie blinked. The images receded, leaving her standing in the entry of the laboratory, staring at the glistening human heart that lay severed and naked on the odd narrow table in the center of the room.

CHAPTER SEVEN

Determinedly, Darcie began to arrange her artist's supplies, secretively glancing at Damien through lowered lashes. He set out his sharp surgeon's tools with careful precision, his studied manner so intense as to make her wonder if he had been as affected as she.

Her gaze slid back to the heart. She would do this because she must. Having committed herself to act as Damien's hands, she would not evince cowardice now that she was faced with this daunting task. Avoiding an unpleasant situation would not make it disappear. In fact, the problem was likely to amplify and expand until it grew out of control.

Selecting a bit of charcoal to begin her preliminary sketch, Darcie quickly became immersed in her work. She forgot to be appalled by the subject matter, and instead began to see a strange beauty in the chambers of the heart.

"These two upper chambers are the atria."

Damien sliced and spread the wall of the heart neatly so she could see the inside. His meticulous movements gave no indication of the fiery passion that she knew had consumed him only moments ago. He walled off his emotions so effectively that he almost seemed like two separate people.

"Do you see the thin-walled, smooth posterior portion? Have you drawn it thus?" He moved his head to look at her drawing.

Darcie nodded mutely, moving her charcoal with rapid strokes.

"Good. Now label this. The *sinus venarum.*"

She labeled the structure he indicated.

"And here. The rough anterior part. These are muscular ridges. The *musculi pectinati.*"

"What is this?" Darcie asked, indicating a small pouch that projected from the heart. "It looks like a dog's ear."

"It does, indeed." Damien glanced at her, his expression contemplative. "It is called an *auricle.* The word *auris* means ear."

Darcie felt strangely pleased at his warm tone, as though her observation had somehow elevated her in his esteem.

"Now look here." Damien made a neat cut through the lower portion of the heart. "These are the two lower chambers, the ventricles. Notice that the right one is thinner walled than the left." He fell silent, allowing Darcie to sketch what she saw.

At length she asked, "Why is the right one thinner walled than the left?"

"The heart is like a pump, Darcie. In fact, you can think of it as two pumps. From the right side, the blood flows to this vessel, the pulmonary trunk, and from there to the lungs, which sit on either side of the heart. From the left side the blood flows to this vessel, the aorta, and then on to the body."

Darcie pondered this for a moment and smiled. "So the left side is thicker because it must work harder, pumping the blood to the entire body. While the right side can be lazy for it only pumps the blood to the lungs, which are close by. Hence the discrepancy in the thickness of the walls," she finished triumphantly.

"Precisely," he said softly. "Do you know, Darcie, that it takes a good deal of thought for some medical students to reach that conclusion?"

"There are no women in medical school." The observation slipped out before she had time to question the wisdom of opening such a Pandora's box.

"No, there are not."

Their gazes met and held. Darcie sensed something in his expression. As he continued to watch her, she felt a warm wave ripple through her, a feeling of pleasure and confidence that blossomed and grew. She sensed that he was genuinely interested in her thoughts and opinions.

"There are no women in medical school," Damien repeated, "yet."

The thought made Darcie give an incredulous snort of laughter. "Yet? You mean to say that you think some day there might be female physicians?"

Damien nodded. "Female physicians. Female surgeons. Do you know what one of my esteemed colleagues said the other day?"

Darcie shook her head.

"He said that women were not suited for higher

education because it would redirect the blood away from their female organs and render them unable to bear children."

Darcie wondered at the intelligence of the colleague that Damien described. "What utter rot," she muttered, and then nearly clapped her hand over her mouth when she realized she had voiced the sentiment out loud.

"Well, I mean, I find the thought ridiculous," Darcie continued. There were women I saw in Whitechapel . . . good women who had fallen on hard times. They worked, tended to their families, and some had enough education that they taught their own brood, or even the neighborhood children to read and write." Realizing that she had been uncharacteristically outspoken, Darcie dropped her gaze and stared at the sketch she had made.

"Go on," Damien spoke softly into the silence.

"I only meant that I think there are women who do many things, brave things, necessary things. Those women bear children."

"And?" He moved across the room, pouring fresh water and scrubbing his hands.

She glanced up and found him watching her intently, his steel gray eyes questioning, probing.

"And I think your colleague was wrong. I think women are capable of many things."

Darcie swallowed as she waited for his wrath, wondering if at last she had found the limit of his patience. Her transgression would draw the anger of most men, she thought. She had openly challenged the widely accepted belief that a woman was a thing of little intelligence, a vessel for the comfort of her husband and the bearing of his children. For a moment, she wondered exactly where her outspoken notions had come from.

Suddenly, Damien's warm hand closed over hers, stilling the nervous movement of her fingers. Her head jerked back and she found him standing close beside her, his expression hard and tense, the firm lines of his lips pulled taut.

Slowly, he raised one hand and moved a stray curl from her cheek.

"What were you fleeing the night my carriage nearly ran you down in the street?" he demanded.

She hesitated, startled by the abrupt change of topic. "Mrs. Feather's House," Darcie replied hesitantly. "I fled my sister's house and the fate that awaited me there."

"And Mrs. Feather sent you to me."

Darcie swallowed. "Yes."

Tracing his fingers along the curve of her cheek, Damien smiled, though there was neither humor nor mirth in the expression. The smile was more a cold curving of his lips, as though they were pulled tight by tension and self-derision.

"She sent you to me in order to save you." He snorted softly. "Did she not consider that Mrs. Feather's House might be infinitely preferable to Damien Cole's?"

Darcie frowned, uncertain of his meaning. There was something peculiar and frightening in his gaze, and she shivered as icy wisps of wariness crawled over her skin, raising goose flesh on her arms.

"How can you ask that, knowing the fate that awaited me there?" she asked, frowning. "You have shown me nothing but kindness." She shifted her gaze and stared at the floor, then slid her eyes to the side and watched him as she spoke once more. "I am happy here."

"Happy?" Damien's hand slid down to the column of her throat, lying flat and warm against her fluttering pulse. His fingers opened, spanning her neck.

She could feel her blood pounding against his fingers. Faster. Harder.

Their eyes met and held.

She gasped and tried to move away, but he caught her wrist and held her, watching her with a kind of wild desperation that shot to her core, sending heated rivulets of molten desire knifing through her, mingling with a nameless unease that ate at the edges of her consciousness.

"I am dangerous to you, Darcie. Run away from this place." His words were at odds with his actions, for he yet held her wrist, preventing her from moving away. It did not matter, for even if he let go his hold, she would stay.

"I cannot," she whispered, all her anguish pouring into those two simple words. So true was their meaning. She could not leave him. To be ripped from him would be to tear her soul asunder. Somehow, he had come to mean more to her than anyone or anything else ever had. And she had no idea how it had happened. "I cannot leave you."

"I will send you away." The words were harshly spoken.

She stared at him in silence. He would force her to leave.

Abruptly, he turned from her. She could read the tension in the muscles of his back and shoulders, as he spoke.

"Or I shall leave. I have a house in the country. You do not understand the danger you court. I am not the man for you, Darcie."

She felt bitter disappointment, then anger at herself for letting her heart open even a little. He would leave her, desert her, just as Abigail had left, and Mama and Steppy.

"I can help you," she said at last.

"Help me?" His voice was strangled. "I am beyond help, Darcie. You can help me with my work, but you cannot help what I have become." The sound of his ragged breathing filled the room.

"Because you drink?" There. She had said it. "You can choose to stop."

He did not turn, and her question hung between them, unanswered.

"I shall help you with your work," she insisted.

Slowly, he turned to face her once more, his expression calm. He had mastered his emotions, as he always did. "Did Mrs. Feather tell you aught about me?"

Darcie shook her head even as her sister's words fluttered insidiously through her thoughts. *Have a care of him. Dr. Cole. He is a man to fear. Stay out of his way. Stay clear of his work. And keep your nose out of his secrets.*

Secrets. A vision of the bloodied shirt, now burned to ashes, fluttered before her, but she thrust it away. She did not want to believe ill of him. He had shown her only kindness, she thought, thrusting aside the tiny seed of doubt that nagged at the edge of her thoughts. Memories of things she had seen assailed her—the men, the chest, the way that Damien disappeared in the shadows, blending with the darkness of the night. She could not deny that there was something faintly sinister hovering about this house. Only fools would refute what they experienced with their own eyes and ears. Still, there was nothing in what she had seen that would condemn Damien, nothing that made a clear case against him on any level.

Staring at his face, as perfect as any sculpture, Darcie quelled her misgivings. All her dealings with him had only served to elevate him in her esteem.

He had shown her only kindness.

Her eyes met his, and she saw the flame of desire flicker there, banked but not squelched.

He had shown her only kindness, she reiterated silently, kindness and the barely leashed power of his desire.

Late in the night, a noise, soft and muffled, but heart-wrenching in its desperation, dragged Darcie from the depths of a dreamless sleep. Blinking, she squinted into the darkness.

"Mary," she whispered, easing from beneath her warm covers. Her toes recoiled as they touched the cold wood floor.

The sobbing stopped abruptly, only to restart seconds later.

In the dimness, Darcie could see the dark outline of Mary's bed, as she crossed the room, following the sound of the muffled sobs. Gingerly, she perched on the edge of the mattress, stretching out one hand to caress the other girl's heaving back.

"Are you ill?"

Her question seemed to send Mary to a new level of despair. The sobs grew louder, harsher, tearing at Darcie's heart.

Moving her hand in slow, soothing circles, Darcie tried to lend the other girl sympathy and support. Her ministrations were met by renewed cries, though Mary tried to muffle them by pressing her face to the mattress.

Darcie reached for the candle.

"No!" Mary cried, her fingers closing about Darcie's wrist with surprising speed, stilling her movements. "No light."

"Are you ill, Mary?" Darcie repeated her earlier question.

"Ill of heart. Ill of soul." Mary's voice was thick with sorrow and despair.

Easing further onto the mattress, Darcie lay down next to her friend and gathered her into her arms. "But sound of mind?"

"Yes," Mary whispered.

"And sound of body?"

There was a dreadful silence as Mary pondered the question, and in the silence, Darcie read the answer.

"What's been done to you, Mary darling?"

"Please, I cannot—" The girl's voice broke into a sob. "I cannot say."

Darcie swallowed as tears filled her own eyes. Her friend had been damaged in some unspoken way. She could feel the pain emanating from her shaking form like bilious smoke from a smoldering fire.

"Don't leave me," Mary begged.

"I won't leave you, Mary. Sleep now. The dawn will be here before we know and we'll be up and about once more." Darcie tightened her arms about her friend, greatly saddened by the other woman's pain. Forcing a bright tone, Darcie chattered aimlessly, hoping her mundane prattle would ease her friend's nerves. "I'm sorry you have to do my share of the work, Mary. I wonder that Poole hasn't hired another girl yet. Perhaps he hopes that Dr. Cole will find fault with my drawings and send me back to my other chores."

She felt Mary stiffen in her arms, apparently dismayed by her words. Frowning, Darcie made soft soothing noises and held Mary until her posture eased and relaxed. She wondered what had caused the other girl's unease, the mention of work, the mention of Darcie's drawings, or the mention of Dr. Cole.

At length, Mary fell into a restless slumber, her shallow breathing punctuated by soft whimpers and cries. Slowly, Darcie eased from the narrow bed. Mary shifted, but did not waken.

Seeking her own rest, Darcie slid beneath her covers once more, her senses tuned to Mary lest she wake and need comfort. The minutes stole past, and still Darcie lay awake in the darkness. Frustrated, she tossed the covers aside and sat up in her bed. She could barely see over the lower ledge of the small window above her cot, but she knew it overlooked the cobbled rear drive and the carriage house beyond.

She wrapped her arms around her bent knees, hugging herself as she stared out at the canopy of dark sky. Suddenly, her blood chilled as a sound carried on the still air, penetrating the glass of the small window. It was a high, keening cry that was cut short with abrupt finality. A bird, she told herself resolutely. An owl, perhaps.

Darcie shifted position, kneeling on her bed and raising herself up to better see the world beyond her attic room. There was a light in Damien's laboratory, on the second level of the carriage house. Losing all sense of time, Darcie knelt on her bed watching Damien's silhouette move intermittently across the drawn shade of the carriage house window until at last he snuffed the flame.

Waiting in the dark, she didn't mark the time as it passed, didn't care to. At length, Damien came into view, crossing the cobbled drive. He stopped halfway to the main house and drew something from the pocket of his coat.

Darcie moved closer to the glass panes, her eyes trained on the doctor's dark form, her senses alert. Her heart began to thud heavily in her chest as an ill wind crept through the cracks and chinks in the wall, making her shiver. Without conscious thought she pressed her face against the glass, watching Damien with intense concentration, trying to discern what it was that he held.

From the way he moved the object in his hands, she could see it was cloth. The color was light, white perhaps, or a pale shade of gray.

Shoving the cloth back into his pocket, he grew still. Darcie held her breath as he tipped his head and his gaze sought her window. She inched back, but refused to allow herself to leap away. Twice before he had looked unerringly towards the spot she had stood hidden. Twice before she had felt this strange attachment as though their thoughts connected, and he knew she was there.

The first occasion had been the night she went to his study with the intention of ripping the page from the sketchbook in order to hide the evidence of her trespass. Then, as now, his gaze had unerringly sought the place where she stood, watching. The second occasion had been the night she had watched him undress, met his eyes in the mirror above the washstand, and known he had sensed her presence.

Reason told her that it was only coincidence that he looked upward, that his glance rested on the place where she pressed her face near to the glass. Surely each of the other instances had been coincidence as well. Her heart continued to pound a steady rhythm. She could hear the sound of her wildly pounding heart, feel the throbbing of her blood pumping through her veins. Then Damien Cole turned his face away, and she watched him disappear into the shadows.

A dreadful sense of menace seemed to fill the small chamber, laughing cruelly at Darcie's pitiful attempts to stave it off. Mary's anguish could have nothing to do with Damien, she reassured herself silently. Still, she could not help herself as she lit the candle and moved slowly across the space that separated her from Mary's bed.

Lifting the light, Darcie stared down at the sleeping form of her friend. Her tossing had dislodged the covers, revealing that she yet wore her work clothes. She had come to bed without changing into her night things, exhaustion, or perhaps despondency, disrupting her regular routine.

Mary shifted in her sleep and Darcie saw that her smock had been torn at the shoulder, leaving the jagged edges of the fabric gaping wide, as though a section of material had been rent from the whole.

Darcie moved a step closer, her gaze traveling over Mary's restless form. She held the candle up just a bit higher, and the flickering flame fell across Mary's face and throat.

With a gasp, Darcie stepped back, her hand falling instinctively, nearly upsetting the candle from its holder. Shaking, she held the light aloft once more, allowing her mind to assimilate the sight revealed by the meager flame. There, low on Mary's neck, near her collarbone, were the faint purple-brown smudges of five oval bruises.

Raising her hand, Darcie stared at her own fingers, slowly curling them into a fist. Her gaze returned to the bruises on Mary's neck. They were precisely grouped, four on one side, a single bruise on the other, positioned in such a way as to make her think . . .

"My collar will hide them."

Darcie jumped at the hoarse sound of Mary's voice.

"Mary, they aren't—" Darcie shook her head and tried again. "I mean, are they . . . did someone . . ." Helplessly, she looked down at her fingers, uncurling them bit by bit, before forcing them to relax.

Sitting up, Mary caught Darcie's free hand, pulling her down until she sat on the edge of the bed.

"Never speak of it," Mary whispered. "We'll never speak of it. Something terrible was—" She blew out a breath, then leaned forward and rested her head lightly against Darcie's shoulder.

Together they sat, each lost in their own thoughts.

Darcie pulled back to stare at the torn edge of Mary's smock, and in her mind she saw Damien turning the scrap of cloth in his hands.

Words churned in her throat, begging for release.

Looking into her friend's eyes, Darcie blurted, "Did Dr. Cole—"

The question was cut short by Mary's soft cry.

"Please. I cannot—" Mary swallowed. "It would mean my death."

Darcie winced at the expression of pain that crossed the other woman's face.

"Something terrible was done to me." Mary raised her hand, gingerly touching her fingers to her throat. "Not just the things you can see, but . . . other things. Unnatural . . . May God forgive me."

"You've done nothing that needs forgiving."

Mary met Darcie's gaze, her normally bright green eyes bruised and dull. "Tell no one. Promise me."

Something in Mary's expression made Darcie think of her sister, not as she had been as a girl, but as she was now. Mrs. Feather. A woman hardened by life and debauchery. A woman without hope.

"Promise," Mary insisted, her voice strident.

"I promise," Darcie whispered fervently, wrapping her arms around her friend. "I promise, Mary."

* * *

Morning brought no respite from Darcie's disquietude. Damien had already informed her that he would be working in his surgery in Whitechapel, and she did not expect to see him that day. Her heart was heavy, her thoughts filled with images of Mary, her bruised throat, her anguished face.

Abruptly Darcie stopped, drawn up short by the memory of Damien standing on the back drive in the moonlight, turning the scrap of cloth over and over in his hands, and overlying that was the image of Mary's torn smock. She stood immobilized, confusion creeping through her thoughts. All was not right in this house on Curzon Street. There was an evil, an aberration snaking through the shadows. She tried to rationalize away her bewilderment and concern, tried to tell herself that the missing maid, Janie, had merely found a better position or had run off with a beau, but the recollection of all that Mary had told her about the disappearance of her predecessor plagued her like a sore tooth.

And what of Mary? She had seen the horrifying bruises with her own eyes. Darcie shivered. Pressing her lips together, she thrust her dark thoughts aside as she entered Damien's study.

Sinking into the chair by the desk, she opened her sketchbook and glanced at her drawings. In a way, she was glad for the time apart from Damien. His presence was overwhelming. Enticing. She needed distance and space to gather her thoughts and bring herself back to a place where she could see him as her employer and nothing more. She knew that no good could come from her insane infatuation. She was a maid. A girl he had rescued from Whitechapel. There could be nothing between them. She could not trust in the illusion of his affection.

She tapped her fingertip rhythmically on the desktop, lost in contemplation. Her sister's warning floated through her thoughts once more. Damien had secrets, and if Abigail Feather thought those secrets were frightening, then how much more wary ought Darcie be of Damien Cole's hidden depths. True, he had shown her only kindness. But more than once he had also shown her a glimpse of his more primitive nature.

He had kissed her. Tasted her. She ran her tongue across her lips. Even thinking about the things he had done made her shift restlessly on the seat. Memories of his naked chest, his hands running the wet cloth over his glistening skin, golden and kissed by firelight, brought a sharp ache, intense and knifelike, to the pit of her belly.

Her mind occupied by sensuous recollections of Damien, Darcie reached for the small bottle of ink that sat on the corner of the desk. Clumsily, she knocked it over. With an exclamation of dismay, she jumped to her feet watching the dark blotch spread across the neatly folded newspaper that lay on the desk. Righting the bottle, she heaved a sigh of relief as she saw that the stain was contained to the newspaper and had not spread to the dark wood of the doctor's fine furniture.

Moving around to the side, she shifted the paper, intending to fold the corners to contain the spill and remove the mess from the room. But the solid black letters, neatly aligned on the page, caught her eye and she bent to read what was written.

Another murder of the same cold-blooded character as those recently perpetrated in Whitechapel was discovered early yesterday. . . . London will talk and think of nothing else except this new proof of the continued presence in our streets of some monster in human form, whose desperate evil goes free and undetected by force of its own dreadful audacity, and by an as-yet-unrebuked contempt for our police and detective agencies. The series of shocking crimes perpetrated in Whitechapel culminated in the murder two nights past of one Sally Booth, who is connected with the other victims only by her miserable mode of livelihood. All ordinary experience leaves us at a loss to comprehend the cruel slaughter of three, possibly four women. The single male victim is now believed to have been the recipient of an unrelated attack.

Darcie stood, swaying, her hands clutching the side of the desk for balance, as the import of the last sentence sank in. The single male victim. Steppy. They knew that someone other than the monster who stalked the unfortunates of Whitechapel had killed Steppy. Deliberately, she looked down and traced the scar on her hand. Of course, *she* had known all along that it was no nameless, faceless villain who had stolen Steppy's life. She closed her eyes tightly, trying to block out the image of her once-beloved stepfather, ragged and broken, his blood pooling on the dirty floor. So much blood.

CHAPTER EIGHT

A sound carried upward from the entry hall, boot heels crossing the tiled floor. Without conscious thought, Darcie folded the ruined newspaper, mindful of the wet ink. Furtively, she hurried from Damien's study and scurried to her bedroom, hiding the paper under her bed. She couldn't explain her urgency, but she knew that she must return to the article and read it in its entirety. There was something in those written words that called out to her, something about the murdered woman.

There was no time now, but later . . . She would revisit the pages later. Conscious of her duties, she descended the stairs once more and returned to find Damien standing by the desk, idly flipping through her sketchbook.

"I'm sorry, sir," she blurted as she skidded to a halt just inside the door.

He turned to her with a perplexed expression creasing his brow. "Sir? I thought we had long-ago established that my name is Damien."

Darcie felt a hot blush stain her cheeks. There was a distance, a certain amount of protection in maintaining the formal address. Calling him by his given name was so personal; it drew her in, made her acknowledge their ever increasing intimacy. She looked away, focusing on the curled leg of the side table.

"And sorry, Darcie? Sorry for what?" he asked.

"I spilled ink on your copy of the *Daily Express*. I'm afraid it was ruined." Her gaze slid back to his. She read no censure there.

"Rather unfortunate. I'll have Poole pick up another copy." He shrugged casually, then returned his attention to the desk and began to examine her sketches, as though he found the matter of the newspaper to be of little consequence.

Darcie cringed inwardly at his words. She could only imagine what Poole would think of the need to fetch a second copy of the *Daily Express*. Though she was no longer directly under his jurisdiction, she could sense the butler's malevolence whenever they chanced to meet. The man hated her. Of that she had little doubt.

"Are you not needed at your offices in the East End today? I had thought you would not be here."

At her question, Damien glanced at the window. "I have worked since before dawn and only now returned. The day is half gone, Darcie. Did you sleep well?" His tone implied mere polite interest, but Darcie could not help but wonder if he had seen her at the window the previous night, if he knew that she had been awake for many restless hours.

She wondered if he knew she had watched him, knew she had seen him with the scrap of material torn from Mary's clothing, knew she suspected that all was not right in this house. Her heart gave a single hard kick, and then sputtered before it began to beat a frenetic rhythm. She stammered an unintelligible reply.

Glancing at her over his shoulder, Damien raised a brow inquiringly. "Are you quite all right?"

"Quite." Darcie choked the word out.

"Mmmm." He ran his finger over one of her sketches.

"There was another woman killed two nights past. I saw it in the newspaper when I spilled the ink."

Damien stilled, his shoulders taking on an unnatural tension, and his hand froze above the pages of the sketchbook.

"Yes, I know." Something in his tone frightened her.

Darcie said nothing, just stood, the fingers of her right hand clasped in her left, her thumb nervously rubbing against her scar.

With the speed of a striking serpent, Damien whirled, catching her hand in his, holding it trapped as he brought his index finger to the raised ridge of flesh and touched the line that marred her hand.

"Tell me," he commanded.

Darcie's gaze shot upward, meeting his, captured there like prey bewitched by a predator's hypnotic stare. Mutely, she shook her head.

Slowly, his eyes trained on hers, Damien lifted her hand to his lips and kissed the scar, tracing the length of it with his tongue.

The contact sent a jolt of lightning slicing through her.

"Tell me," he whispered, no command this time. A request.

Tearing her hand from his, Darcie made to move past him, to flee his presence before she gave in to the desire to do exactly that, to tell all, to free herself from the terrible truth of what had been done to her, and what she had done in return. But to tell him meant she must share a little of her trust, a little of herself, and she was afraid.

Damien shifted his stance, his broad shoulders blocking her path. Wordlessly, he pulled a second chair closer to the desk, so that two stood side by side, angled towards each other. He guided her to the one further from the door, and then sank into the other, obstructing her path and her hope of escape.

"I don't know where to start," she said simply, hedging.

He watched her, making no comment, merely waiting.

He would listen. He would not judge. A feeling of serenity settled over her. Yes, she would tell him. Likely he already suspected something worse even than the truth.

"The old man that the newspapers talk about, the one who was killed by the Whitechapel murderer . . . h-h-he was killed by someone else." Darcie watched him carefully, to be certain that he understood.

"Yes, I am aware of that."

She frowned. He knew that someone else had killed Steppy? How? How could he know that?

Perhaps he only meant that some newspaper articles claimed it was so.

"Go on," he commanded softly.

Darcie licked her lips nervously, but didn't drop her gaze. She would watch him as she spoke, gauge his reaction to her words. Somewhere in the darkest corner of her mind, a warning bell tolled, but she thrust her unease aside. The secret had been kept long enough. Now she felt as though it might burst free of her chest, writhe out of her body like a live thing, so desperate was she to share the terrible tragedy of it with another living soul.

No, not true. Not just any living soul. She wanted to share her pain with Damien, to let him catch a glimpse of the fires that had forged her, to let him heal her tortured heart as she so desperately longed to heal his.

"The old man who was killed. He was my stepfather."

There. One secret out. But so many still hidden within. "My life was once different," she continued. "I lived in a pretty house, wore pretty dresses. Abigail played with me, teased me, dried my tears when I cried."

"Abigail?" he asked.

Darcie nodded. "Abigail, my sister. Mrs. Feather."

Damien's expression did not change. His face remained a mask of cool compassion. His doctor's face, Darcie thought.

"I lived a sheltered life, and my dreams were those of any young girl. Country balls. A handsome suitor. Marriage. Children. Then my mother became ill." Darcie's voice caught as she said the words. Ill. Such an innocuous word. It seemed to imply a mild sniffle. Perhaps she should have been more dramatic in order to fully convey the horror of her mother's death.

Sucking in a deep breath, she continued. "She coughed away her life."

"Consumption," Damien murmured.

Darcie nodded.

"A terrible disease."

He did not rush her. They sat, face to face, he waiting for her to continue, she waiting for the courage to do so.

Finally, she spoke, the words barely above a whisper, wrenched from her in harsh syllables. "We buried her on a cold wet day, gray clouds and a chilly drizzle marking her passage. It was that same day that the news came. Steppy had lost everything. We were destitute." Darcie shook her head slowly and twisted her fingers together. "At first, Steppy kept up a cheerful front. We'd get it back, he said. He'd find investors. But the creditors took the house, the silver, my mother's pearls. There was nothing left."

As she spoke, her voice gained strength, and her palms came to rest calmly on her lap, as though in the telling of the tale she was exorcising the demons that gnawed at her thoughts.

"Steppy found me work through a business acquaintance. They were a nice family, the Grants. I was happy there for a short time. Then Mr. Grant was sent to India, and I was sent back to Steppy. He had acquired a small flat in Whitechapel."

She could remember the flat, rank with the

smell of mildew and decay, and the stench of the desperation of the inhabitants who had passed through over the decades. Closing her eyes, Darcie tried to push aside the image of Steppy, unshaven, unwashed, stinking of liquor and misery.

"Where was Abigail?" Damien's quiet question insinuated itself into the sad image, weakening it, making it fade.

Darcie stared down at her hands for a long moment, remembering.

"She had a secret suitor. At least, she believed at the time that he was a suitor. Mere months before our world collapsed, she fled, went to the man who had promised her everything, only to find he had been toying with her. He already had a wife and two small children, or so he claimed. I don't know exactly what happened to Abigail then, only that she somehow became who she is today—Mrs. Feather. She never came back and wrote only once. The letter came just before they took the house, and by then she had already been gone for nearly a year." Darcie smiled sadly. "I kept it. The letter. That was how I found her that night. Funny, I had lived in Whitechapel for a good long while before I came to know that Abigail was Mrs. Feather. I'd heard of Mrs. Feather, but I had not encountered her. Not until that night."

"The night I found you."

"Yes." *The night you saved me,* she thought.

"Tell me about your stepfather's flat."

"It was cold. And gray. Cheerless. He didn't care. Most of the time he barely knew I was there. We had no money for coal, for clothes, for food.

But somehow, Steppy always found coin for drink."
Her voice held no rancor. She was long past the
wasteful luxury of resentment and blame.

"One day, I came home to find him in a state.
His eyes were bloodshot, his hands shaking. There
was vomit on the floor. He had found no money
for many days. No coin meant no drink." Darcie
looked away, focusing on a small smudge on the
desktop. "Two men waited on the far side of the
room, standing by the open window. Steppy caught
my wrist as I came through the door. He shoved me
across the floor, and I fell at the feet of those men."

Damien made a rough noise, low in his throat.
Turning her gaze on him, she found that his mask
had been wiped away, replaced by an expression of
cold fury. He looked primitive, feral.

"They tossed Steppy a bag of coins. I heard
them chink as they hit the floor. Then one of them
grabbed my wrists and dragged me to my feet. They
took me to an empty warehouse near the dock. I
heard one of them say I would fetch a good price,
being a vir—" She looked away, embarrassed. "Being untouched. When they left me, my wrists were
bound, a dirty cloth tied across my mouth. They
locked me in a small, empty room."

"Your stepfather sold you." Damien's voice came
low and hard.

Darcie shrugged, as though it were of little consequence, yet the truth of his observation was a
terrible thing. She had loved Steppy, trusted him
with the open honest heart of the child she had
been until that terrible night, and he had betrayed
her.

Taking her hand, Damien sandwiched it between

his callused palms. She could feel the heat of him, smell the fragrance of soap and endless summer sky. Strange, that she could think he smelled of summer. What, exactly, did summer smell like? Leaning closer, she breathed in the scent of him. She longed to lay her head on his shoulder, to be enfolded in his warm embrace.

Idly, Damien ran his thumb along the scar, waiting patiently for her to continue.

The feel of his hand on hers reassured her. She sucked in a shaky breath, drawing strength from his implacable calm.

"There was a small lamp. They left it for me. A tiny kindness, or perhaps an oversight, but it proved to be my salvation. The flame faded and died, leaving me in darkness. I wiggled over and banged the lamp as hard as I could with my elbow. I heard the glass shatter."

Her voice caught as she forced herself to go on. She didn't want to tell this story, didn't want to remember that terrifying night. But a part of her wanted to tell it very much, to share it with him, to let him in.

"I picked up a shard and began to saw away at the rope. But it was dark. My hands were numb after being bound for hours on end. I-I couldn't hold the piece of glass steady, couldn't aim it where I wanted it to go. It cut the rope, but it cut my skin, too. And the muscle underneath. All the way to the bone before I was free." There were tears streaming down her face. Darcie could feel them on her cheeks, taste their salty tang on her lips. "There was blood everywhere. My hands were slick with it. At last I was free."

Pulling her hand from his grasp, Darcie jumped to her feet, pacing to the window. Damien made no move to stop her.

"I ran." She gave a hollow laugh and spun to face him, her voice rising. "And can you imagine? I ran to Steppy's flat. Can you imagine a more stupid girl?"

Damien rose from his chair and crossed to her, gently brushing the tears from her cheek.

"I cannot imagine a more brave girl."

She blinked, his words penetrating her mind, lending her calm reassurance. He thought her brave. Desperate now to finish it, she continued. "Steppy was passed out on the floor, a nearly empty bottle on the table. I gathered my folio of drawings and tried to tie some stale crusts of bread in a cloth, but my hand was almost useless. Though I had wrapped an old cloth about the cut, there was so much blood, and my thumb would barely move at all." Darcie swallowed, and her voice dropped to a whisper as she continued. "I thought that if a seam would hold with the help of good, even stitches, my hand would do the same. I took a needle and some thread and sewed it up as best I could."

Damien caught her hand and turned the scar to the light, examining it closely. "You stitched your own wound." His voice was flat, his lips pulled in a taut line.

Darcie nodded.

Slowly, he raised his head, and she saw his thoughts mirrored in his eyes. Terrible rage mingled with boundless admiration. For her. She felt stronger now, buoyed by his silent support.

"I heard a sound. It was the men, the ones Steppy

sold me to. They banged on the door. I was clumsy. I knocked over the bottle on the table, spilling the last of the liquor over my wound."

At her words, Damien sucked in a sharp hiss of breath.

"I would not have thought the pain could get worse, but it did. The men were pounding on the door. Then they kicked it." Raising her hands, she covered her ears as though, even now, the sound of the pounding echoed in her mind.

"I turned. Steppy was awake, watching me, his eyes wretched and sad. 'Hide in the shadows. Run, girl, run,' he cried, and I knew he was resigned to his fate. He had sold me once, but could not bring himself to do it a second time. So I did as he bid. I climbed out the open window, hid in the shadows. I left him there to die. They stabbed him, over and over. The blood—" she covered her face, desperate to block out the sight that haunted her still.

Turning her head, she found Damien staring at her, and in his liquid silver eyes, she read indescribable emotion. He blinked, and it was gone. His expression became shuttered, his thoughts and emotions hidden behind his habitual mask.

"I am so sorry," he whispered, folding her in the warm cocoon of his embrace.

Sheltered in his arms, Darcie experienced a feeling of safe harbor, and she reveled in the momentary freedom from the terrible weight that had dragged her down since her mother's death.

"Why do you apologize?" She ran her hand along the hard angle of his jaw. "You didn't even know me then."

"Perhaps that is why I am sorry."

Darcie rested her head on his shoulder, allowing herself the luxury of feeling cared for and protected, imagining what it would be like to be loved by this man. She thought of his words, of the way he touched her, embraced her. Mayhap he cared for her on some level, loved her just a little.

Then her eyes fell on the miniature of the dark-haired girl, and a great sadness washed over her. While she had shared her deepest secrets with him, he had shared nothing of himself with her. With that realization came comprehension of the thickness of the walls he had built around himself.

Dry-eyed now, Darcie sat in Damien's embrace, her heart wringing silent tears of sorrow for her lack of ability to offer him comfort, to ease his pain as he had eased hers. She had offered him her trust, but he had denied her his. So where, then, did that leave them?

The sound of Mary and Tandis laughing together echoed through the house when Darcie returned from a walk late the following afternoon. Damien had gone to an anatomy lecture, and bid her do as she would for the remainder of the day. John Coachman was at her disposal. Hence, the afternoon had been her own, and she had spent it taking a brief ride through Hyde Park, then walking, enjoying the sunshine and the fresh air.

Darcie hung her bonnet on a peg before following the sound of cheerful voices that led her to the kitchen. In a way, she was envious. The laughter implied closeness, camaraderie. She felt a bit left out now that she no longer held the place of maid in the below-stairs hierarchy of the house.

On the other hand, she was glad that Mary seemed in better spirits today. Last night, Mary had cried herself to sleep, burying the sound in her pillow as best she could, mourning whatever horror had left those bruises on her body. She still refused to speak of it, and Darcie did not force the issue, sensing that such a tack could prove disastrous.

Darcie found the two girls polishing silver in the scullery next to the kitchen. They looked up as she entered.

"Hello," Mary said with a smile.

"Might I help?" Darcie began to roll up her sleeves, even as she voiced the suggestion.

"Help would be much appreciated." Mary nodded her head.

"You mustn't even think of it!" Cook exclaimed at exactly the same moment. Standing in the doorway with her fists planted firmly on her ample hips, she sent Mary a quelling look, before returning her stern gaze to Darcie. "What would the doctor say if we had you scrubbing and scrubbing till your hands were blistered and sore? You wouldn't be able to draw pretty pictures then! No, no! That wouldn't do at all."

Cook said the words kindly, but Darcie felt the sting of them all the same. She was excluded now, an outsider, neither servant nor employer. That was how the rest of them saw her. How she saw herself. The painful bite of terrible loneliness gnawed at her, but she pushed the feeling aside.

"Perhaps I could dust, then. Or wash the windows?" She had no wish to sit idle. Having nothing to do gave her mind too much time to roam in areas that were better left unexplored.

"No, and again, no." Cook was firm. "Now off with you. We've work to do. I've a special pudding I want to make the doctor for his supper."

"But you could use my help," Darcie insisted. "Poole still hasn't hired another maid, and I have two good hands right here."

Suddenly, a peculiar ripple surged through the small room, and all eyes turned to Darcie.

"We've been short-handed before. It seems that this household has made a habit of losing its staff," Mary said softly, exchanging a quick glance with Cook.

"We have indeed been short-handed before," Cook agreed. "But there will be no more talk of lost staff, Mary Fitzgerald." Pressing her lips together in a thin line, Cook stood silent and somehow forbidding.

Tandis put extra vigor into her polishing and spoke not a word, her head bent low over her task.

Confused, Darcie looked from one to the next, wondering how to restore the convivial humor that had laced the women's actions when she had first arrived. At a loss to explain the changed atmosphere, she decided that perhaps she should simply remove herself and let them get on with their work.

"Well, I'll go find a chore in the doctor's study, then."

Cook nodded. "Perhaps that would be best."

Mary flashed her a strained smile, saying nothing.

Darcie crossed to the door, edging past Cook, who shifted to the side and let her pass. She hesitated for a heartbeat, wanting to say something to the other women, to somehow regain her place within the fold, but she had no clear idea of how to accomplish her goal. With a sigh, she moved along the hallway, determined to go to the doctor's study and retrieve a book. That would cheer her, she thought.

She pondered the cryptic statements of Mary and Cook as she walked in the direction of the stairs. Yes, they had been short-handed before, when the maid, Janie, left without a word of farewell. She already knew a portion of that story from the things Mary had told her the other night. Still, there had been an inexplicable undercurrent of fear beneath the women's taciturn behavior just now. Shrugging it off for now, she decided to ask Mary about it later. There were questions here that begged answers, and though she had not wished to press Mary the last time they had spoken of Janie's disappearance, perhaps the time had come to search for a solution to the riddle of the missing maid.

As Darcie started up the stairs, a cold voice stopped her in her tracks.

"Finch."

Slowly, she turned and found Poole standing at the foot of the staircase.

"Good afternoon, Mr. Poole," she said calmly, though she felt the same discomfort in his presence that she always had.

"I would have a word with you."

"Yes, of course." Darcie made no move to descend the stairs. Ordinarily, Poole towered over her, looking down his long, thin nose at her. Today, from her vantage point on the stair, it was she who stood taller than he.

With a jolt, she realized that Poole no longer intimidated her as much as he once had. In fact, it seemed that lately she was less and less likely to allow herself to hide beneath a meek and frightened exterior. She wondered if sharing her burdens and heartache with Damien had somehow freed her from the terror and anguish that had dogged her since her stepfather had sold her for a bag of coins. The thought deserved further consideration, but right now she had Poole to deal with.

"I have been watching you." He moved a step closer as he spoke. "I saw you with Dr. Cole. The other day, outside the carriage house."

So it had been Poole who twitched the curtain aside, she realized with a sinking sensation. He had watched her and Damien together in passionate embrace. The thought sent a shiver of disgust across her skin.

"I am often with Dr. Cole," she said coldly, praying that he wouldn't hear the slight tremor in her voice.

Poole inclined his head slowly, a tiny nod that acknowledged her bravado. "We are both aware of the occasion to which I make reference."

Darcie held her breath for a moment. The air left her in a whoosh. She decided to brazen it out, though her heart pounded horribly in her chest, and her mouth felt dry as five-day-old bread.

"I cannot see that my actions are any of your affair, sir. I am in Dr. Cole's employ—"

"But did he employ you for *that?*" His harsh tone cut her off.

Darcie felt her cheeks heat up at his implication.

Holding up his flattened hand, Poole warded off arguments or excuses. "Dr. Cole is a man of many faces, not all of them as pretty as you might think. I have been in his employ many years, seen many things. Watch yourself, Finch. For I cannot always watch you."

Her mouth fell open as she sought a reply, but no words came to mind. With a curt nod, Poole turned and strode away, leaving Darcie standing on the stair, frowning in confusion.

"For I cannot always watch you . . . What could he possibly mean by that?" she murmured, bewildered. Turning the words over and over in her mind, she continued her ascent to the upper floor.

Lost in thought, she settled in the doctor's study, a copy of Charles Maturin's *Melmoth the Wanderer* lying open on her lap, but she was unable to concentrate on the words that seemed to blur and waver on the page. At last, she gave up. Closing the volume and staring at nothing at all, she wondered what Poole had meant when he said that Dr. Cole was a man of many faces, not all of them as pretty as she might think.

How long she sat there, she could not say, but when next she looked about her, she found that the hour had grown late.

"Oh! I must have dozed off!" she murmured aloud, shifting uncomfortably on her chair as she drew the back of her hand across her brow, pushing aside the wayward strands of hair that had escaped the neat roll at the base of her neck. Rising, she smoothed her skirts, rolling her shoulders to work out the kink caused by sleeping at an awkward angle in an upright position.

Darcie crossed to the window, pushed aside the heavy velvet drapery and peered out. A sliver of bright moon peered back at her. She suspected the time was well past the supper hour.

After carefully replacing her book on the shelf, she left the study, her destination the back stairs that led to her chamber. Her steps took her past Damien's closed bedroom door. A thin line of light showed through the narrow crack at the bottom. Pausing, Darcie listened for any sound that might indicate Damien's presence in his chamber, but silence reigned.

The feeling of isolation that she had experienced when she returned to the house from her walk crept over her once more. She stood in the hallway, hovering uncertainly outside Damien's door, feeling inexplicably lonely and bereft. She turned away, intent on seeking her bed. She took only three steps before drawing to an abrupt halt and whirling back towards the closed door. Her hand raised, she froze just before her knuckles touched the wood.

Good heavens! What was she doing standing outside her employer's chamber in the dark hours of the night? Did she intend to rap on his door and seek entry? And once inside, what exactly did she intend to do?

Turning away once more, Darcie wrapped her

arms tightly about her chest, admonishing herself silently, shocked by her own behavior. She must take herself off to bed, she decided, and be done with this foolishness.

"Darcie." His voice, pitched low and warm, caressed her, sending tiny chills cascading along her spine.

She pressed her eyes shut, freezing in place as the sound of her name on his lips told her she was no longer alone in the dark hallway. At a snail's pace, she turned to find that he had opened the door of his chamber, the well-oiled hinges allowing the portal to swing wide without a hint of sound. She could not help but wonder, as she had on more than one previous occasion, whether he possessed some mystical knowledge, some preternatural power that allowed him to know her exact whereabouts.

The sight of him, standing framed in the doorway with the light of the fire flickering behind him, made her heartbeat quicken, her breathing grow shallow. His linen shirt hung loosely on his muscled frame. It was open at the neck, revealing a vee of golden skin. She stared at his chest, recalling the night she had seen him shirtless, his muscled torso bared to her gaze. Sucking in a quick breath, she dragged her gaze to his face.

The corners of his mouth curved ever so slightly and his eyes glittered with a primitive light, beckoning to her in silent invitation. Darcie stood frozen, pinned in place by a desperate desire to be with him, even while her common sense bid her to flee as far from him and his carnal sensuality as was humanly possible.

"Have you supped?" He cocked a brow questioningly, his query posed so casually, as though in denial of the intoxicating spell that he wove about her senses like a heady wine.

Darcie shook her head. "No, I'm afraid I fell asleep in your study and missed the evening meal."

"Did you?" He drew back from the door, sweeping one hand before him in a gesture of welcome. "Cook left a tray piled with cold meat, bread, fruit, and cheese. There are even some berry tarts. More than enough for both of us."

"Oh, it would be improper . . . I should not."

He sent her a guarded look. A strange, tight smile graced his lips, and he raised one hand revealing a bunch of plump red grapes. Taking the small round fruit between his teeth, he tore it from the stem, his eyes never leaving hers.

"No, you should not," he said, his voice a velvet caress.

CHAPTER NINE

"Run away, Darcie, to your safe bed."

The sound of Damien's voice made her shiver, more in anticipation than in fear. Every instinct warned her that sharing a meal with him in the privacy of his bedchamber was a dangerous thing to do. Yet, even as her common sense screamed against accepting his invitation, warned her to follow his last directive and seek her own bed, the secret yearning of her heart bid her enter. She looked intently at his face, wetting her lips nervously. His eyes glittered with a silvery light as his gaze dropped to her mouth.

"You know what I want," he said softly.

She knew what he wanted. The breath left her body in a rapid huff, leaving her lightheaded and panting for air. Her legs felt weak and boneless. One hand jerked upward in a gesture of supplication as she sank against the doorsill.

"I want you, Darcie. In my arms. In my bed." He caught her wrist and pulled her against him, his expression hardening with passion. "I want to do all manner of things to you, and have you do them to me. Wonderful things. Pleasurable things." He ran the pad of his thumb across her lips. "Wicked things."

His words made her feel hot and flustered.

Dr. Cole is a man of many faces, not all of them as pretty as you might think. A memory of Poole's warning intruded, and Darcie frowned in bewilderment, her thoughts a maelstrom of unfamiliar emotions. Fear, anticipation, confusion.

Desire.

With a soft cry, she raised her mouth to his, welcoming the firmness of his lips, the thrust of his tongue. He tasted of wine and fruit and promised pleasure.

Bracing his forearm around her waist, Damien turned her into the bedroom, kicking the door closed behind him.

There was nothing subtle or sweet about their kiss. It was a frantic and wild melding, a conflagration of heat and need.

Darcie thrust her fingers into his soft golden hair, reveling in the silky feel of it. Molten desire shot through her veins, tugging at her breasts, her belly, until she thought she would scream aloud at the intensity of her hunger.

Frenzied, she clawed at his shirt. She wanted to feel the warmth of his flesh, to run her tongue over the naked planes of his muscled chest, to taste the golden perfection of his skin.

"Shh. Shh." He caught her wrists, holding her still. "Slowly. We have all night."

She leaned against him, pliant, and he let go of

one wrist, and then shifted his hold on the remaining one so their fingers intertwined. With a gentle tug, he led her to the bed, then stood unmoving, gazing down at her. The edge of the mattress pressed against the backs of her legs. Finally, he pulled his hand from hers, leaving her alone, unfettered, free to run away from him, away from the white-hot hunger that gnawed at her more viciously than any lack of food ever had.

She liked it, this hunger, this hard-edged pleasure.

Sinking her teeth into her lower lip, Darcie dragged in a shaky breath, feeling as though she was struggling to expand her rib cage against some invisible constriction. She wanted him, and that wanting, the strength and emotional depth of her compulsion, made her afraid.

Her gaze slid to the closed door. Would he stop her if she tried to flee?

"Run away, Darcie." Damien's whispered words echoed her thoughts, even as the liquid silver of his gaze bid her stay. "Go while you can. I am not fit to be friend or lover."

As she gazed up at him, she read a wealth of emotion in his eyes. He would not stop her flight, if that was the path she chose. Instead, his words encouraged it.

Darcie cut off his warning, pulling him down to her and touching her lips to his, leaning forward until the tips of her breasts rested lightly against him. Her decision was final. She would not vacillate, would have no regrets.

The hunger undulated in her belly, a live thing seeking to burst free of the confines of her body.

She swallowed, moving her legs restlessly beneath her skirt, shifting her weight first to this limb, then the other. The movement only served to fan the flames.

"What I give, I give freely, Damien." She found it difficult to find adequate breath for speech. "Do you think that after living for so long on the streets of Whitechapel that I have no idea of the ramifications of the decision I make? You want to be my lover."

"Yes," he rasped. The sound of his voice, low and rough, stroked the heat in her belly until it cascaded through her.

In a single fluid motion, he stripped the shirt from his body, baring the golden skin of his torso to her hungry gaze. He pulled her against him, and she inhaled the scent of his skin, touched the hard ridges of his abdomen.

Resting his palms against her cheeks, Damien turned her face upward and pressed his lips to hers, softly, gently. With a groan of frustration, Darcie pushed her tongue into his mouth, tasting him. She had no need for sweet kisses. She wanted the hard, lusty thrust of his tongue, the firm press of his mouth to hers. She wanted the wild desire that she could feel coursing beneath the thin veneer of his control.

With a growl, he gave what she demanded, angling his lips over hers, devouring her.

He tumbled her onto the bed so she lay beneath him. The hard ridge of his arousal pressed to the juncture of her thighs. Darcie wriggled against him, reveling in his response, the sharply indrawn breath, the hard pounding of his heart.

Their eyes met and held as he raised his weight on one arm, using his free hand to slowly unbutton the front of her dress. Without conscious thought, she snaked her hand upward, her fingers closing around his wrist, halting his movement as he continued to unfasten her garments. The sensations he aroused were new and strange. Suddenly, she felt lost, uncertain of her place in this unfamiliar tableau.

"I want to see you. Your breasts. Your legs. Your hair unbound and free, spread across my pillow." His touched each part he named, dragging her hand with his as he did so, for her fingers were yet curled in a vice-like grip around his wrist.

"No, I—" Darcie bit her lip as he deftly drew the pins from her hair, freeing the length of it.

He trailed the tip of his index finger across her cheek, dragged it over her sensitive lips. She opened her mouth and sucked on it, laving the rough callus at the tip with her tongue. The glow from the coals was the only illumination in the room, casting Damien in shades of light and dark, accentuating the chiseled planes of his features. The chamber faded in the shadows. There was only this bed, only Damien, solid and warm against her.

Pulling his hand free of her grip, he leaned forward and caught her wrist, drawing her fingers to his lips. She thought he would imitate her actions, lick her, caress her. He did not. Instead, he bared his straight, white teeth and sank them gently into the mound of flesh at the base of her thumb.

With a low cry, she came off the bed, arching her back, extending her neck. Liquid heat coursed through her, throbbing at the pit of her belly. Her

thighs pressed against each other, moving of their
own accord, seeking some surcease to the burning
pressure that built in the wet folds of her feminine
core.

A chuckle rumbled in Damien's chest as he let
loose her hand, moving his mouth along the white
column of her throat where he licked and sucked
until she felt as though her skin would burst into
flame, and she would be enveloped in an un-
quenchable blaze.

"Damien." His name was a sigh, a whisper that
escaped her.

The cool air kissed her skin as Damien freed her
from the confines of her clothes. Looking up, she
found him watching her, his eyes dark in the meager light.

"You are beautiful." He palmed her breast, running his thumb over the sensitive tip.

She gazed at him mutely, unable to speak, to tell
him that it was he who was beautiful. She had
thought so from the very first.

Damien shifted, his mouth seeking her breasts.

A keening cry escaped her as the tug of his
mouth grew insistent. The rough lap of his tongue
against her nipple sent an exquisite bolt of pleasure shooting to the pit of her belly, making her
liquid and warm.

As though reading her most secret thoughts, he
slid his hand between her legs, pressing his fingers
between the wet folds of her feminine flesh. The
part of her mind that was still sane cried out for
her to move away, to close her legs against the
foreign invasion of his fingers, but the part of her
that was enraptured by his touch urged her to

press herself against him. Bending her knees to allow him better access, Darcie ground her heels against the soft coverlet, allowing him to touch her body in ways she could never have imagined.

The sound of Damien's breathing, harsh and rough, stroked her senses as surely as his fingers caressed her, driving her towards some unknown destination.

Sliding her palms along the smooth skin of his flanks, she found him naked, his trousers gone. She couldn't remember when he had removed them. Every thought focused on the exquisite sensations he created, the reactions he coaxed from her willing body.

Darcie traced the curved bone of his hip around to the front of his body where her fingers closed around the smooth, hard length of his jutting erection. She liked the way he felt, liked the sensation of his velvety skin, smooth beneath her touch. Slowly, she pumped her hand along the rigid rod, feeling the pounding of his blood as if it were her own. Perhaps it was her own. She had lost track of where her pleasure ended and his began.

"Hnn-hn." Damien gave a soft grunt as he shifted over her, pulling himself from her avaricious grasp, seeking entry to her body as he replaced his fingers with his rigid member.

"Darcie," he whispered, prodding gently at her opening.

She stared into his eyes, inviting him to take what he wanted. He sank himself fully in her welcoming warmth with a single long, hard thrust.

She had expected pain. There was none. Instead, she felt only a pinch, a momentary discomfort as he sheathed himself within her body. And then she felt only the heat of him, the width of him, pulsing at her core.

He began to move, slow, languid thrusts that stroked her to a fever pitch.

"Oh. Oh! I don't think—"

"Don't think," he whispered against her ear. "Feel. Let yourself go, Darcie."

"Yes-s-s-s." She sighed as he angled his hips, increasing the friction, the pressure, until she writhed beneath him, meeting each thrust, striving for some amorphous goal she could not name.

Her fingers curled, clutching his buttocks, pulling him closer, tighter. Her heels pressed against the bed and she rocked her hips, thrusting her pelvis to greet him.

Higher, higher she climbed. She could feel the tension in his body, and she sensed that with each thrust he was drawn with her towards the distant pinnacle.

Her senses narrowed until they were filled only with Damien. His touch. His scent. The taste of his skin on her lips and tongue.

He pushed deeper, harder and at last she flew, her soul crashing free of earthly restraint as the sky exploded into a million points of light. And she felt him there, with her, joining her on her glorious voyage. She was alone no more.

They were one.

"You are beautiful." Darcie rolled onto her side, her bent elbow resting on the mattress. She propped her cheek on her palm, gazing at him in the light of the coal fire.

Damien lay on his back, unashamed of his nudity, legs splayed, one forearm resting across his eyes.

He laughed softly. "It is I who should say that to you."

"I would love to draw you." Reaching out, she ran one tentative finger along the hard plane of his chest.

Raising his head, he caught her hand and nipped lightly at her fingers. With a small cry, she snatched her hand away.

She watched the even cadence of his breathing, wanting to touch him again, but too shy to overstep her bounds. Shadows of insecurity gnawed at her. "Why did you choose me?"

His arm snaked out and caught her, drawing her down against his side. She lost her vantage point for studying his form, but she enjoyed the sensation of being cuddled against his long, lean body.

"Why me?" she asked again, tentatively, running the tip of her finger against his jaw as she tipped her head back to look at him.

Cocking his head to the side, Damien sent her a curious glance. His brow furrowed, and he looked puzzled.

"I have asked myself that question since the night I found you, wet and starving, looking like you might not last the night."

Darcie sat up, suddenly wary. "Is that why? Because I am some foundling you feel sorry for?"

Pushing himself up on his elbows, Damien regarded her with an amused smile.

"I feel pity for Mrs. Brightly with her drunken husband and her gouty great toe. Ah, and Mrs. Anderson. She's prone to fainting spells and fits of melancholy. Poor woman. There. I feel sorry for her as well."

He flopped back down on the bed, and closed his eyes, leaving Darcie feeling that he had shared a wealth of information while at the same time giving no answer at all. She was not acquainted with the women he spoke of, but she had a suspicion that they were not the sorts of women that a man would fall desperately in love with. For that matter, neither was she. She smacked him lightly on the shoulder. One eye popped open and he gazed at her balefully.

"That was no answer," she said primly.

Damien sighed, curling upwards until he reached a sitting position. Darcie couldn't help but admire the play of his muscled abdomen as he carried out this attractive feat.

"I want you." He leaned forward and kissed the tip of her nose. "You are beautiful. Intelligent. Brave." He shrugged. "Yes, very brave. I don't know. I have no explanation." A question flickered in his gaze, a thoroughly uncharacteristic uncertainty. "Had I an explanation, an understanding of the fascination, perhaps I could have guarded against it."

"There are other women. More beautiful. More intelligent." Darcie bit her lip, feeling foolish and gauche. Instead of declaring her undying devotion and passion for him, assertions that hovered on the tip of her tongue just bursting to be vocalized, she was haranguing him like a crass fishwife.

His expression cleared and Damien shrugged once more, seemingly unperturbed by her behavior. "But I don't want them, Darcie. I want you."

She bit the inside of her cheek, half insulted, half amused that he did not notice the unwitting insult in his lack of denial of her assertions that there were women who surpassed her. Clearly, he did not think it mattered.

He rolled her beneath him, bringing his mouth to hers. She felt the stirring of desire, even as she felt his renewed hardness as he nudged her thighs apart.

"I want *you*, Darcie," he whispered against her lips. "And with your sweet acquiescence, I shall have you."

How very wicked she felt. Strange how being wicked was so wonderful; she would never have imagined.

Darcie rolled onto her back and stretched languidly. The sun streaming through the small attic window above her bed told her that it was morning. She lay there, listening to the silence, knowing even before she looked about that Mary was not in the room. That was for the best. Darcie wanted to savor her memories, to acclimate to the changes in both her body and her emotions, and that adjustment was better done in solitude.

Images of Damien floated with radiant clarity through her mind. She was a different woman than she had been yesterday. Her lips curved in an irrepressible smile. Recalling every glorious detail of the night she had spent in Damien's embrace, she wrapped her arms around herself, hugging the memories close.

She had left him in the earliest hours, though a part of her had wanted to stay in his arms forever, to never leave the secret joy of his chamber. But as the dawn had crept mercilessly closer, Darcie had slipped from his bed. Glowing with a private rapture, she had crept through the sleeping house silently in stockinged feet, wishing she could surrender to the bubbling urge to dance, to twirl, to sing. Instead, she had noiselessly ascended to her chamber, avoiding the third stair, which she knew would creak and betray her wandering.

Damien had not wanted her to go.

"Stay," he had said simply, holding one hand out in invitation, watching her intently as she dressed. She was reminded of the first time she had brought him a tray to his study. He had bid her stay that day as well. "I have no care for what small minds think. Come back to bed and the world be damned."

"You have the luxury of such sentiment. I do not. The reality remains that it is I, rather than the world, who will be damned." She had said the words with the sincerity of truth, and with a complete lack of rancor. She had made her choice with eyes wide open, and she harbored no regrets. In fact, she was wickedly delighted with her decision.

"You shall not be damned for this choice, Darcie. Never will I let you suffer for it." Damien had stared at her intently, his eyes burning brightly as he spoke. "Now come back to bed."

Ignoring his softly voiced command, Darcie had

kissed his beautiful mouth and slipped away. She was not ready to share their passion with the world, not willing to have the household staff intrude on their secret liaison.

Now, with eyes closed, she lay on her bed, reveling in gorgeous thoughts of Damien, his lips, his hands, his—

"You worked late last evening."

Darcie's eyes popped open. She had not heard the other woman's approach, but Mary stood over her now, a frown marring her brow.

"I thought you'd gone down already," Darcie said, her cheeks hot with embarrassment at having been caught in her secret imaginings.

"I went down hours ago. But now I've come up. To tell you that the doctor was called away. Said he'd return quite late. He left you this." Mary extended her right hand, offering a sealed note.

Darcie sat up and reached for the folded sheet. "Thank you, Mary. I feel bad that you had to come up to give it to me. You have more than enough to do already."

"I didn't 'ave to come up. I was curious." Mary shrugged. She leaned forward a bit to peer closely at Darcie's face and pressed one palm to her brow. "Are you feeling poor? You look flushed . . . but you feel cool."

"I-I feel very well, thank you." Darcie fanned herself with the folded note.

Mary glanced down and skewed her lips to the side. "Well, what's it say?"

Lowering her head, Darcie stared at the note in her hand, unwilling to open it in front of the other woman. She wanted to savor the message in private, but Mary couldn't know that. She thought the note was just a missive from employer to employee. As she slowly slid her thumb under the seal, Darcie recalled that Mary could not read. Should the need arise, she would simply dissemble, she decided.

Carefully unfolding the sheet, she stared at the bold masculine writing, wishing she could press the page against her heart, while at the same time battling the surge of disappointment that tugged at her when she realized that the words were not those of a lover.

> *Darcie,*
>   *The day is yours to do with what you will. John Coachman is at your disposal. Perhaps you wish to have a carriage ride in the park. I expect to return late.*
>
>   *Damien Cole*

So much for love words and heartfelt emotion, she thought, her brows rising then falling, her shoulders slumping slightly. She felt deflated, like a bellows with all the air forced out. Though she had enjoyed a previous outing to the park, the idea held little appeal this morning.

Mary cleared her throat, reminding Darcie of her presence.

"The doctor will be away for the day," Darcie said, slowly refolding the page and carefully pinching the crease between her thumb and forefinger. Dropping her gaze, she ran her fingers back and forth, accentuating the fold. "He will return quite late."

"Oh. Well, I told you that already," Mary said with a huff and an inflection to her voice that implied she thought the note rather odd. "Why did he need to leave the note at all?"

Darcie wondered the same thing herself, and her mood brightened a bit. Perhaps he had left it just so she would know he was thinking of her. Her disappointment over the distinctly unlover-like tone of the missive evaporated at the thought.

"I'd best get back downstairs." Mary turned to go.

Drawn out of her reverie, Darcie reached out and caught her friend's hand. "Thank you, Mary."

"For bringing up the note? It was nothing. Like I said, I was curious." Her tone clearly implied that her interest had been for naught.

Darcie shook her head. "For being my friend," she said softly.

Mary stared at her for a moment, tears welling in her green eyes. She ducked her head and cleared her throat, then gave Darcie's hand a reassuring squeeze. Turning, she took a step towards the door.

"There's a plate of food for you in the kitchen," she said over her shoulder as she departed, her voice thick. "I covered it to keep it warm."

For a long moment after Mary departed, Darcie stared at the empty doorway, wondering why she had not taken the opportunity to talk with her about so many things, the questions and suspicions surrounding Janie's disappearance, the bizarre conversation with Poole. Well, not about the entire conversation. She did not feel she could share the private matter of her embrace with Damien outside the carriage house. That was something she preferred to lock away in her heart, to cherish secretly and silently. Besides, bringing up that embrace might lead to a conversation about other stolen moments, and Darcie was not ready to talk to anyone about the night she had spent in Damien's arms. Those memories were her own private treasures. With a sigh, she realized it was a question of trust.

Rising from her bed, Darcie quickly performed her ablutions. She ran her hand over the plain black bombazine of her dress, and for a moment, she felt utterly sad at the thought that Damien had only ever seen her in this, a plain, serviceable old dress, or worse, in the rag she had arrived in. She recalled the pretty dresses of her youth, soft and ruffled, adorned with lace. Little girl dresses. She shrugged and thrust all regret from her mind. Wishing that she had a beautiful gown to wear for him wouldn't make it so. As she slipped the dress over her head and fastened it, she smiled as she recalled that Damien had, in fact, seen her in something other than an ugly black dress.

He had seen her in nothing at all.

The thought should have given her pause. She was a woman raised with the expectation of marriage and children, reared with a keen sense of propriety. But the reality of a harsh life had intervened. Her current circumstance ought to be abhorrent to her, yet as she thought of Damien's embrace, his caresses, she refused to feel ashamed.

Darcie reached up and wound her long hair into a smooth coil, humming softly to herself as she moved, her thoughts far from her attic room.

Scratching up her hairpins from the small stool by her bed, she slid them between her teeth and closed her lips around them, then took one at a time to push into the thick mass of hair, securing it in place. As she removed the last pin from her mouth, it slipped from her fingers and fell to the floor. Getting down on one knee, she reached under her bed to retrieve the hairpin, but found nothing. She rested one hand on the mattress, and ducked her head down so she could see beneath the bed.

"There you are!" she murmured as her fingers closed around the pin.

From the corner of her eye, she spied a pale mass shoved far beneath the bed. Frowning, she looked more closely and found that it was the ink-stained newspaper that she had thrust there days ago. She had saved it with the intention of revisiting the article about the Whitechapel murders. Straining forward, one arm extended to the fullest, she reached far into the shadows and brought forth the stained and folded paper.

Darcie sat on her bed, placing the newspaper down before her. Carefully, she opened it and smoothed the creases until it lay flat on the coverlet. The small window above her head filtered in the daylight, and she shifted the newspaper until it lay directly in a beam of sunlight. The large ink stain from the spill obscured the bottom half of the newspaper, but stopped short of rendering unreadable the article of interest. Hitching up her skirt, she crossed her legs and leaned forward, her attention fixed on the article. She began to reread the text she had started days ago.

Another murder of the same cold-blooded character as those recently perpetrated in Whitechapel was discovered early yesterday. . . . London will talk and think of nothing else except this new proof of the continued presence in our streets of some monster in human form, whose desperate evil goes free and undetected by force of its own dreadful audacity, and by an as-yet-unrebuked contempt for our police and detective agencies. The series of shocking crimes perpetrated in Whitechapel culminated in the murder two nights past of one Sally Booth, who is connected with the other victims only by her miserable mode of livelihood. All ordinary experience leaves us at a loss to comprehend the cruel slaughter of three, possibly four women. The single male victim is now believed to have been the recipient of an unrelated attack.

Darcie tapped her finger lightly against the page, lost in thought. There was something about the words she had just read that nagged at the edges of her consciousness. The first time she had read the paragraph, days ago in Damien's study, the part about Steppy, the single male victim, had upset her greatly—blotting out all other considerations. But as she read the sentences now, there was something else that bothered her.

Her eyes were drawn to the name, Sally Booth, and the reference to the woman's miserable mode of livelihood. Suddenly, she felt as though an icy deluge had drenched her skin.

The name. Sally Booth. The reference to her miserable mode of livelihood could only mean that she was a prostitute. Darcie slammed her eyes

closed, trying to block out the realization that over-
took her. The girl that she had met at Mrs. Feather's,
the one that Damien had treated. Her name was
Sally.

No—she shook her head against the implication
of her reasoning. The name was common enough.
Surely there were many women of the night called
Sally. But even as she tried to reassure herself, the
terrible certainty lodged in her chest, making each
breath heavy and choked.

Returning her attention to the newspaper, Darcie
read on, unwillingly drawn into the recitation of
the deadly fiend's horrific acts.

*The details of Booth's murder need not be re-
ferred to here at length. It is enough to say that she
was found, early on Wednesday morning, lying,
with her head nearly severed from her body and mutilated in a most revolting way, her heart torn from
her breast. She was found in the backyard of 10
Hadley Street, Spitalfields. She was an occupant of
the house, which is known as a house of ill-repute.
It is nearly certain that, for the purpose of privacy,
she made her way, together with her murderer, into
the yard, which is easily accessible through the house
at all hours of the night. She was most likely not
killed in another place and then carried to the spot
where she was found. The fact that no cry from the
poor woman reached any of the inmates of the house
shows that the assassin knew his business well. The
wounds inflicted by him were carried out with a
precision and knowledge that lead authorities to
suspect the perpetrator to be a man of medical
knowledge.*

Darcie read the words a second time, then a third—10 Hadley Street. Oh, God! Mrs. Feather's House. Sally Booth was the girl she had met when she accompanied Damien there. She wanted to doubt the assumption, but the facts substantiated the terrible truth. A massive shudder racked her frame, and her teeth began to chatter as though she were caught in a chilly wind.

Burying her face in her hands, Darcie moaned softly, thinking of the terrible fate that poor girl had suffered. She drew in a trembling breath.

Her eyes scanned the words once more.

. . . found, early on Wednesday morning, lying, with her head nearly severed from her body and mutilated in a most revolting way, her heart torn from her breast.

The room seemed to spin, and Darcie's stomach rebelled as she reread the words slowly, fixing her utmost concentration on the small, black letters that blurred and swam before her eyes. Sally's heart had been torn from her breast.

Her heart . . .

With a cry, Darcie jumped up from her bed, flinging the newspaper from her as though it was some vile insect, and began to pace the narrow confines of her chamber. Her throat felt tight and strangled, and her stomach churned, rolling with a terrible nausea. *Sally's heart. Sally's heart.*

Darcie had spent the day on Wednesday making endless sketches of a human heart. She remembered asking Damien whose heart it was. Frowning, she tried to recall what his answer had been.

Does it matter? he had asked, unconcerned.

At the time, she had thought it did not. Now, she thought it mattered more than anything in her life ever had. Frantic, she paced three steps forward, then whirled and paced three steps in the opposite direction.

Oh, dear God! Did the heart in Damien's laboratory belong to Sally? And if it did, how had he—

Suddenly, she recalled the night that she had watched Damien through the open door of his chamber. What night had that been? Monday? No, Tuesday. Tuesday night.

With trembling hands, Darcie poured water from the pitcher on the washstand into the chipped basin. Leaning forward, she splashed the tepid liquid onto her face, trying to calm her racing pulse, to cool her fevered brow.

Finally, she straightened and dabbed her face with a folded square of linen that lay beside the basin. Tuesday night she had watched Damien through the open door of his chamber. She recalled the bloodstained shirt and the way he had drawn it from his shoulders, and then thrown it in the fire. The assumption she had made at the time was that he was destroying a shirt that was stained beyond repair, but now nagging doubt plagued her. She had seen Damien in a blood-soaked shirt on Tuesday night, and Wednesday morning someone had found Sally's mutilated remains.

Once more Darcie began to pace the cramped confines of her chamber, fighting the nausea that roiled and writhed and climbed to sting the back of her throat with its acrid taste. She had spent the night in Damien's bed, in Damien's arms. His hands had roamed freely over her naked skin. The hands of a healer? A murderer?

She could not bear it.

Snatching the newspaper from her bed, Darcie folded it, again and again, until it was only a small square, approximately the size of her hand. She ran her fingers across her brow then down along the curve of her cheek, feeling trapped within the small chamber. She turned this way and that, searching for some release from the gnawing anxiety that festered in her thoughts.

She must go to Mrs. Feather's House. Her sister's warning, the words she had uttered when she first sent Darcie to Damien Cole, pounded loudly through Darcie's mind. . . . *have a care of him. Dr. Cole. He is a man to fear. Stay out of his way. Stay clear of his work. And keep your nose out of his secrets.*

CHAPTER TEN

Holding the folded newspaper in her hand, Darcie hastened from the room, quickly making her way down the stairs and out the back door. She was intent on finding John and asking him to take her to Whitechapel, to Mrs. Feather's House. She did not stop in the kitchen on her way. The breakfast that Mary had told her about earlier held no appeal. Her stomach was clenched in tight little knots, the pain sharp, but it was the ache in her heart that was nearly unbearable.

The days spent living under Damien's roof had lulled her into a false sense of security. She had come to feel safe, to feel that she had a place, to believe that she was cared for. Now, the harsh lesson of Whitechapel must be recalled, she thought. She had allowed herself to hope, to dream. It was too dreadful to conceive that just as her fantasies and expectations had begun to bubble and grow, they must crash to the ground in a horrible conflagration and burn away to cold, dead ash.

So frenzied were Darcie's thoughts that she did not see John moving across the drive toward her. It was not until she slammed up against him that she was pulled from her reverie.

"Whoa, there girl," he said, as though speaking to one of his horses. His hands closed around her upper arms, steadying her.

"Oh, John!" Darcie exclaimed looking up into his kind eyes. "I'm terribly sorry."

"No harm done." He let go his hold of her arms and dropped his hands to his sides. "Where were you heading in such a hurry?"

"I was looking for you. Damien—I mean, Dr. Cole, said that I might ask you to take me somewhere today."

"To the park then? Like last time?" John asked with a smile.

Darcie swallowed. "No, to Whitechapel. To the place you took us once before. Mrs. Feather's House."

The coachman looked startled. "Why would you want to be going there, Missy? 'Tis not a fit place for a young girl like you."

"Please, John." Darcie felt a cloying panic begin to ferment deep inside of her. She had not considered that he might refuse to take her there.

John gazed down at her and slowly shook his head from side to side, and with his denial her panic grew, squeezing her chest in a vice-like band. She must go to Mrs. Feather's. She must have her answers. What if she had bedded a murderer—

No, she could not think it, not until she questioned her sister. Damien was good. He was kind. He had shown her only goodness, yet—

Abruptly, she thought of an apple that she had held in her hand the day before, ready to bite into the glossy red surface and taste the tender flesh beneath. Suddenly, she had spotted a small wormhole, and instead of tasting the fruit whole, she had sliced it open with a pearl-handled fruit knife. The inside had been riddled with worms, rotten to the core.

Darcie caught John's arm as he began to turn away.

"Please," she whispered once more, but as he turned his face back towards her, and she saw his resolute expression, she tried the only argument that could possibly sway him. "Please, John. I must go. For you see, Mrs. Feather, she is . . ." The words seemed trapped in her throat. She could read in his eyes that he would not agree to take her, and sucking in a single shallow breath, she said in a rush, "Mrs. Feather is my sister."

John blinked, clearly astounded by her admission, and for a long moment he said nothing. His expression remained guarded, and for a solitary interminable heartbeat, Darcie thought he would turn her down. Abruptly, he nodded.

"Right, then. Off we go," he said, turning in the direction of the carriage house. "I'll have the carriage ready in a few minutes."

Darcie sagged in relief. He would take her. She would go to Mrs. Feather, to her sister, and demand answers. Darcie closed her eyes, struggled to rein in her emotions. Her sister may well refuse her demand, in which case she would beg. Beg for answers, beg for reassurance that the man she loved was not a cold-blooded killer.

Loved.

Darcie sank to her knees on the cobbled drive and buried her face in her hands. The enormity of it crashed over her in merciless waves. She had fallen in love with Damien Cole, a man of secrets, a man she knew little about. She loved him, even in the face of damnation. She loved the man she glimpsed behind the walls of his rigid self-control.

She thought of Steppy, how he had been such a wonderful father for most of her life, only to turn into a monster at the end. She had lived with Steppy for years, but had not known him at all.

How, then, could she be certain that her heart was right, that Damien was a man worthy of her love? Could love survive without trust?

She closed her fingers tightly over the folded newspaper, crushing it, wishing she had never seen the terrible article about the Whitechapel murders, wishing that she was still cocooned in the glowing aftermath of the night spent in Damien's arms. Forcing herself to her feet, she moved woodenly to the front of the house to await the carriage.

True to his word, John had the horses ready in short order, but the trip to Hadley Street seemed to take forever. Darcie unfolded the newspaper, which she still clutched in her hand, smoothed the crumpled surface and read the article once more. The dates, the times, everything seemed to point towards Damien's involvement. There was the matter of the bloodied shirt, and even more damning, the disembodied human heart that he had dissected in his laboratory the morning after Sally's heart had been ripped from her body.

And why, oh why, did he have that laboratory at

all? Why did he not carry out his dissections at the medical school?

Darcie shivered, trying to reconcile the tender lover of the night before with the image conjured by the horrifying newspaper article. The two seemed incompatible in the extreme. The door to the carriage swung open, and she looked up to find John waiting patiently. She was back in the East End. She was back in Whitechapel, in the cauldron of human suffering that had spawned a demon who preyed on the weakest and poorest.

"I'll wait here," John said gruffly as he helped her down.

"Thank you," Darcie whispered.

She had taken but a few short steps, when a thought struck her. Turning, she faced John once more.

"John, you have been in Dr. Cole's employ for many years, have you not?"

"Yes, Missy. Many years."

"Do you know"—Darcie hesitated, then rushed on—"how is it that Dr. Cole made the acquaintance of Mrs. Feather?"

John's expression was closed, remote. "Can't rightly say, Missy. You'd have to ask the doctor that."

Opening her mouth to say more, Darcie thought better of it. She would get no answers here.

"I don't think I'll be long," she said. Turning away, she made her way to Mrs. Feather's door.

She knocked, and after waiting several minutes with no results, knocked again with a great deal more force. Shifting her weight from foot to foot, Darcie waited impatiently for someone to answer.

No one came.

With a sigh, she raised her hand and rather than rapping smartly with her knuckles, she turned her fist and using the flat side of it pounded on the door.

"What is it?" The words were spoken in a tone that was hardly friendly.

The portal swung open to reveal none other than Mrs. Feather herself, her complexion devoid of paint, her hair hanging loose and scraggly over her shoulders. When she saw Darcie her face took on a distinctly unwelcoming expression.

"Told you not to come back here," she said sullenly.

Darcie nodded. "I know. I'm sorry, but I had to speak with you."

Through narrowed eyes, Mrs. Feather peered at her, as though seeking to look deeper than her skin, all the way inside of her to her very core. "How'd you get here, then?"

"By coach. I came in the doctor's coach."

"Well la-dee-da!" Mrs. Feather gave a harsh bark of laughter. "In his coach, no less. Just like a lady." She closed strong fingers over Darcie shoulder and gave her a rough shake. "You didn't heed my warning, did you, foolish girl?"

Uncertain of her meaning, Darcie stared at her mutely.

"You're in love with him," Mrs. Feather clarified.

Darcie's composure faltered at her sister's words. How could she know such a thing merely by looking at her?

As though reading her thoughts, Mrs. Feather shrugged. "If I could turn back the years, I'd be in love with him myself. And it'd be a painful mistake. Heartbreaking to love someone who cannot love you in return." She stepped back from the door and motioned Darcie to enter. "The girls are asleep," she muttered, leading the way through the narrow hall towards the back of the house.

Darcie struggled to maintain an outward show of calm. She had no wish to show her sister that her observations had landed with unerring precision, that the idea of loving someone who could not return her affection was terrible indeed, but even worse to love a man she could not trust.

When she reached the kitchen, Mrs. Feather sat on one of the simple wooden chairs and motioned for Darcie to take another. The scarred table was barren save for a half-empty bottle of whiskey and a chipped glass.

Mrs. Feather lifted the bottle and poured some of the amber liquid into the glass. Her hand shook, and a small puddle sloshed onto the tabletop. Darcie watched as her sister tossed back the liquor in a single gulp.

"You're mourning her," Darcie said softly, moving her hand tentatively across the table, closing it over Mrs. Feather's.

The other woman seemed to deflate before her eyes, as though Darcie's small expression of sympathy had somehow poked a hole in her defenses, sucking the bravado out of her. A single tear traced a path down her pale cheek.

Mrs. Feather nodded slowly. "Yes, I'm mourning her. She was a good girl, always smiling."

Darcie watched in stunned amazement as Mrs. Feather buried her face in her hands. Suddenly, she wasn't Mrs. Feather anymore. She was Abigail. Just plain Abigail. Rising from her chair, Darcie crossed to her sister and sank to her knees by the other woman's side. She wrapped her arms around Abigail's heaving shoulders and held her while she sobbed.

At last, her tears exhausted, Abigail quieted. "Why did you come here?" Her voice was a raspy whisper.

Darcie rose and hitched her chair closer, then sat by her sister and smoothed the crumpled sheet of newsprint over the table. She pointed to the article about the Whitechapel murders. "I had a terrible thought that it might be Sally. Your Sally."

"My Sally," Abigail echoed, her tone unutterably sad. "Yes, he killed her. So much blood—" She broke off, shaking her head.

Darcie felt her heart constrict at the confirmation of her worst fears. Of course, she had known as soon as Abigail herself opened the door, rather than one of the girls or a maid. But hearing her sister affirm that the dead girl was Sally, the same Sally that she and Damien had treated only days ago, was terrible.

"I'm so sorry for your loss, Abigail," she murmured, her voice catching.

Her sister jerked her head up and stared at her, her blue eyes puffy and red from crying, dulled by her grief.

"You really mean that, don't you? You *are* sorry for my loss!" She was quiet for a moment, studying Darcie's face as though searching for some clue as to her true thoughts and motivations. "You have changed. Years ago, you wouldn't have given Sally any notice. You would have twitched your skirts aside lest they be soiled by touching her."

Darcie chose not to take offense at her sister's words. The statement was nothing but the truth. "Yes, of course you are right." Taking Abigail's hand between her own, she squeezed gently. "You, too, would have twitched your skirts aside. But that was a long time ago. You have changed. I have changed. Life has buffeted us to and fro, like leaves caught in the wind. But we have survived, and that must count for something."

Abigail cleared her throat. "It does count for something," she said fiercely. With an awkward jolt, she surged to her feet and cleared away the whiskey bottle and glass. "Enough of this."

She moved across the small kitchen and put the water on to boil. "Would you like tea?"

Darcie smiled despite the sadness that still hung in the small room.

"Yes, I'd like tea."

Abigail nodded and slowly set about preparing a pot and two cups. She moved like an old woman, or someone who was terribly battered and bruised. Darcie's heart went out to her sister. Darcie knew the grief that she, herself, felt at Sally's death, and she could only imagine the greater intensity of her sister's sense of loss.

Silence reigned as Abigail tended to her small chore. At length, she carried the pot and cups to the table, and then sat down once more to pour.

"Sugar?" she asked, in the same polite tone they had used in their mother's parlor.

"Yes, thank you."

"And milk?"

Darcie nodded. "Please."

They sipped in silence.

"You've come to ask me about him."

"Yes." There was no point in pretending otherwise. Darcie put her cup onto the tabletop. Abigail had provided no saucer. "Abigail, when you first sent me to Dr. Cole, you warned me about him, warned me to stay out of his secrets, out of his work . . ."

"But you didn't listen, did you?" Abigail challenged, her expression mutinous. "You couldn't just take it for what it was. A decent wage and a roof over your head. You had to climb into his life."

"I didn't mean—"

Abigail cut her off with a sharp slash of her hand. "We never mean for it to happen, Darcie girl. It just does. I never meant for things to end this way. I thought he loved me . . . thought he'd marry me . . . Instead, he made me into this." She made a choked sound. "And I let him."

"Not Damien?" Darcie asked in horror. Surely the man who had seduced her sister then left her to fend for herself was not Damien Cole.

Abigail stared at her, puzzled, until Darcie's meaning sank in. "Oh, no. I never loved Damien Cole. By the time I met him I had long ago given up such dreams. I only meant that men are fickle creatures, loving you, cherishing you until they get what they want. Then their love evaporates like morning dew."

Her heart gave a pathetic lurch at Abigail's words, but Darcie forged on bravely. "No, Abigail. Not all men. I cannot believe that all men are so callous." Oh, but she could believe it. She thought of Steppy, the way he had turned on her like a rabid dog. Thrusting the memory aside, she steeled herself, choosing not to believe that Damien would purposely betray her heart.

"Believe what you wish. You will learn." Abigail nodded sagely. "You will learn."

Darcie pressed her lips together and held her silence, drawing her emotions under rigid control. She had come here for answers, not arguments.

Suddenly, Abigail looked at her sharply. "When you knocked on my door weeks ago, you were a timid little mouse, scared of your own shadow, barely able to raise your eyes and look in my face. You are different today. Less timid, less afraid." She narrowed her eyes and leaned closer. "Don't think he will protect you, stand by you. If this bravery comes from him, then it is a false bravado, my girl. He'll be gone, or worse, he'll send you away, and you'll be the timid mouse once more. And you'll be brokenhearted, to boot."

Darcie digested Abigail's words for a moment, wondering at their veracity. Was her confidence just a shallow reflection of Damien's support? Or had she truly come into her own, regained some of the self-assurance that had bled out of her that long-ago night when Steppy had sold her? She thought it was the latter that was true. She hoped it was the latter.

"Abigail, was Dr. Cole here that night? The night Sally was killed?" The questions tumbled from her lips. She thought that if she did not ask them aloud in a rush, she would not find the courage to speak them at all.

A faraway look came into Abigail's eyes, a look of unbearable heartbreak and dread.

"He was here," she said softly, her confirmation sending Darcie's spirits plummeting. "In spirit first, then in body. He was here." Abruptly, Abigail rose from the table. "Come with me, and I will show you the legacy of blood he left me."

Abigail's words fell like leaden weights on Darcie's hope, squelching it beneath the load. Her heart hammering in her breast, Darcie rose and followed her sister from the room.

"You wonder how I came to be acquainted with Dr. Damien Cole." Abigail paused on the landing, her expression shuttered as she turned to watch Darcie ascend the remaining steps behind her.

She *did* wonder, but did she truly want to know? Darcie pressed her lips together in consternation as she slowly made her way up the narrow staircase at the back of the house, pondering her sister's assertion.

"The night I met him was clear and cold. There was no wind." Abigail moved along the cramped hallway, speaking over her shoulder, her tone clipped. "Curious the things a person remembers. I don't recall the exact date, or even the month, but I can see the stars winking down at me as clearly as if I were looking at them right now."

She glanced back at Darcie, a sharp piercing look, before she continued. "I was hurrying back after visiting a sick friend. I was late. The house was about to open for the night and I knew the customers would begin to arrive in just a few moments. As I came round the corner there was a noise, pitiable really, so faint and desperate. Following the sound of that soft cry, I found a woman ..." Abigail's voice trailed off and she paused for a long moment, saying nothing.

Though it was a warm day outside, Darcie rubbed her hands along her arms, feeling a chill settling in her bones, a premonition of what was to come. There was nothing threatening about the dark-paneled walls, the simple carpet whose threads were worn from the passage of so many booted feet. Nonetheless, she felt a darkness, a frightening aura descend upon her. She could not help the furtive glance she cast over her shoulder.

A dog barked in the distance, the sharp sound cutting the silence. The noise jolted her from her contemplation. Abigail shook her head and led Darcie the rest of the way along the hall, to the door at the far end. There, she paused before continuing her story in a subdued tone.

"She wasn't a woman, really. She was little more than a girl, doubled over, clutching her belly, huddled in a puddle of blood. I couldn't leave her there in the alley, so I brought her home. Here. Half dragging her, half carrying her." Waving her hand in the direction of the closed door before her, Abigail stepped aside. "Go on, open it."

Darcie moved forward to rest her hand on the door handle, the vague feeling of unease growing stronger. She hesitated, not sure that she could face what she might find.

"He came here that long-ago night," Abigail said, moving closer as she spoke. Darcie felt the whispered words on her skin. "He came to this very room where she lay on the bed, her blood soaking the sheets."

"Dying?" Darcie whispered, questions rioting in her mind, her fingers curling painfully tight around the handle of the unopened door.

"Yes, she was beyond the hope of recovery." Abigail laid her hand on Darcie's arm as though to steady her inner turmoil. "The girl was with child. I suppose the father refused to do right by her, for she came to Whitechapel in search of a way out."

Frowning, Darcie turned her head and met her sister's steady gaze. "You mean she visited someone who would—who could—"

"Who could end her pregnancy? Yes, I found her in the back alley, bleeding, too weak to move. It was obvious that she wasn't from these parts. No stink of whiskey on her, and her clothes were clean. Her cloak was too fine, her hands soft and smooth. Quality." Abigail gave a harsh, self-mocking laugh. "I suppose I recognized the signs because I'd left them behind myself, not so long ago. She was out of her head, weak, and in pain. I brought her inside, here to this room, laid her on the bed. Too late. With her last breath, she gasped a name. Dr. Damien Cole."

Darcie recoiled as though she had been dealt a physical blow, feeling a sharp pain knife into her heart. No, not Damien. Whatever she had expected Abigail to tell her, it was not this. He could not have fathered a child with an innocent girl, then left her to fend for herself. She refused to believe it of him. "He would never—"

"I sent for him," Abigail continued, ignoring Darcie's whispered objection. "He came through the door, gaunt, and drawn, looking as though the demons of hell gnawed at his heels. Took the stairs three at a time. Flung himself on the bed, kissing the girl's cold cheek, touching her hair, whispering his love. Foolish man. A dead woman hears nothing." She shrugged, the motion nonchalant, seemingly uncaring, but in her eyes Darcie saw compassion, sadness.

"Who was she?" Darcie knew the pain in her chest would not kill her, but, oh, the heartache was near unbearable. Had Damien fathered a child, deserted the mother, only to realize, too late, that he loved her? No, no, a thousand times no.

Abigail shook her head. "He never said who she was, and *she* was far beyond any communication. He just gathered her in his arms and carried her to his carriage. I never knew more than that. He paused at the door, the dead girl limp in his arms. I'll never forget the look on his face, his beautiful features twisted by grief, his eyes cold and flat. Still, he spoke to me as civilly as you please. Thanked me for trying to help her, polite as if I'd served him tea."

Nodding, Darcie pictured Damien, cool, controlled, doing exactly as Abigail described.

"And he said that if ever I needed a favor, I had only to ask. Then, months later, he began to come round regularly—oh, no, you can take that look from your face. He came round to see to the girls if they were sick or hurt. Talking to them, to me, as though we were his equals. Imagine."

Stunned, mesmerized by the terrible story, Darcie tried to assimilate its meaning. Suddenly, an image of the small miniature on Damien's desk crossed her thoughts. "The girl who died . . . did she have dark hair?"

Abigail looked at her quizzically. "She did."

A sick feeling curdled in Darcie's belly. She recalled with striking clarity the way Damien had
spoken of the girl in the miniature. There was no
doubt in her mind that he had loved her. Darcie
shivered, a deep chill permeating her bones. She
had come here for answers, but instead seemed to
find more questions. The only answer she had,
she'd already known before she came here. Damien
had loved that girl, and he loved her still.

Perhaps the girl had taken all Damien's love
with her to the grave. A knife twisted in her gut at
the thought.

"What about the night Sally died? You said that
Damien was here . . . in spirit first, then in body.
What did you mean by that?" Darcie demanded,
staring at her sister intently, searching for answers
in her eyes.

"One of my girls, Mayna, made a mistake. Got
caught, if you know what I mean."

"With child?"

Abigail nodded. "Not many men will pay to lie
with a pregnant whore. So she went and found
someone to get rid of it. Never asked me or I
would have helped her. The woman she went to
see was a back-alley butcher. . . ." She paused, snort-
ing derisively. "Maybe the same one who did that
young girl wrong. But Mayna made it here on her
own. She was in a terrible way. Lying on this bed,
crying and bleeding. Looking at her, I thought of
that night, thought of Damien Cole and the girl
who died in this room, on this bed. That's what I
meant when I said he was here in spirit."

"Then in body . . ." Darcie prodded.

"Yes, he came as though he knew something was amiss. Came to this chamber, did what he could." Abigail shook her head. "There have been times . . . Sometimes I wonder if he has some strange way of foretelling the future, or sensing tragedy as it unfolds."

Darcie shivered as Abigail voiced her own thoughts aloud. She herself had wondered if Damien possessed some inexplicable otherworldly knowledge. "Did . . . did he save her?"

"Mayna? She'll never have a child," Abigail said gruffly. "But she survived."

"Why did you say he left you a legacy of blood?"

Abigail brushed Darcie's hand aside and twisting the knob, she pushed open the chamber door. Darcie stumbled back in horror from the sight that greeted her.

"Oh, my God," she whispered, pressing her knuckles to her lips. The light-colored walls were stained crimson, as though someone had taken a bucket full of dark red paint and tossed it against the pale surface, then let the rivulets flow unheeded to the floor. The color was darker in places, paler in others, suggesting that someone had tried to scrub away the stain.

"Surgery is messy work," Abigail said dryly, shaking her head. "We tried to clean it, but those walls will need fresh paint. The carpet was good for nothing but the rag bin." She jutted her chin toward the naked floor.

Darcie whirled towards her, grasping her arms. "What of Sally? When was she killed? When exactly did Damien leave?"

Frowning, Abigail froze, her brow furrowed as

Darcie's fingers curled about her arms in a frantic grasp. She pressed two fingers to her lips in silent contemplation.

"I don't know," she said slowly, squinting slightly as she tried to recall. "I stayed alone here with Mayna. The other girls went about their business. I never knew about little Sally until the constable banged on my door the next morning."

Darcie's hands shook as she slowly dropped them to her sides. She felt drained, bruised. The explanation she so desperately desired eluded her, and she was left in a knotted turmoil of helpless confusion. With a last lingering glance at the horrific sight of the bloodstained walls, she acknowledged that she would find no further answers here.

Damien had been here that night. He had saved one woman's life. Could he possibly have killed another? The thought of it was both intolerable and incredibly implausible.

"I must go." She gazed searchingly into Abigail's eyes, but found no further answers there.

"Yes, I understand."

The two women made their way along the narrow hallway, and then descended to the main floor. Darcie paused in the entryway. With a soft cry, she flung her arms around Abigail, holding her tight.

"You are my sister, and I love you. No matter what has happened, no matter what the future brings, I love you. I should have said it before, should have come to find you long ago."

Abigail's arms closed tightly around her.

"What I said, about never coming back here," Abigail began, her voice choked with emotion. "I hope . . . that is . . . if you should wish to visit, I would be glad to see you any time. I mean, any time during the daylight hours. It wouldn't do for you to come at night."

"I will come back," Darcie promised, glad that from the depths of all this sadness, one good thing had arisen. Her sister was returned to her. Oh, not the sister of her youth. That woman was gone. But this Abigail who stood before her—this brave woman who had survived despite life's treachery—this woman had invited her into her life, and Darcie had no intention of turning down that invitation, regardless of how society might view Abigail now.

"You saved me, you know. That night you sent me to Dr. Cole." Darcie whispered the words against her sister's shoulder. "Thank you."

Drawing back, Abigail stared at her, her expression infinitely solemn. "Never think it, Darcie girl. I might have given you a push, but it was you who saved yourself. You are a woman of great strength. Never doubt it."

Darcie nodded, wishing she could feel as certain as Abigail sounded. She didn't feel particularly strong, only horribly confused and afraid that she had become tangled in a web that was more complicated than she could ever hope to comprehend.

"You remember, Darcie girl. Damien Cole is not an easy man to understand. I have known him for years, yet I know him not at all. But one thing I do know . . . he has terrible secrets and even more terrible guilt."

"But *how* do you know that? What are these terrible secrets?" Darcie demanded.

Abigail shrugged. "I know men. And I can recognize another tortured soul when I see one. There are rumors that he was ejected from the university for strange experiments, and worse tales that he cares not where his bodies come from. . . ."

Sucking in a deep breath, Darcie fought the cold fingers of dread that crept along her spine. "They are only rumors."

"Suit yourself," Abigail said, the uncaring words belied by her concerned tone. "But take care."

"I will take care, Abigail. And I'll return another day."

With a last quick hug, Darcie hurried from Mrs. Feather's House, back to John who paced beside the waiting coach.

CHAPTER
ELEVEN

The ride back to Curzon Street seemed interminably slow. Darcie wanted to be away from Whitechapel, away from the harsh memories that haunted those streets. She felt overwhelmed by all she had learned, and even more confounded by all she had been unable to unearth. She knew that Damien had been to Hadley Street the night of Sally's murder, knew that he'd had his surgical tools with him. She had seen his bloodstained shirt. So, too, had she seen the disembodied heart in his laboratory. While those facts seemed damning, there was Abigail's assertion that he had saved Mayna's life. Could a man save one woman then turn around and kill another? It made no sense at all.

Then there was the question of why Damien would slink through the streets, killing women of the night. She wondered if a man could be mad one moment and sane the next, in one instant a horrific murderer, in the next a dedicated doctor. She had no proof that Damien Cole was anything other than he appeared, and her heart argued that he was a good man.

Pressing her palm against her forehead, rubbing absently against the dull ache that throbbed there, Darcie agonized over her suspicions. She was enamored of Damien, entranced by him. How could she suspect him of any involvement in such a repugnant crime? He was a doctor, a healer. And though he was an anatomist, one who, perhaps, bent the rules more than a little, that in itself could not be used as evidence of his involvement in Sally's murder. He had made no secret of the fact that he dissected bodies. In fact, quite the opposite. It was an open and accepted part of the daily doings of the household on Curzon Street. Yet, even that was suspect, for why did he carry out his work in the laboratory above the carriage house? Why did he not perform his dissections at a medical college? Abigail's suggestion that some dark secret held the answer to those questions bore further consideration.

Darcie's mind spun with conjecture and despair, and with each terrible question that jumped to the fore, she was simultaneously confronted by the memories of the night she had spent in Damien's glorious embrace. She refused to believe that she had lain with a murderer. Heartsick, she stared unseeing out the window as the coach drew to a halt in front of the house. The question was, could she trust Damien Cole, did she dare to trust him?

John opened the door and helped her down, narrowing his eyes as he examined her for a long, intense moment.

"Your visit with your sister upset you," he said, his brow furrowed in concern.

"No, John. Not at all. I just have a great deal on my mind."

"You be careful, Missy." He held her fingers for a moment longer than necessary, and gave them a reassuring squeeze. "I'd hate to see you hurt."

Cocking her head to one side, Darcie pressed her lips together, and tried to decide how to phrase her response. She was tired of trying to guess at the cause of the cryptic warnings she had received. First her sister had warned her about Damien Cole, then Poole, and now John was cautioning her about *something*, but he hadn't said exactly what she was to be careful of.

Tired of the monsters conjured by her imagination, preferring whatever awful things the truth might reveal, Darcie caught John's arm as he made to move away. Best to just confront the issue head on and be done with it, she decided. "What exactly am I to be careful of, John?"

His eyes widened in surprise, dropping to the place that her fingers curled about his forearm. Clearly he hadn't expected her query.

"You be careful of Dr. Cole, be careful or you'll find yourself mired in the muck."

For a moment, Darcie was stunned speechless. She wondered at John's meaning, unsure if he was cautioning her to be careful of Dr. Cole in the general sense, or if he knew about her personal involvement with Damien.

"Why should I be careful of Dr. Cole?" she queried, trying to maintain a calm facade. "And how will I become mired?"

"Well, you're helping him with his work. It ain't right. A body should be buried right and proper, shrouded and shriven, not poked and prodded and cut up on a table. Bad enough that the doctor feels the need to carry on so. But to involve a wee thing like you. . . ." John shook his head. "A woman . . ."

Darcie barely restrained the sigh of relief that hovered in her chest. So, he knew nothing of her liaison with Damien, and his warning was simply a caution that she remember her place.

"Thank you, John. For taking me to see my sister," she said, squeezing his arm gently for a brief second.

He patted her hand, then nodded brusquely and moved off to drive the carriage round back.

Inside the house, Darcie hung her bonnet on a peg and hurried upstairs to Damien's study. She knew he would not be there, did not expect him to return from his lecture for many hours yet, but she wanted to be near his things, to touch his desk, his chair, his books. There was a certain comfort in the familiar, and she needed that right now.

"Ah, here she is."

Darcie stumbled to a halt as the deep timbre of Damien's voice greeted her arrival. She was surprised that he had returned before her. She paused in the threshold, her eyes meeting his, and she found him watching her with an intent expression. For the briefest moment, she felt they were the only two beings on earth, and her heart resounded with joy at the sight of him. The sensation was a primitive thrill that overrode all her fears and misgivings.

Damien rose at her entry, and as he did so, she

realized for the first time that they were not alone. A second man pushed himself up from his chair, his movements hampered by his rotund girth. He was a man of middle years, short in stature with bushy side whiskers that bristled along the angle of his jaw. Darcie smiled uncertainly, her gaze gliding back to Damien.

"Miss Finch, may I present Dr. William Grammercy. Dr. Grammercy, Miss Darcie Finch, the artist responsible for the excellent illustrations we have been discussing."

"Remarkable drawings, Miss Finch." Dr. Grammercy's shaggy brows crunched together as he peered at her intently. "Bit odd for a woman to be doing such work, but I cannot argue with the results. I daresay I'm well pleased with your rendition of my heart."

"My rendition of your heart?" Darcie asked in confusion, glancing quickly back and forth between the two men.

"The heart we dissected the other day was given to me by Dr. Grammercy," Damien clarified. "After I told him of the skilled artist I had employed to illustrate my specimens, he decided that the heart would fare better with me than it would with him."

"And it turns out I was quite right. Quite right. Excellent job, my dear. Most excellent."

As the doctor bobbed his head in punctuation of his effusive praise, waving his arms in an all encompassing circle, Darcie drew back, half fearing that in his eagerness to express his enthusiasm for her work, Dr. Grammercy might actually clap her on the back. Her gaze shot to Damien, and she found him regarding her with amusement.

"Well, my boy, I'll be on my way. A pleasure, my dear." Dr. Grammercy inclined his head to both Darcie and Damien. "No need to see me out."

"On the contrary," Damien objected. "I have one last question for you, regarding the matter we spoke of earlier."

"Mmmm," Dr. Grammercy nodded, his gaze sliding to Darcie, then quickly away.

The two men took their leave and departed the study. She could hear the soft murmur of their conversation and the occasional word that drifted back to her . . . *Whitechapel . . . sexual insanity . . . Bedlam . . . Thank you for coming . . . Yes. Good-bye.*

The words floated over her. Sexual insanity? Bedlam? She could not fathom what they were discussing.

Darcie sank into a chair as the reality of what she had learned penetrated fully. Her emotions floated to the ceiling like butterflies set free as she digested the information that Dr. Grammercy had supplied the heart. Dr. Grammercy's heart. She wanted to jump up and dance. Good heavens! To think she had suspected Damien, actually considered the possibility that he could have been responsible for Sally's death. . . . The heart was not Sally's. Of course it was not Sally's!

Her thoughts went to the bloodstained shirt that she had watched Damien burn. The stains had not been made by Sally's blood as Damien tore her heart from her body—oh, how could she ever have thought it so! Obviously, the stains had arisen as Damien struggled to save Mayna's life. She nearly giggled with the euphoria of her relief.

His footsteps sounded on the stairs heralding

his return, and Darcie leaped to her feet. She longed to catapult herself across the room, to fling herself into the shelter of his arms. Instead, she fisted her hands at her sides, feeling uncertain of exactly what her place was in his life.

He paused in the doorway, his heated gaze raking over her, and then he held out his hand.

"Damien," she breathed, gliding across the space that separated them, drawn by the need to be close to him.

Pushing the study door closed with his booted foot, Damien pulled her against him and lowered his lips to hers. She kissed him with all the pent-up emotions that had built and churned throughout the day, her mouth open and seeking, her tongue twining with his. His own ardor answered her in kind. Breaking the kiss, he drew back and looked into her eyes.

"Was the day so very long?" he asked gently.

"Yes," she whispered, thinking of her ghastly suspicions, her disturbing trip to Mrs. Feather's House, the bloodstained walls in the upstairs chamber. "So very long."

"Did you ride in the park?"

"No." She shook her head. "I went to see my sister."

His brows rose in surprise. "You went to see Mrs. Feather?"

"Yes."

"I see," he said, though his tone and his quizzical expression suggested that he did not see at all.

Clasping her hands nervously together, she ran her finger over her scar. Darcie glanced at the desk where the miniature rested, a silent witness, a wraith from the past. Now was the time. She had to ask.

"Damien, the girl in the picture, who is she?"

He drew a sharp breath, his brows elevating in surprise, and she saw that her question had stunned him. "Where did that question come from? I thought we were discussing your visit with Mrs. Feather."

Darcie moved to the desk and lifted the miniature, examining the small dark-haired figure, searching for enlightenment. There were no answers to be found in the minute brush strokes.

Raising her eyes, she found Damien watching her intently, his expression shuttered, his thoughts hidden behind the polite mask she knew so well, his features arranged to give no indication of his secret contemplations.

"Perhaps this *is* a discussion of Mrs. Feather," he observed dryly. "Exactly what did your sister tell you?"

"She told me that a girl died with your name on her lips. She told me that you came and carried her away."

He turned from her and crossed to the window, resting one shoulder against the frame, staring out toward the carriage house. She pressed her lips together, waiting. With a soft sigh, she replaced the picture on the desk.

"Please," Darcie whispered forlornly, "I have shared with you the darkest secrets of my soul. Will you share nothing with me?" One heartbeat, two, Darcie lost count as she waited for his answer. Drawing a shaky breath, she stared at his broad back. "Will you not entrust your secrets to me?"

He did not turn to her, did not acknowledge by word or movement that he even recalled that she was there. The silence blossomed and swelled, a dark flower winding tight tendrils about them both.

Slowly, she began to back away, intent on leaving him to his reflections. Her heart was heavy at his unspoken rejection, his unwillingness to let her into his inner sanctum, to share his secrets with her. Oh, he had shared his body. Beautifully, gloriously. But now she understood that though he had cleaved through her walls and barriers, leaving her defenseless, she had had no similar impact on him. She had not touched his soul, had not gained his trust.

The realization was like a physical blow, the pain as swift and great as though she actually had been struck. She loved him, with all that she was and all she would ever be. There was no doubt in her mind. The thought was both wonderful and terrifying, filling her with unspeakable joy and desperate longing. Still, she could not deny the one dark truth that cast a pall on her emotions. Despite the love that burst through her defenses, flouting her carefully erected guards and the darkness of her past, there was a kernel of reserve, a part of herself that did not fully trust him. How then could she condemn his reticence?

"Why do you wish to visit my own personal hell?" he asked curtly.

Darcie licked her lips, searching for the right words. A partial truth was best, for she sensed that confronting him with her newly recognized sentiment would only serve to alienate him. At length, she spoke. "Because you toured my hell, walking hand in hand by my side as I confronted my demons, and you made me less afraid. Those memories have dulled for me. I would do the same for you."

"Nothing can change the ugly truth, Darcie. I killed her." His voice lashed through the room with the vicious speed of a whip, cracking the still air.

"K-killed her?" Darcie stammered, disconcerted by his abrupt admission. Her thoughts skittered this way and that, and she leaped to the most obvious conclusion. Sally? Did he mean Sally? Her heart lurched and twisted, then settled into a steady rhythm once more as reason returned. They had been talking about the girl in the miniature. His wretched admission must relate to her. "You mean the girl in the picture?"

"Yes," he rasped as he turned from the window, his expression bleak, tortured.

Darcie stared at him, feeling his pain, suffering at the realization that he believed with a bone-deep certainty the words he spoke, truly saw himself in such a terrible light. But she could not believe it of him, and she had Abigail's story as her proof.

"But Abigail said she breathed her last breath before you came. How then do you take the blame for her death?"

Damien laughed, a hollow sound. In three long strides he closed the distance between them, and curled his hands around her upper arms, pulling her close until their lips were mere inches apart. She could see the wildness, the haunted grief that churned and roiled, his storm gray eyes a reflection of his soul.

"I killed her with my neglect," he said, the cold certainty grating over her. "Run from me, Darcie. I will cause you only harm. There is a darkness in me that I cannot control, a disgust over my own failings." His fingers tightened around her arms, not enough to hurt her, but enough that she felt the barely leashed turbulence of his volatile emotions. "I have no love left to give."

Shaking her head, Darcie made no move to draw away. Her head fell back, and she met his tormented gaze, feeling his terrible pain. "Tell me," she whispered. "Let me help you."

She leaned forward, resting her lips against his. Her lids drifted shut and she focused all her concentration on him, willing his suffering to flow away like the ebb of the tide. She felt him shudder against her.

"*Darcie.*" Her name was wrenched from him on a harsh whisper.

Suddenly, he thrust her from him, stepping back, as though their proximity was too intimate, too tempting to bear.

"She was my sister, and I am responsible for her death." The vowels and consonants were strung together, enunciated with careful precision, impeccable diction, as though by focusing on the sound of them, Damien could distance himself from their meaning.

Darcie stifled a gasp. Whatever admission she had expected, it was not this.

"I promised my mother on her deathbed that I

would care for Theresa, guard her with my life. I failed." The words were clipped, bitten off with harsh exactitude, falling like leaden weights from his lips.

Moving towards him, Darcie held out one hand, slowly, gently letting it come to rest on his arm. He stiffened and she thought he would pull away. Then his shoulders slumped in acceptance of her silent support.

"Tell me, Damien. Share your burden with me and together we will carry it. I promise it will be lighter for the sharing."

"Theresa was headstrong, volatile. With our mother's death, she went a little wild. Parties and balls were very well and good, but she had in her mind a fairy tale dream of a prince who would whisk her away and make all her dreams come true. If not a prince, then a title at the very least. With Father gone, Mother gone, and an older brother who was caught up in the euphoria of his studies and his own youthful folly—in fact little more than a rake himself—she longed for hearth and home, the promise of a man who would never leave her. She was a naive innocent, easy prey for the first unscrupulous man who came along." Damien sat on the edge of his desk. Catching Darcie's hand, he pulled her against him, looping one arm about her waist and resting his forehead on her shoulder.

"I had such dreams myself, once upon a time," Darcie said softly, running her hand in a gentle caress along the length of Damien's golden hair. *You are my dream,* her heart whispered.

"She met her *prince*," Damien continued derisively. "Met him secretly, told no one his name. He was no prince. Within weeks, she was ruined and pregnant." He tightened his hold on her, and Darcie thought her closeness offered him some comfort. "My sister did not tell me of her plight. Perhaps she feared that I would refuse to help her, or worse, that I simply would not care. I cannot say that I acted the part of protector. Mostly, I paid her pretty compliments and little else, leaving her to her own devices. She trusted me to protect her, and I failed."

Damien tipped back his head to meet Darcie's gaze. His emotions were naked and clearly etched in his expression. "She sought the services of a back-alley abortionist. Mrs. Feather found her that night, bleeding, near death."

Darcie swallowed, feeling faintly ill. He blamed himself. She could hear it in his words, feel it in the guilt that emanated from him in undulating waves.

"It was not your fault." She squeezed his hand, her heart heavy as she wished with a fervent, silent prayer that she could take this terrible pain, this gnawing guilt from him.

With a snarl, Damien rose from the edge of the desk, his face a mask of anguish. "She was too afraid to come to me. My own sister. She did not tell me of her plight, and I killed her with my ignorance. I should have paid closer attention to her comings and goings, should have known where she was, what she was doing, who she was with. I would have helped her. My God, I would have helped her. If only—"

Raising her hand, Darcie pressed her fingers to

his lips. "There is no 'if only,' Damien. She is dead. A terrible, terrible loss. An unbearable waste of a young life. But there is no 'if only.' If I have learned one thing in my life, it is that lamentation and regrets only make things worse. A person must move on, move forward, never forget the past, but learn from it. If you ponder the 'if onlys' of life, they will drive you mad."

Damien caught her wrist, and his lean fingers curled about her small bones. Slowly he drew her arm down until it rested by her side, his grip solid and unyielding, his gaze holding hers in a swirling pool of molten silver.

"How do you know that I am not quite mad already?" he rasped. "There are nights . . ."

Darcie held her breath as his voice trailed off. What terrible secret was prefaced by those words? No secret, she admonished herself firmly. Just a man wracked by guilt over his sister's tragic death.

Was that the reason he had taken her in? "When Abigail sent me to you, that night in the carriage, I asked you if you would please do this one favor for your old friend Mrs. Feather. You looked at me so queerly, and your whole demeanor changed. You took in a total stranger on the request of a notorious madam. Why?"

Damien stared down at her. "A sister for a sister. She tried to help mine, and then asked me to help hers. A fair trade?" he asked gently, his fingers tangling in her hair, his expression shifting to one of desire.

"A fortuitous trade, for me," Darcie whispered, confused by his mercurial moods, entranced by the glittering intensity of his gaze. Gone was the torment, the angst. The face he turned to her mirrored a burgeoning hunger.

"I had another reason for keeping you in my employ." His lips were a hair's breadth from her own.

Her pulse raced at his declaration, a steady, heavy pounding in her veins. Oh, please, let him care for her just a little.

"What reason did you have?" Darcie's heart pounded as she willed him to voice an avowal of his affection. Oh, she was not foolish enough to expect declarations of love or undying devotion, but she sensed more in his regard for her than mere attraction. The words came out in a whisper. "What reason?"

He laughed harshly. "If I could name it, perhaps I could have defended myself against it. I have no rational explanation. I only know that I am drawn to you in a way I cannot deny. You are a fire inside of me, Darcie, licking at the edges of my soul." He kissed her then, a hard press of his lips to hers. Possessive. Hungry. Leaving her gasping for breath when he pulled away.

"Damien." Darcie raised herself up on the tips of her toes, molding her body against his, welcoming the closeness of their contact.

He needed no further invitation. With a low groan, he took her lips once more, plundering them with the heat of his desire, open-mouthed, and wild. She gave what he demanded, and demanded his conciliation in return.

Her skin tingled everywhere he touched. She felt as though she would burst into flame.

"Come," he whispered. Taking her hand, he

edged the door open and peered out into the
empty hallway.

Damien led her to his bedchamber, drawing her
inside.

She glanced at the window, at the beam of sunlight that surged through the partially open drapery to land with unerring precision upon the
cream-colored satin coverlet of his bed.

"The sun yet shines," she whispered. An observation, not a protest. Strangely, the thought of
standing unclothed before him in the bright light
of day held a certain appeal, adding to the intensity of the sensations rioting inside of her, for he
too would be naked, allowing her to gratify her
craving for him. Catching her chin between his
fingers, he tilted her face for his kiss, a possessive
caress of his lips.

"I want to see you. I want to touch, to taste, to let
my senses feast upon you." He undid the buttons
of her dress, his fingers skimming lightly over her
heated skin. A gentle stroke of his palm moved her
collar aside, baring the tops of her breasts to his
fervid gaze.

His words, his touch, stoked the fire, sending
her careening over an unseen precipice into the
boiling cauldron of her desire. Hands trembling
with the rampant urgency of her passion, Darcie
forced the top button of his shirt through the
buttonhole, then the next and the next. Her fingers fumbled and she tamped down the compulsion to simply rip the garment open. She ached to
run her tongue along his sun-drenched skin, to taste
him, to inhale the scent of his body.

At last he stood shirtless, glowing with golden

perfection. Darcie exulted in the quickening rise and fall of his chest as she ran questing hands over the hills and valleys of his muscled torso, reveling in the feel of his warm skin. Then her hands drifted lower, her fingers working earnestly at the fastening of his trousers. He neither helped nor hindered, merely allowed her free rein in her explorations. But the sharp hiss of air that slid from him as her hand closed about the hard thickness of his erection attested to the strength of his reaction.

She gloried in the surge of pleasure that coursed through her. She did this to him. She engendered this raging need.

He kissed her lips, her throat, parting her bodice so his mouth could taste the valley between her breasts. Her dress slid from her shoulders, then pooled at her feet.

"No," she whispered a soft protest as he sank to his knees before her, pulling himself from her avaricious grasp, denying her the velvety feel of him cradled in her palm. He wrapped his arms about her waist, his tongue probing the hollow of her navel.

Slowly, he pulled the remainder of her clothing from her trembling limbs, rolled her gartered stockings down over the smooth curve of her calf, his fingers stroking, teasing. Her hands curled over his muscled shoulders, her fingers digging deep.

She cried out in shock, in ecstasy, as he kissed the soft brown curls at the juncture of her thighs, his fingers sliding smoothly into the moist furrow that welcomed him. Nudging her legs apart, he leaned forward, his tongue flicking over the sensitive bud of her desire. She wriggled—horrified, enticed. Her legs threatened to collapse from beneath her, would have collapsed if not for the support of his warm hand grasped firmly around her hip, his long fingers splayed across the round globe of her buttock.

Caught in the throes of pleasure, she thrust herself forward to meet each rasping stroke. There was only Damien. Her world had narrowed to the touch of his hand, the scrape of his tongue against her overheated flesh. She was wild for him. She shifted her hand, weaving her fingers through the thick strands of his hair, melding him to her as firmly as she could.

"Oh, please, Damien. Please . . ." She wanted to feel him against her, to delight in feeling his fullness between her thighs, to share all of herself with him.

He surged upward at her frantic plea, tumbling her backward onto the smooth coverlet.

"Open for me, Darcie." His hands guided her legs to do as he bid.

Following his lead as he urged her knees up, she tilted her pelvis toward him. With a single fluid thrust he came into her, then again, and again. She held nothing back.

Her high, keening cry was muffled in his shoulder as she bucked and jerked beneath him, her world splintering into a thousand points of pleasure. And with his hoarse cry she knew he joined her there, sharing the pinnacle of ecstasy.

They lay together, a tangle of limbs and unspoken emotions, uncaring of the passage of time. Darcie felt as though she floated on a haze of contentment, and her lids fluttered, drifting shut. She slept, wrapped in the safe haven of Damien's embrace.

Much later, she stirred, opening her eyes, taking in her surroundings. The sun had moved with the passage of time, no longer casting its rays upon the bed. Now, the watery light of evening filtered through the glass panes.

Damien rose up on one elbow and gazed down at her.

Darcie licked her lips, waiting for him to speak, uncertain of what he might say. She expected that the sharing of their secret thoughts and wounded hearts and the melding of their bodies would have a lasting effect on the harmony of their budding relationship, but she did not know what to expect from her lover by way of overt demonstration of his feelings. He had shown her, with every touch, every gentle caress, but even in the peak of passion he whispered no words of affection.

Her lover. The thought was strange, exciting, and baffling all at once.

"I am famished," he stated.

She blinked, taken off guard by his statement. The words could by no means be construed as a statement of fondness.

He smiled. "Come on. Cook should have a fine meal just about ready to serve. I'll have them set a second place."

Startled, Darcie surged to a sitting position, clutching the rumpled sheet over her breasts. "A second place?" she asked. "In the formal dining room? With you?"

One eyebrow rose questioningly. "Do you prefer to eat there alone?"

"Yes . . . No . . . I mean, I eat with the other servants." She felt a hot blush steal into her cheeks.

Damien's expression hardened. "A situation I should have remedied the first day I brought you above stairs. My oversight left you in an awkward position. You are not my servant." He kissed her, trailing his fingers through her disheveled hair. "You were never meant to be a servant."

"But, Damien, what will they say?" Even as the words left her lips, she realized that she did not think she cared what the others said. She wondered if that meant she was brave, or merely foolish.

"This house belongs to me," Damien stated with quiet determination. "Any who disagree with the way I choose to live my life may leave. Besides, do you honestly care what anyone says?"

Darcie thought about that, thought about all she had lived through, and realized with certainty that whispered condemnation could not harm her. Her life had been so unorthodox, her position in society so depleted, that she could never again hope to be the innocent, naive girl who had shopped and gossiped and entertained polite company. For heaven's sake . . . she was Mrs. Feather's sister!

Still, a tiny corner of her heart bled at the thought that her place in Damien's life would surely be transient, that she would be his mistress, not his wife. There was a small part of Darcie Finch that remained the wide-eyed girl, the innocent who dreamed of hearth and home. And children.

With a small shake of her head, Darcie pushed aside those dangerous thoughts. In her present situation, she could hardly offer a child the kind of life she would wish to provide.

Damien read her movement as a negative answer to his question. "Good. You should have no care for small minds and wagging tongues."

He caught a stray strand of her hair, running the length of it through his fingers before tucking it behind her ear. Bounding from the bed, Damien began to dress.

"Come on, then." He sent her a roguish grin over his shoulder. "Unless you have a mind to lure me back to bed. . . ."

Darcie laughed, allowing herself to enjoy his infectious good humor. She would not spoil her time with him by worrying about what was yet to come. While tomorrow might bring heartache, today was truly lovely.

CHAPTER
TWELVE

Seated to Damien's right at the formal dining table, Darcie finished her raspberry tart, and looked up to find him watching her, a frown creasing his brow. His own tart sat untouched.

"You will never forget."

Darcie placed her cutlery on her empty dessert plate, and dabbed her lips delicately with her serviette. "Forget?"

"What you suffered in Whitechapel. The hunger. The deprivation."

She was about to answer, when Poole entered the dining room and began to clear away the dishes. As he moved to Damien's side she glanced at the butler in the same instant that he turned his attention to her. Darcie felt certain that he knew what had passed between Damien and her, certain that he would make no attempt to hide his anger, his disgust of her, his condescension. He had been unkind to her from the moment of her arrival. To her surprise, she felt no consternation, no concern.

His opinion meant nothing to her. And then, as she held his gaze, she saw that Poole's expression held none of the emotions she expected to see. For an instant, she thought she read concern in his eyes, and then he looked away, breaking the connection.

How odd. She felt disoriented for a moment, and her attention remained fixed on Poole as he silently exited the room.

Deliberately returning her thoughts to Damien's earlier comments, she resumed their dialogue. "Forget Whitechapel? No, I would not even try. It is part of who I am. I shall never forget what it was like to be desperate, alone, hungry." She smiled ruefully. "Which is why it may be a good idea to ask Cook to avoid serving pudding. You do not seem to favor sweets, and I have this terrible urge to eat everything that is served. If I continue my consumption at this pace, I shall soon be the size of a house."

Damien examined her, unsmiling. "You will not return there, Darcie. To the streets of Whitechapel. You will never again know hunger, or cold. Never be destitute. That is your past."

She stared at him, confused by his declaration. Was this Damien's avowal of affection, his version of loving words? Did he mean that she could trust in him to protect her, or did he mean to imply that she was stronger now, that she would never allow those terrible things to happen to her again? Pressing her lips together, she acknowledged that whatever his intent, she had learned that she could fully trust only in herself.

Suddenly, Poole returned to the dining room,

casting a furtive glance over his shoulder. He leaned down and spoke quietly in Damien's ear, and when he straightened she saw a look of agitation cross the butler's features. He turned and strode briskly through the door.

Poole had barely exited, when there was a shuffling sound, a huffing, and Damien's friend, the man Darcie had met the previous day appeared in the doorway. Dr. Grammercy. His boots were mud splattered and he yet wore his coat. Darcie wondered at the urgency that had prevented him from handing the garment to Poole.

"Cole—" Dr. Grammercy huffed and puffed as he strode across the room, one hand pressed to his side as he fought to catch his breath, the other coming to rest on Damien's shoulder. He glanced at Darcie, and bobbed his head apologetically. "Miss Finch. So sorry to interrupt your meal." He wheezed. "Cole, I've come to warn you. I've had a visit from an Inspector—*huh . . . whooo . . .*" His reddened cheeks worked like a bellows as he sucked in air and blew it out again. "He was asking about that terrible misunderstanding at the University, the dead girl, your dismissal . . . I told him nothing. That business in Edinburgh, as well . . . What did the man say his name was? Inspector . . . Inspector . . ."

"Trent. Inspector Trent."

Darcie whirled in her seat as an unfamiliar voice supplied the information that Dr. Grammercy was struggling to find. A man stood in the doorway, his sharp gaze taking in the lot of them. His bearing was erect, military. He was dressed in a tweed suit, but Darcie could easily picture him in a uniform.

Their eyes met, and his attention lingered on her for a moment, before moving on to Damien.

Poole hovered in the hallway behind the newcomer. "I am sorry, sir," he intoned. "The gentleman refused to wait until I announced him. Shall I call the constable?"

"That would hardly prove beneficial, Poole. The man is an officer of the law," Damien observed dryly as he rose and strode to Darcie's side, offering his hand and helping her to her feet.

His fingers squeezed hers reassuringly before he dropped his hand to his side.

"I am Dr. Damien Cole."

Inspector Trent inclined his head politely. "I would like to have a word with you, Dr. Cole."

"Perhaps we could adjourn to the comfort of the front parlor?" Damien suggested.

"By all means," Trent agreed equitably. "We should *all* adjourn to the parlor." His gaze rested pointedly on Dr. Grammercy, before shifting to Darcie.

She felt as though she were being examined under a quizzing glass. For a moment, she was acutely aware of her worn and mended day dress, her plain hair, the lack of adornment on her person. Raising her chin, she forced herself to meet the inspector's gaze squarely, forced herself to recall that she was a woman tempered by life's fires. She refused to feel awkward or ashamed of her choices. Like a tide ebbing from the shore, the feeling of inadequacy passed.

"My assistant, Miss Darcie Finch," Damien performed the introduction.

"Your assistant, you say? Most unusual. In what capacity does she assist you?" the inspector asked.

There was an undercurrent, an implication, in the man's tone that made Darcie uncomfortable.

Damien stepped in front of her, shielding her from Trent's perusal. "She assists me in my laboratory. And she is a lady under my protection."

The tension in the room was palpable.

"A *lady* under your protection, you say?" Trent drawled.

Darcie had the peculiar thought that the man was purposefully trying to irritate Damien, to intentionally raise his ire.

"So I say," Damien replied, his quiet tone at odds with the edge of steel underlying the words.

"To the parlor, shall we?" Dr. Grammercy interjected. "I would welcome a glass of your fine brandy, Damien, my boy."

The tension temporarily contained, they proceeded from the room.

In the parlor, Damien seated Darcie in a chair by the fire, positioning himself behind her, his hand resting on the carved wooden chair back. Inspector Trent took a seat on the small velvet settee to their right, and Dr. Grammercy sank onto the overstuffed cushions of the large brocade sofa across from them.

Damien offered brandy first to Dr. Grammercy, who accepted a glass gratefully, and then to Inspector Trent, who declined.

Darcie noticed that Damien took nothing for himself. She shifted uncomfortably on her seat, feeling inexplicably wary, even afraid.

"I may wish to speak with each of you privately," Trent began, "but for the moment, I simply wish to inquire if any of you recognize this."

For the first time, Darcie noticed that Inspector Trent carried a long thin sac. He untied the twine that secured the top and used his handkerchief to carefully withdraw a slim metal instrument. It was a scalpel, similar to the one she had seen Damien use for dissection, as well as during their visit to Sally. Trent placed the instrument on the low table that was between them.

"Good heavens, man. It's a scalpel. Of course we recognize it." Dr. Grammercy's tone was incredulous, and he dismissed the object in question with a wave of his hand.

The inspector's keen gaze remained fixed on Damien. "And you, sir? Do you recognize this instrument?"

"As my esteemed colleague pointed out, it is a scalpel." There was a brittle edge to his voice.

Inspector Trent rubbed his chin thoughtfully. "Is it common for surgeons to engrave their initials on their instruments?"

"Yes, yes, indeed. Some do. Some don't." Dr. Grammercy nodded his head vigorously.

"Miss Finch . . ."

Darcie jumped at the sound of her name on the inspector's lips. She felt as jittery as a cornered fox.

"Have you seen this instrument before?"

"I have seen a scalpel," she affirmed.

"*This* scalpel?"

"I cannot be sure."

"Please, look closely if you wish." He gestured at the table.

Leaning forward, Darcie stared at the instrument. The blade was dirty, caked with dried blood. She shivered. There was something terrible about this blade. She could sense it. Mesmerized, she leaned even closer, stretching out one hand to touch the handle.

Suddenly, she found her wrist caught in the inspector's rough grasp.

"Do not touch it, if you please."

Damien stepped from behind her, and Inspector Trent glanced up at him before letting go his hold.

"Do you see the initials on the handle?" he asked.

Darcie swallowed, and being careful not to touch the scalpel, she leaned close enough to see what was engraved there. But she knew even before she saw the letters. With a cold and certain dread, she knew.

DWC. Damien Westhaven Cole.

"This instrument was found in the yard of 10 Hadley Street," Inspector Trent said conversationally, as he stared intently at Damien. "Is there anything familiar about it?"

"The scalpel belongs to me." Damien bit the words out impatiently.

Darcie's fingers curled involuntarily into the wooden arms of her chair. The muscles of her shoulders knotted and bunched, and her stomach lurched with dread. So great was her tension that she thought she might lose the entire enormous dinner that she had eaten.

The inspector rose from his seat, staring fixedly at Damien. "Perhaps you should come with me, Dr. Cole."

Darcie half rose from her chair, but Damien's hand on her shoulder stopped her.

"Yes, that might be for the best," he said. "Grammercy, if you would stay and keep Miss Finch company for a short while, I would be in your debt."

The older man's florid face reflected his concern. "No trouble at all, my boy. None at all."

Darcie watched with a sense of unreality as Inspector Trent packed the scalpel away in his sac. Rising she faced Damien. He smiled at her, and she knew that he meant to reassure, but his expression was strained. Resting his hand gently on her shoulder, he guided her back into the chair she had just departed. His fingers tightened momentarily, conveying to her a message of comfort, and then he was gone. Darcie pressed her fingers to her lips, watching Inspector Trent warily as he followed Damien from the room.

"This is not possible," she whispered into the ensuing silence, dropping her hand to her lap. "There must be some explanation—"

Her gaze shot to Dr. Grammercy, who stared back in gloomy silence, his jowls sagging, his expression cheerless.

"Please, Dr. Grammercy. I must know. What happened at the University? You made reference to an episode. . . ."

He shook his head. "I cannot say."

"You *will* not say," she challenged. Darcie looked down at her hands, clasped in her lap, the right fingers closing and unclosing with obsessive repetition about the left, then sliding across the raised ridge of her scar. She hadn't even realized she was doing it.

Taking a deep breath, she purposefully moved her hands back to the arms of the chair. She rested them there, consciously choosing a calm demeanor, forcing the agitation from her thoughts. Panic would do her no good. She must think clearly.

She rose and crossed to Dr. Grammercy, staring down at him in silence. He watched her apprehensively. After a long pause, she spoke.

"Please." The word was more than a plea. It held all her desperation and fear.

Dr. Grammercy sighed. "You could easily hear it elsewhere."

Darcie perched on the edge of the sofa, twisting so she had a clear view of Dr. Grammercy's face.

"So I might as well hear it from you," she prompted.

"Yes, well. I suppose that is true." He shook his head, a gesture of sorrow and despair. "First there was that poor girl in Edinburgh. Damien was visiting. Attending the lectures of the anatomist, Dr. Barrow. The man is quite well-known. He sells tickets to his dissections. The gentry often attend. Quite the spectacle, I have heard."

Darcie waited impatiently as Dr. Grammercy stared at the far wall, lost in his memories.

"I know of this only through hearsay, you understand," he continued. "There was some confusion at a lecture that Damien attended. He challenged Dr. Barrow. Challenged his ideas and his science. Damien was never one to allow an audience. He allowed medical students to view his work, but never gawkers. Damien and Dr. Barrow had words. Later that night, Barrow's daughter was found with her throat crushed."

"Surely you don't think—" Darcie exclaimed.

"*I* don't think," Dr. Grammercy interjected. "But the authorities did. They took Damien in for questioning, but naught was proven. In fact, his alibi was indisputable. He was at a pub with a dozen medical students. No question as to his whereabouts that night." His gaze slid nervously away from hers.

"No question? Are you certain?" There was something not right here, she thought.

"They were all well into their cups. At first, they said they couldn't recall, but then after a bit . . ." Dr. Grammercy cleared his throat and gave a short sharp nod. "There was a London lordling there for a visit. Lord Ashton . . . No, perhaps Lord Alton . . . I cannot recall. He swore that Cole was there all night. The constable agreed that there was no evidence that Damien was anywhere but in that pub."

Darcie rose and strode across the room, fumbling with the brandy decanter as she sought to busy her hands while her mind sorted through this new and troubling information. "May I offer you more brandy, Doctor?"

"Yes, that would be fine."

Returning to the man's side, Darcie took the snifter from him and refilled it. The motions felt odd, unfamiliar. She was standing in Damien's parlor acting the part of hostess while Damien was being interrogated regarding a terrible crime. Was it truly only a handful of hours past that she had lain in his arms? Feeling as though she was caught in some frightful dream, she turned away from Dr. Grammercy and returned the brandy decanter to its place on the table as she struggled to maintain her composure. A fit of tears would serve no good purpose here.

"There is more," she said softly, staring at the glittering crystal facets of the decanter, not daring to face Dr. Grammercy, afraid of what she might see in his eyes.

"Yes." His acknowledgement hung heavy in the air.

Darcie closed her eyes against the pain of it, taking a long, slow breath as she fought to maintain a calm façade, though her emotions roiled and churned.

"It happened here, in London, at the University. Damien went a bit mad after—" He stopped abruptly. "Do you know about Theresa?"

"Damien's sister? Yes, I know she died a tragic, needless death." At last Darcie found the strength to face Dr. Grammercy once more. She crossed to the sofa and sat on the edge of the seat, though in her agitation she was sorely tempted to pace the length and breadth of the room.

"There was an episode. Damien's sister. He brought her body. There was an experiment with electricity being carried out at the University." His voice was low and rough. Suddenly, he reached out and grabbed her hand. "Do you understand?" he rasped.

Darcie stared at his fingers where they curled over her wrist. She shook her head. "Right now, I feel as if I understand too little."

"Theresa's body was cold, lifeless. Damien, by all

accounts was calm, collected, devoid of emotion as he carried her through the corridors to the laboratory on the top floor. The night watchman tried to stop him, but he walked past as though he heard nothing, saw nothing. I was working late that night reading old journals of the Royal Society. I heard the hue and cry the watchman raised. By the time I got to the laboratory, Damien had laid his sister's body on the table, attached wires. Allowed an electrical charge to flow through her flesh."

"You can't mean—" Darcie jumped to her feet, no longer able to force herself to sit still. Terrible images of a book she had read, Mary Shelley's *Frankenstein,* quivered to life in her imagination.

Dr. Grammercy still held her hand, and his grasp stopped her mindless flight. She stood over him, looking down into his ravaged expression.

"I do mean," he said solemnly. "Damien didn't really think . . . he didn't imagine he could bring her back. It was the grief that did it to him. I'll never forget the look on his face, that terrible hopeless void that reflected in his eyes." His voice trailed away, and Dr. Grammercy sat for a moment, silent, lost in his memories. " 'What is the point of scientific study,' he asked me as I tried to talk to him that night, 'what is the point of scientific study if it has no practical application to the human condition?' "

Darcie stared at him, horrified by the thought of what Damien had done, yet empathetic to his actions. What good were the experiments conducted in closed laboratories if they were not used for the good of man? She understood that he could not have lived with himself had he not tried to save his sister by any means possible, even if those means were horrific in the minds of many.

"The night watchman had sounded the alarm," Dr. Grammercy said. "Damien was dismissed from the University. There were those on the board who were looking for an excuse." A huge sigh escaped him. "And a second dead girl, so close on the heels of that terrible tragedy in Edinburgh . . ."

"It seems a harsh punishment," Darcie mused. "You would think he would have been allowed some latitude for his situation, some acknowledgement of his loss. And with the equipment in place . . . You mentioned that experiments were already being done?"

Dr. Grammercy grunted, and then took a sip of his brandy. "There were those who whispered that Damien was mad. An intense youth, he was, always caught in the what-ifs. He thought he could change the world, if only he could change the minds of his professors. Brilliant, but combative. There were those who were glad to see him go."

"Then he was hounded out without good cause," she exclaimed.

Dr. Grammercy peered at her, unblinking. "Without good cause? He was found in the laboratory with the body of his sister. He was using equipment for an unauthorized purpose. On a human corpse. Until that night, the experiments were used to make animal parts reanimate. The most interesting was the limb of a dead simian that would clench into a fist with the application of the current. Before that night, there was never any involvement of human parts."

"I see." Darcie grimaced at the thought of the

severed simian limb. She clasped her hands in her lap, pondering the revelations of Dr. Grammercy. "But that hardly makes Damien a killer," she blurted. "He was trying to restore life."

"You do not need to convince me, my dear. I am firmly in Damien's court." Dr. Grammercy gulped down the last of his brandy. He set the empty glass on the small side table beside the sofa. "But in the eyes of the authorities, there was that matter of the dead girl in Edinburgh." He held his hand out, palm forward, as she opened her mouth to protest. "Nothing was ever proven, but suspicion is a weighty enemy. A dark cloud like that can hang over a man for the rest of his life."

Darcie shivered. Suspicion. Inspector Trent had taken Damien away for questioning. She had little doubt that in the inspector's mind, Damien was a viable suspect. But what about her mind? Could she honestly say that she harbored no doubts, no questions, no suspicions?

With a heavy heart, Darcie buried her face in her hands, barely aware of Dr. Grammercy as he laid his hand on her shoulder in a gesture of comfort. Oh, to turn back the hands of time, to restore her faith, her trust. She wished away her reservations, but they were not so easily dispelled.

The grandfather clock in the hallway chimed the midnight hour, and still Damien did not return. Darcie shifted uncomfortably in her chair; in her mind, the sound of the clock's chime was akin to a death knell. Elongated shadows crept from the corners, and every sound made her skin prickle from nerves. The fire had burned low in the massive fireplace, leaving the parlor in semi-darkness.

She had not thought to light a lamp, for all she truly needed to see was in her heart. The hours of silent contemplation had led her round and round a single question. Had she given her love, her body, her very soul to a murderer? The idea was beyond reason.

She knew Damien Cole to be a man who answered to his own conscience. He was unorthodox, unconventional. She had seen only good in him, but she knew from her own bitter experience that a man could be something other than he appeared. Steppy had gone from loving father to vile demon, his sanity chased away by drink.

Darcie recalled the one time she had gone to Damien's study and found him sequestered there with the smell of alcohol hanging heavy in the room. But she had not seen him drink it, neither that day nor any other. There was only his own intimation that there were nights when he succumbed, but exactly what did he mean? she wondered. Did he lose control of his actions or his emotions? Frustrated by her own confusion, she fisted her hands in the worn material of her skirt, willing her restlessness under control. She was reasoning herself in circles.

As the clock's twelfth chime echoed through the still house, Darcie strained to hear the click of the front door opening, wishing that this nightmare of waiting would end. She longed to hear the sound of Damien's booted feet on the stairs, to feel his arms pull her close. Her breath hung suspended, held still by hope. But no masculine footfall answered her unspoken prayer. Only lonely silence.

She rose, arms wrapped tightly about herself, her gaze roaming the darkened parlor, resting momentarily on the dim outline of the large, ornate mantel above the fireplace, then sliding to the silhouette of the mahogany writing desk on the far wall. The distinctive shape of an oil lamp's glass chimney caught her eye, and she crossed to the desk, her tread muffled by the thick, woven carpet that covered the floor. Striking a Lucifer match, she lit the lamp, filling the parlor with a soft glow. The smell of sulfur stung her nostrils.

Dr. Grammercy shifted noisily, his sonorous snore rumbling through the quiet. Darcie glanced anxiously over her shoulder at him, for she had not intended to rouse him with her actions. She felt a pang of empathy, thinking he would have a sore neck come morning. He sprawled, half reclining on the sofa, his head tipped at an odd angle, his mouth hanging open.

Darcie took a step toward her recently vacated chair, but found the prospect of returning to it distinctly unappealing. The thought of sitting idle for even one more second was maddening. Seeking a distraction from her uneasy thoughts, she crossed to the tall window overlooking the street. She pushed aside the heavy velvet drapery and faced the night-darkened panes of glass. The reflection of her face, pale and taut with tension, stared back at her.

"Oh, Damien," she whispered brokenly.

Extending her arm, she rested her fingertips against the glass. Her chin dropped, and she closed her eyes in a futile attempt to block out the terrible thoughts and wretched doubts that assailed her. Her imagination tortured her with vivid images of the murder scene in the yard of Mrs. Feather's House. That terrible picture haunted her, undulating at the edge of her consciousness, until it shifted and coalesced into a memory of the small flat where Steppy had died. She could taste her fear, as she had that long-ago night; she could feel the terror and despair. Sally had known fear a hundredfold greater. And while Darcie had survived, Sally had died.

Shivering, Darcie tried to imagine Damien plunging a knife into Sally's heart, tried to conjure a vision of him committing murder. The image refused to form. She could not conceive of such a thing.

How could Damien be the monster responsible for those foul crimes in Whitechapel? The very idea seemed preposterous.

She caught her lower lip between her teeth, her frantic thoughts whipping about at an exhausting pace. The man who had held her in his arms and cherished her with his body was not a man who could do murder. The caring doctor who had tended to Sally's leg, apologizing for the pain he caused her, was not a man who could rip out a woman's heart, snuffing her life. There must be a reasonable explanation for the presence of Damien's scalpel at the scene of the murder at 10 Hadley Street. There must.

Dropping her hand to her side, Darcie lifted her head and stared absently out the window. With heavy heart, she caught the edge of the curtain, ready to pull it across the casement and close out the night. Suddenly, a faint sound, the rattle of carriage wheels on the cobblestones, caught her attention. Frowning, she quickly extinguished the lamp. The room thus darkened, the view of the street became clear. Expectation flickered at the sight of a cart rolling slowly along the street.

Damien. His name was a silent cry of hope.

As the cart drew near Darcie saw that it was not a carriage meant to carry a person, but rather an oddly made pull-cart that resembled a backward wheelbarrow. Not Damien, then. Her heart sank at the realization.

She was about to turn away, when the wagon stopped directly in front of the house. Her curiosity roused, she watched as a tall, roughly garbed man lowered the wooden handles of the cart to the ground. His shorter companion swaggered to his side and cuffed him on the shoulder. A tremor of recognition shuddered through her.

There was no doubt in Darcie's mind as to their familiarity, for accompanying the cart were the two men she had seen that night she had stood in Damien's study, watching as they dragged the chest to the carriage house.

The resurrectionists had returned.

CHAPTER THIRTEEN

Icy tendrils curled around Darcie's heart as she wondered what business the resurrectionists had here on this grave night. Hidden by the voluptuous folds of the velvet drapery, she watched, unseen by those on the street. Reaching into the cart, the two men hefted the familiar trunk to the ground, and taking up its weight between them, they looked up and down the street as though to confirm their solitude. Apparently satisfied, they proceeded from Darcie's line of sight at a slow and unsteady pace, their progress hampered by the heavy bulk of the chest, which caused them to stagger this way and that. Or perhaps their gait reflected drunkenness. She could not discount the possibility.

Darcie whirled away from the window, her thoughts a maelstrom of confusion. She could not help but wonder if the appearance of those men on this night was some portent of doom, a harbinger of tragedy. Frantically, she glanced about, unsure if she should follow, perhaps even confront them, and demand to see the contents of that chest. The thought of facing down the two unsavory characters, alone, in the dead of night, brought a twisting knot of panic to her belly.

"Dr. Grammercy," she whispered urgently, then spoke more loudly when there came no reply. "Dr. Grammercy."

He groaned and shifted to one side, but did not awaken.

She moved to stand beside him, intending to shake him awake. Plagued by indecision, she hesitated.

There was nothing sinister in that trunk, she insisted silently, trying to convince herself of the fact. There was nothing that would warrant concern.

She shivered as another possibility begged consideration. Mayhap there *was* something to fear in that trunk, and if that proved to be the case, did she want Dr. Grammercy to bear witness to whatever she might find?

Though it was common knowledge that anatomists regularly paid good coin for fresh cadavers, there was no need for Dr. Grammercy to see proof of Damien's involvement with the resurrectionists, if indeed she did discover a body in the trunk when she confronted the two men. While purchase of a cadaver did not make a man guilty of murder, she had no desire to provide Inspector Trent with fodder for his suppositions. Best not to involve Dr. Grammercy, she decided.

Darcie sucked in a shallow breath, and then blew it out. Determined to seek out the answer to at least one question this night, she marched resolutely toward the door, throwing one last glance over her shoulder at the sleeping form of the doctor.

Heart pounding, she crept through the darkened house. The sound of a board creaking overhead stopped her in her tracks. She froze, waiting, wondering at the madness that had taken hold of her, for surely it was madness to follow those men to the carriage house. She knew it with certainty, yet was unable to choose a different path. She felt an inescapable compulsion to learn the contents of that trunk, a burning need to solve the riddle at hand, to be in control of one small factor in her life.

A moment passed and she heard no further sound. Darcie continued on her way, hastening on silent feet to the servants' entrance. Carefully, she slid the bolt and let herself out. Up the narrow flight of stairs she went, to the wrought iron gate that led to the road. It groaned eerily as she pushed it open.

Every sense alert lest the two men return unannounced, Darcie stole toward the cart. Peering over the wooden slats that formed the sidewall, she saw the gouged and uneven boards that served as the floor of the cart. She reared back as a wave of revulsion rolled over her. The boards bore a large irregular stain, darkened to a deep russet brown. Then the smell hit her full force—damp rot and the distinctive sweetly rank odor of old blood. Revulsion rose in her throat, and she gagged.

Whirling away, she pressed the back of her hand to her lips as she struggled to overcome the dizzying nausea that threatened her self-control. A hideous image of rivulets of blood, glistening and slick, leaking from the bottom of the chest to stain the floor of the cart, filled her mind.

Here was her evidence, then, but it was not enough. She needed to see with her own eyes the contents of that chest, for her instinct whispered that it had some important secret to tell, though whether for good or for ill she could not be certain.

Gathering herself, she walked woodenly to the side of the house and along the drive. The moon was a bright flat disc against the backdrop of endless night. Darcie surveyed the shifting shadows as she crept forward, ever watchful. She much preferred to come upon the two resurrectionists, rather than have them leap out at her unannounced.

A part of her wanted to flee, to run back to the safety of the parlor. She touched her scar, memories of the past rearing up, threatening the thin thread of her composure. On the night of Steppy's death, she had fled the clutches of two unsavory men, barely escaping with her life. Why then was she seeking out this peril, choosing to pursue these rough and frightening characters?

Rationally, she acknowledged that it was sheer lunacy to confront them, even as her heart whispered that it was madness to let the opportunity pass.

The need to learn the truth twisted like a live thing inside of her. Darcie stiffened her resolve. Hugging the shadows, she crept forward. As she reached the far end of the wall, she drew up short.

Directly in front of her were the resurrectionists, sitting close together on the top of the trunk at the foot of the carriage house stairs. Even as she saw them, they looked up in unison and saw her. Their faces mirrored their surprise.

The tall man sat gawping at her while his stout companion leaped to his feet.

Darcie let out a choked cry and stumbled back, losing her footing. Her arms flailing, she struggled to right herself. Oh, God. They would be upon her in seconds. *Run, girl, run.* Steppy's warning from a lifetime ago.

A rough hand grasped her upper arm. She felt blind panic claw its way to the fore. Struggling to pull free, she kicked back at the man who held her, her heel connecting with some part of his lower limb.

"Gor! What you go and do that for?" The short man let go his hold and hopped about on one foot.

"Ye flippin' mad, Robbie?" barked the second man. "Get yer mawleys off her!"

"They're off, Jack. You can see I'm not holding her no more. I was only tryin' to stop her fall."

Darcie staggered backward, her breasts heaving with exertion and fear. She did not scream, for her time on the streets of Whitechapel had taught her that a cry for help might bring a worse fate upon her, drawing the attention of an accomplice rather than a rescuer. She had learned to fend for herself.

The temptation to flee was nearly overwhelming, but she held her ground, for she had yet to find the answers she sought. Besides, they might easily overtake her if she tried to run. Better to brazen it out.

"What do you want here?" she demanded in what she hoped was a stern and forbidding manner. "I shall call the constable if you do not state your business at once."

"Here now, Robbie. Looks as though the doctor got himself a *trouble and strife.*"

"Naw, Jack. He ain't married. You know it."

Darcie shook her head as she recognized the rhyming street cant often heard in Whitechapel. *Trouble and strife* was a slang term for wife. She looked from one to the other, the feeling of menace dissipating somewhat as they made no move to approach her.

"State your business," she repeated.

"We got the swag an' Dr. Cole always pays us ready gilt," said the one called Jack, punctuating his statement with a brisk nod of his head.

Darcie turned to the shorter man, Robbie, hoping for a translation. From the way he was eyeing her warily, she had the distinct impression that he was as mistrustful of her as she was of him. The thought was somewhat heartening.

Snatching off his hat and twisting it nervously in his hands, Robbie bobbed his head at Darcie. "We brought our weekly delivery. The doctor always pays cash money."

"You . . . you come here every week?" she stammered, wondering how she could have been unaware of a fresh cadaver being delivered each week. Where on earth had Damien been keeping all those bodies? The only human organ she had seen was the heart that Dr. Grammercy had given to Damien.

"Every week, like clockwork," Robbie assured her proudly. Then his face fell. "Though lately, he hasn't seemed to have as much need for us. I'm wondering if he's using someone else."

"We do a slap job," Jack piped up eagerly.

A slap job of what? she wondered. Gravedigging, or something more sinister? Darcie shot him a sidelong glance. He stood with one foot resting on the large trunk. She winced at the casual pose. It was as though he was resting his foot on a coffin.

"Is it in there?" She gestured in the direction of the trunk, a mixture or fear and revulsion coiling within her.

"Right enough, it is." Jack grinned, revealing several dark gaps where his teeth had once been.

Darcie realized he was older than she had originally thought. The man looked to be positively ancient. Her fear cooled to a low simmer.

"The doctor is unavailable to meet with you gentlemen right now," she said stiffly. "Perhaps you could return another time."

"No troubles. We'll just carry it up the *apples and pears,* and come back for the ready another time."

"*Apples and pears?*" Darcie echoed, mystified.

"The stairs. We'll just carry it up the stairs," Robbie clarified, "and the doctor can pay us next time."

Darcie couldn't imagine unloading the body from the trunk and leaving it unattended in Damien's laboratory. She had no idea if he carried out some special preparation on it, or even how long it could be kept. No, this wouldn't do at all.

"The laboratory is locked and I have no key." She shook her head, imagining the two of them hauling the body away and leaving it in the trunk until Damien's return. The thought was ghastly. "Perhaps you could take it elsewhere?"

"Elsewhere?" Jack parroted, looking confused.

Robbie rubbed his palm along his grizzled chin. His expression brightened. "We could leave it in the kitchen."

"Ugh!" A startled cry escaped her. "This kitchen? I think not!"

"Why not? It's clean." Jack gestured toward the trunk.

"You wash it?" Darcie asked incredulously, feeling as though she had stumbled into a strange dream. These two men wanted to leave a freshly washed cadaver in the kitchen. She pressed the back of her hand to her lips and inhaled slowly through her nose, trying to make sense of it all.

"Well, that's the point, ain't it?" Robbie cackled, a hoarse rasping sound that made Darcie nervous.

"What point?" This conversation was as slippery as an eel wriggling from her grasp. She held up her hand, putting a halt to the flow of words. "Wait. Please. Explain why you wash the body."

Robbie and Jack looked at each other strangely. "What body?"

"The body in the trunk."

"She's a bit tetched in the head," Robbie said sagely, tapping his temple with his forefinger.

"Like my Aunt Gertie," Jack replied.

"We don't wash no body. We wash the linens from Dr. Cole's laboratory and from the surgery in Whitechapel. Or, at least, my wife washes 'em. And then we bring 'em back. Dr. Cole says that the last time he gave the bloody linen to the maid, she fainted. We been taking it away for nigh on two years now. Don't know where he sends the linens from his surgery here. Wouldn't mind if he gave us that too." Robbie leaned closer and lowered his voice as though imparting some great confidence. "Tell you the truth, we can use the blunt. I've got nine grandchildren now, and I like to help out when I can."

He was delivering linen to support his grandchildren. Darcie felt her sense of reality shift and tilt.

Jack gestured to the trunk. "So can we leave 'em in the kitchen?"

"No!" Darcie cried.

Jack looked disappointed, but Robbie shrugged fatalistically. "Right, then. We'll be back next week. Tell Dr. Cole that he'll have to make do with the linens he has. Come on Jack."

The two men hefted the trunk between them and staggered toward the front of the house.

"Wait, please." Darcie hurried after them. She could not simply accept their word at face value. "I want to see what is in that trunk."

"Right, then," Robbie said. "Put it down Jack."

They set the chest on the ground and flipped open the lid. Darcie stared at the stack of folded linens. Slowly she leaned forward and touched the top of the pile. Her mind circled around the possibilities. Was a chest of linens truly heavy enough to make two men stagger about so, even two men clearly past their prime?

"What else is in here?" she demanded.

Robbie shrugged. "Man's got to make a living. We do a bit of delivery work for a particular gent." He winked. "French brandy that ain't exactly legal. Don't like to leave it unattended in the cart, so we carry it with us till our next stop."

"I see." Darcie took a moment to assimilate that information. "Does Dr. Cole purchase your brandy?"

Jack sent Robbie a sly look. "A man's got to have his secrets."

The two men lifted the chest once more and moved haltingly toward the cart. Darcie followed.

"Your cart," she said, watching as they loaded the trunk in back. "It bears the distinct smell of blood."

"That it does," Robbie said jovially. "During the day we do deliveries for the butcher. We tried lye and salt and even vinegar. But it still smells of the slaughterhouse." He peered at her hopefully. "Don't suppose you know a remedy?"

Darcie shook her head mutely.

He shrugged, and raised a hand in a farewell salute. "Well, good-bye."

"G-good-bye," Darcie stammered.

She stood on the street long after they had disappeared, pondering the astonishing fact that the two men she had long-assumed to be resurrectionists were nothing more than laundry deliverymen! A soft exclamation escaped her, and her heart lightened.

Rather than damning evidence that proved that Damien paid coin for fresh bodies ripped from the grave, she had found only proof of his kindness. He hired those men and paid them for a job he could easily have instructed the laundry maid to do. She smiled, hugging to her heart this further proof of Damien's decency.

Making her way back to the gate leading to the servant's entrance, Darcie paused, her hand resting on the railing. The hairs on the back of her neck prickled and rose, and the suspicion that she was no longer alone slithered through her thoughts. Nervously, she glanced over her shoulder, but only shadows greeted her. The street was deserted.

She shuddered, suddenly acutely conscious of the fact that she had been painfully foolish to chase Robbie and Jack out into the night. They could have proven to be dangerous, violent thugs. Glancing about once more, she saw no one about, but the feeling that she was being watched did not resolve. The sensation was chilling, and she recalled the long-ago night when she had hurried through the back alleys of the East End, certain that she was not alone.

Suddenly desperate to return to the parlor and the safety of the house, Darcie pushed open the gate and hurried down the stairs.

Returning to the parlor, Darcie lit a lamp once more. Now that she was safe inside the house, she wondered at the eerie sensation of being watched that had come upon her as she stood by the gate. Rational consideration dictated that she was overtired, overwrought, and in all ways hard-pressed to form a valid opinion about almost anything. In all likelihood, there had been no one there.

What if there *had* been someone there? a voice whispered on the edge of her consciousness. She wrapped her arms about herself, feeling chilled. Seeking a distraction, she focused her attention on Dr. Grammercy, who was reclined on the sofa, exactly as she had left him.

Poor man, she thought. He looked terribly uncomfortable. It was truly beyond the bounds of friendship to expect him to stay here on the sofa for the entire night. When Damien had made the request that Dr. Grammercy offer her his company, he had likely thought that his absence would be brief. The time had come to send Dr. Grammercy home. She pressed her lips together, fighting the deep melancholy that threatened to overcome her composure, for she suspected that Damien would not return this night.

"Dr. Grammercy," she said, shaking him gently.

"Yes, yes, a brandy," he muttered as he bolted upright.

"The hour has grown late." Darcie dropped her hand from his shoulder and took a step back. "I cannot imagine that Dr. Cole meant for you to remain here all night when he asked you to sit with me for a short while. 'Tis time for you to seek your rest in your own comfortable bed. This sofa will not do."

"Not sleeping." He scrubbed one hand over his face. "Resting my eyes, you know."

Despite her heavy heart, Darcie smiled. "I know you would stay here until Dr. Cole's return, for you are most kind. I thank you for your company, but I feel terribly guilty denying you your rest." She hesitated, unsure of the appropriate etiquette. She was acting the part of hostess in the parlor of her employer, who was also her lover, and quite possibly the prime suspect in a series of hideous murders. Salty tears of frustration and despair pricked her eyes.

Inspector Trent would not have kept Damien so long unless he believed he had good cause. She could only pray that Damien was not being subjected to any physical form of coercion. The thought brought a bubble of nausea to her throat. Whatever just cause the inspector thought he had, he was mistaken. She would gladly forgive the inspector his error, if only he would send Damien home.

Impatiently wiping her tear-dampened eyes with the back of her hand, Darcie glanced at Dr. Grammercy as he heaved himself from the deep cushions of the sofa. She was glad that his attention was elsewhere so he did not notice her distress. She felt bad that he had sat here half the night and could not justify keeping him on the uncomfortable sofa till morning. His presence would not hasten Damien's return.

Besides, she longed for a moment of true privacy, for the chance to unfold her convoluted thoughts and sort through them one by one.

"If you're certain, my dear?"

Darcie tried to muster a smile, but from the answering flicker of concern in Dr. Grammercy's eyes, she suspected she had failed dismally. "I am certain."

"I'll be on my way then." His voice was brisk with false joviality.

"Thank you for staying with me."

Suddenly, Dr. Grammercy grabbed her hand, staring intently into her eyes. She started in surprise. He opened his mouth, leaning close, as though

ready to impart some important information. Darcie
tensed as she waited for whatever he might say.
Then his expression shifted, and he closed his mouth
abruptly, leaving her feeling deflated, and more
than a bit puzzled.

He sighed. "It will be fine," he said, nodding
once as he offered Darcie his arm. "Come see an
old man to the door."

"Of course. Let me bring the lamp."

Holding the lamp high to illuminate their way,
Darcie linked her arm through his. She welcomed
the warmth of human contact, found it comfort-
ing.

Together, they made their way through the
darkened house. Darcie wondered what had become of Poole, and why he had left no lights burning in anticipation of his master's return. *Unless he
did not anticipate such a return.* The thought made
her stumble.

Dr. Grammercy looked at her with concern. She
shook her head mutely, and they continued on
their way.

After seeing him out and carefully locking the
front door, Darcie stood in the hallway, feeling
lost. In that moment, the silent house seemed to
echo her own loneliness. Without Damien, it was
like a tomb—soulless, a shell without a heart.

What was her place here? Was she to sleep in
her bed under the eaves, or was she expected to be
waiting for Damien in his chamber upon his return?

Darcie blew out a long, slow breath. It was positively ludicrous that she was faced with a question
of etiquette in regard to whose bed she ought to

choose. Rubbing her hands up and down her arms, she snorted at the ridiculousness. The decision was irrelevant, really. Whichever bed she chose, she doubted she would be able to sleep.

"Upstairs with you now," she whispered aloud. Slowly, she climbed the stairs, and walked along the shadowy hallway, her lamp sending a soft glow ahead of her. She paused outside Damien's chamber, staring at the closed door. She longed for Damien, longed for his touch, the comfort of his presence, but she knew that was not possible.

Tentatively, she pushed open the door, feeling torn. She had no wish to invade his privacy, but she longed for some physical connection to him. Surely their earlier intimacy had meant something? He had seemed to indicate that it did.

Darkness shrouded the room. There was no fire in the empty hearth. Darcie entered, the light from the lamp she carried throwing flickering shadows across the walls. She walked to Damien's large canopied bed, and pushing aside the heavy velvet bed hanging, she laid one hand on the cool surface of a pillow, her fingers sinking into its softness. Placing her lamp on the night table, she lifted the pillow, pressing her nose to it, inhaling the scent of sandalwood and sunshine that was Damien's. She felt a tight band of sorrow squeeze her chest.

The bed sheets were tidy, she noticed. Mary, or perhaps Tandis, must have been here since her afternoon tryst with Damien. The thought brought a heated flush to her cheeks. Carefully, she placed the pillow back on the bed.

Taking her time, Darcie moved through the room, lightly running her fingers across Damien's shaving brush, the front of his armoire, the drapery that adorned the window. With a melancholy sigh, she returned to his bed and sank down on the inviting surface, trailing her hand over the polished wood of his night table. Inadvertently, she brushed against a small volume of poetry he kept there, and she heard it fall to the ground with a dull thud.

Carefully balancing the lamp as she moved, Darcie knelt on the floor and looked for the book. It lay, half hidden by the far leg of the small table. Bending forward, she lowered the lamp to get a better view, and extended her arm, reaching for the volume. Her fingers closed around it just as her eyes were drawn to a crumpled cloth on the floor near the bedskirt. She pulled the book free, keeping her eyes fixed on the bit of cloth.

Frowning, she reached up with one hand to place the volume on the nightstand, and then angled forward, straining to reach as far back as she could. Her fingers closed around the wadded material from the floor. Resting back on her haunches, she smoothed the cloth flat on the floor, tracing her index finger around the edges of its odd shape. The jagged outline brought to mind a woman's boot.

The appearance of it tugged at her memory, and then the recollection came to her. This appeared to be the cloth she had seen Damien turn in his hands the night she had found Mary weeping in her bed. The night Mary had been attacked.

Darcie pictured the torn edge of Mary's smock, and suspected that this would be a perfect match. She shivered. A terrible image of Mary pulling frantically away from the man who had harmed her formed in Darcie's mind. She imagined the sound of rending cloth, imagined Mary's cry as she broke free. The vision was horrifying.

Damien could not have been that man. She knew that with bone deep certainty. Who, then, had done something terrible to Mary, and how had this scrap of her smock come to be in Damien's possession?

Feeling confused, Darcie rose to her feet, tucking the piece of material into the pocket of her dress. She moved from the night table to the window, staring down at the back drive as she had the night Mary was attacked. She leaned her forehead against the cool glass, wondering if it truly was only mere hours since she had lain in Damien's warm embrace, only hours since she had known such joy. Now she was haunted by questions and worries, and a gnawing fear for the man she loved. Taking up her lamp once more, she turned and left Damien's chamber as she had found it, deserted and silent as a tomb.

CHAPTER FOURTEEN

"Did you sleep at all, poor lamb?" Cook jumped up from her place and patted Darcie's arm reassuringly as she entered the kitchen the following morning. "Come and have a spot of breakfast. A good strong cup of tea will brace you up a bit."

She could feel the weight of everyone's eyes upon her. The smell of bacon and eggs permeated the air, but rather than making Darcie feel hungry, it made her feel slightly nauseous. Sliding into her seat, she mustered a weak smile for Cook's benefit. She was grateful for the other woman's welcoming presence.

Glancing up, she met John's concerned gaze across the table. He nodded at her encouragingly. Darcie marveled that only last night she had been elevated from the servants' table to the master's table, and this morning she had returned to the kitchen to take her meal. How strange that she felt comfortable in both worlds.

She helped herself to scrambled eggs and toasted

bread, and though the food was like dust in her mouth, she forced herself to chew and swallow.

Glancing around the table, Darcie wondered what the other servants thought about the previous evening's events. At the very least, Poole knew that Damien had left in the company of Inspector Trent. She could only guess at the story circulating among the others.

She took another mouthful of egg and hazarded a quick look at Cook from beneath lowered lashes. The woman appeared to be her usual unflappable self.

Swallowing her food, Darcie turned her attention to Mary, who sat on her left. She opened her mouth to inquire how her friend was feeling this morning, but found the other woman looking at Poole with a strange, almost soft expression on her face. Even more odd was the way Poole was looking at Mary. Tipping her head to the side, Darcie watched the peculiar interaction in confusion. Poole was always condescending, unpleasant, or nasty. She had never seen him with anything other than a sneer contorting his features, but at this moment, his gaze fixed on Mary's green eyes, he looked almost agreeable.

Shifting her attention to the coachman, Darcie spoke softly, feeling the weight of the morning hush. "John, will you take me to see Dr. Cole?"

The coachman's head snapped up, and he stared at her, chewing thoughtfully. "At the jail?"

She swallowed against the lump in her throat. Would Damien be in a cell, caged like some wretched beast, or would he be held in an office at Bow Street? She had no idea, though she had héard tales of what went on below the Bow Street Station. Men in Whitechapel spoke of the holding cells, and the strong room, and the interrogations done there. She could feel the eyes of the other servants boring into her, and she thought that they, too, must know the terrible stories.

"I wish to go to Bow Street," she said. "And I can only hope that Inspector Trent will see me. And see reason, as well."

"What will you do there?" Tandis asked shyly, surprising Darcie with her softly voiced question, for the young maid rarely spoke. "I ask because I thought that Dr. Cole might be hungry and want some food. My Uncle Jack landed himself in Fleet for his debts. Ten long months he was there, and I don't know as he'd have been fed a morsel if my Da hadn't paid good coin to make certain he had food and bedding." She looked around at the other servants, nervously gauging their reactions.

"That's a wonderful idea, Tandis," Darcie said, feeling warmed by the little maid's concern for Damien. "Thank you."

"It is a fine idea," John agreed. "Don't know as Dr. Cole will 'ave been brought to a holding cell. Might be in a room with that inspector asking him questions all night."

"Either way, I expect he'll be tired and hungry," Cook said.

"He'll want a fresh shirt." Darcie turned in surprise as Poole made that statement.

"I'm sure he'd appreciate one," she said quietly.

The butler stared at her from his lofty position at the head of the servants' table, and the concerned expression in his eyes made Darcie frown in confusion. Gone was the chilly superior, replaced by a man who joined in her concern for Damien.

The support of the staff bolstered her determination to confront Inspector Trent and attempt to convince him to allow her to see Damien.

"Trent is questioning the wrong man," Poole said brusquely, echoing her thoughts. "The sooner he comes to understand that, the sooner he can move toward arresting the perpetrator of this terrible chain of crimes."

"Yes," Darcie agreed, though her attention had shifted to Mary, who had slumped low in her chair and was nervously twisting her napkin between her hands, wringing it tighter and tighter. Reaching out, Darcie closed her hand around Mary's, stilling her anxious movements. The other woman made no move to pull away, nor did she reach out to Darcie. After a long moment, she lifted her head and met Darcie's gaze, her green eyes haunted and fearful.

Darcie frowned as Mary withdrew her hand, wishing that her friend would share her concerns. She wondered once more if whoever had harmed Mary on the night she was attacked was somehow linked to the murders. She had no specific reason for connecting the two, save for instinct.

"Right," John said, drawing her attention. Tossing his serviette on the table beside his now-empty plate, he rose and nodded at Darcie. "I'll go harness the horses. About twenty minutes, then, Missy?"

"That will be fine, John. Thank you."

She watched as he strode from the room. Picking

up on the suggestion that Tandis had made, Cook rose and took down a large wicker basket from a high shelf. She began to gather bread, cheese, and cold meat. After a brief hesitation, she added several small pink-iced cakes to the basket.

"Dr. Cole has no liking for sweets," Darcie said, feeling forlorn as she recalled her conversation with Damien.

"Usually he doesn't, but today might be the day." Cook smiled at her reassuringly.

Darcie took up a clean serviette, rolled it into a cylinder, and tucked it into the basket.

"What do you think the place is like? Dark and dingy . . . damp, I'd guess," Cook commented.

"I expect so," Darcie said glumly. The words conjured the dismal picture of Damien locked in a cold, dark cell, or the strong room in the bowels of Bow Street Station. She hated to think of Damien there, he of sandalwood and sunshine and freedom.

Her gaze fell on an unopened rose that Cook had sitting in a jar on the windowsill. "In fact, you've given me an idea, Cook. Tell John I've gone to the park. I won't be long."

Cook blinked owlishly. "The park? Whatever for?"

"Flowers. There is always a flower girl by the gate."

"Flowers!" Cook repeated in amazement, as though Darcie had said she was going to purchase diamonds, and then a smile spread across her face, and she resumed packing the basket. "Flowers. Yes, what a lovely idea."

"Perfect." Darcie smiled, feeling heartened. She

would take a basket of food to Damien at Bow Street, and a fresh posy of sweet-smelling flowers to brighten his day some small measure. And then she would have a word or two with Inspector Trent, she thought resolutely.

Hurrying upstairs, she retrieved her shawl, for it was quite early, and she suspected the day would not begin to warm for another hour. She left the house, noticing the overcast sky. Darcie had taken only a handful of steps when she heard the baker's bell signaling his arrival on the street.

"Hot loaves!" his voice boomed out. "Hot loaves!"

Across the street, she saw a milkmaid carrying a pair of churns suspended from a shoulder yoke, her large round straw bonnet shielding her face from the early morning sun. Darcie's throat tightened, the small measure of cheer she had felt only moments ago evaporating like the morning dew. Life, it seemed, went on, regardless of the fact that her heart was tight with apprehension and worry. The baker sold his loaves, the milkmaid her milk, and all the while Damien might be suffering in a moldering cell.

She quickened her pace, striding along the street toward nearby Hyde Park. The sound of the baker's call faded behind her, and turning a corner, Darcie found herself alone.

The rhythmic click of her boot heels on the cobbled road marked her passage. Then a ripple, a current, some small sound alerted her, and she stopped, looking about for the source of the sudden unease that tiptoed along her backbone. She saw no one on the deserted street. Nothing unusual caught her notice. How strange. Perhaps she was merely testy in her worry over Damien's circumstance.

With purposeful stride she continued on her way, anxious to complete her task and reach Damien's side as quickly as possible. She could only begin to imagine how he must feel. Suddenly, the hairs on the nape of her neck rose, and a cold shiver crawled along her spine once more, the feeling reminiscent of the unease she had felt as she stood in front of the house the previous night. Stopping dead in her tracks, she whirled about, but again found the street deserted.

Shaking off the strange feeling, Darcie proceeded to the park. She was rewarded with the sight of the flower girl waiting near the gate to hawk her wares.

"Hello, miss." The girl grinned at her, holding out a small bouquet of roses. "Care for some pretty flowers? I have red or pink or white."

Fishing a coin from her pocket, Darcie hesitated, suddenly realizing the meaning of her actions. She was using her earnings to buy flowers. She stared at the flower girl, then at the coin.

"Good heavens," she whispered softly, the magnitude of her changed circumstance pummeling her, leaving her winded.

Only a few short weeks ago, she could never have dreamed of spending good coin on flowers. She could barely have imagined having enough money to buy a morsel of food. She looked at the penny resting on her open palm.

"Something wrong, miss?" the flower girl asked.

"No, nothing." Darcie thrust her hand into her pocket and pulled out a second coin. "For the flowers," she said, placing the first penny in the girl's outstretched palm, "and this one is just for you." She laid the second coin atop the first.

The flower girl's eyes widened. "Thank you kindly, miss." She offered the bouquet of red roses.

"You are most welcome," Darcie said absently as she considered the roses. No, red was wrong. The color reminded her of—

Shaking her head, she gestured toward another posy. "I'll take the white ones instead, please."

Bouquet in hand, Darcie turned back toward Curzon Street. Within moments, the feeling that something was not quite right returned, stronger than before. She quickened her pace, clutching the flowers in her fist.

Was that a footfall close behind her? Stifling her unease, she glanced over her shoulder, nearly running now as she sought the safety of home.

Home. Yes, the house on Curzon Street was home, and despite the odd comings and goings, she felt safe there.

A large shadow fell across the stones in front of her. She glanced up in dismay, and then heaved a sigh of relief as she saw the looming shape ahead. It was the carriage. John had come to find her. He climbed down from the box and peered at her, his brows raised questioningly.

"No hurry, missy. No hurry," he said, opening the door of the carriage for her.

"Oh," she breathed. "Of course. Thank you, John. Do you have the basket from Cook?"

"Right there on the seat." He pointed into the carriage.

"Then we can be on our way," Darcie said with

forced brightness. She climbed inside, struggling to calm her racing pulse.

John cast her a searching look, his brow furrowed in concern. "Is aught amiss?"

Darcie shook her head. "The only thing amiss is the fact that Dr. Cole sits at the jail while a killer prowls the streets."

"I'll agree with that." John closed the door of the carriage.

Settling herself on the seat, Darcie tucked the posy under the linen square that covered the food basket. A cold whisper slithered across the nape of her neck, and she jerked her head up, turning to look out the carriage window.

There, across the street, a man dressed in a long, black cloak. Darcie frowned. The weather was warm. She barely needed her shawl. Leaning forward, she strained for a clear view of the man's face. There was something familiar about his black-clad figure, but as she strove to make out his features, he turned away. She caught only a glimpse of his profile and the dark color of his hair. He was of medium height, and there seemed nothing remarkable about him. Still, something nagged at her. Some vague, almost forgotten memory.

"John," she called loudly, intent on halting their departure. He did not hear her. The coach lurched into motion, traveling in the opposite direction of the man she had seen.

Darcie pushed the curtain back as far as she could, endeavoring to catch a last glimpse of the stranger's departing back. His cloak moved with each long stride, and something in the manner of his gait, or perhaps it was the way the material of the cloak swirled about his limbs, called up the memory of an old fear. Clutching at the shadows of recollection, she watched until he disappeared from view.

As they rounded a corner and she lost sight of the stranger, Darcie leaned back against the velvet upholstery of the seat, and put the dark-haired man from her mind. She focused her thoughts on the wording of her appeal to Inspector Trent.

Some time later, the carriage rolled to a stop in front of a large brick building. Darcie leaned forward and examined the façade of the Bow Street Police Station. A series of granite steps led to the front door. The double windows lining the front of the building boasted granite lintels, as did the arched entryway. Several people loitered near the wide steps, and Darcie wondered at their purpose.

John opened the carriage door and helped her down.

"What do you suppose all those people are doing here?" Darcie dragged the basket of food closer, then lifted it, and looped the handle over her arm.

John grunted and gave the assembled group a cursory glance. "Waiting for Her Majesty's carriage, I'd wager."

Amazed, Darcie stopped in her tracks and whirled to face him.

"Her Majesty's carriage? The queen would come to the Bow Street Station? Whatever for?"

The tension left John's face, and he smiled, the lines of worry softened by his momentary amusement. "Her Majesty's carriage is the cart they use to bring the felons, Missy."

"Oh, of course." Darcie smiled at her own naivety.

Hefting the basket so the handle rested in the crook of her elbow, she took several steps toward the front door of Bow Street. With a sigh, she stopped and turned to face John.

"I am afraid, John. What if they won't let me see him? What if they've—" She hesitated, unwilling to voice her concerns aloud. Forcing herself to continue, she said, "What if they have hurt him?"

John nodded, his lips pressed together. Reaching into his coat, he drew forth a small, black velvet bag. "Even honest men have a fondness for money. We'll use these coins if we need them."

Darcie thought about the story that Tandis had told at breakfast. They very well may have need of those coins.

Together, they ascended the stairs and entered the Bow Street Station. Darcie looked around the large public room. There were many people standing about, and she tried to ascertain the most likely candidate to answer a query as to Damien's whereabouts. She had just decided to approach a pompous-looking man on the far side of the room, when she saw a familiar figure dressed in tweed striding away from her.

"Inspector Trent!" she called out, hurrying after him.

He stopped, turning as she approached, a flicker of recognition sparking to life in his eyes. Unwilling to lose sight of her quarry, she did not spare a glance to ensure that John followed.

Sidestepping a rather rotund man with an enormous beaver hat, Darcie planted herself directly in front of Inspector Trent.

"I have come to see Dr. Cole," she stated boldly, though her insides quaked. "Please see that I am taken to him directly."

Inspector Trent raised a brow at Darcie's demand, as if to mock her.

Drawing on heretofore-unknown reserves of composure, Darcie spoke quickly, lest the inspector lose interest and leave before she accomplished her goal. "Inspector Trent, I understand that you have a job to do. In fact, we have a similar goal. Sally Booth, one of the unfortunate murdered women, was a friend of my sister. I would like nothing better than to see the vile fiend responsible for her death apprehended. Hence, it is incumbent upon me to clarify a rather important point. Dr. Damien Cole is not the man you seek."

"A friend of your sister, you say?" His gaze sharpened. "Who is your sister? I may wish to speak to her."

Darcie wet her lips. "I believe you have already questioned her. My sister is Abigail Feather." She paused. "Mrs. Feather of 10 Hadley Street," she clarified when he showed no sign of recognition.

To his credit, Inspector Trent made no derogatory remark. "You are correct. I have already spoken with her," he stated inscrutably.

"I assumed you had." Darcie glanced over her shoulder, looking for some sign of John. A sinking feeling accompanied the realization that he was nowhere in sight. She was alone with Trent, had only herself to rely on if she hoped to convince him to take her to Damien. She thought of the black velvet pouch full of coins that John had shown her as they stood beside the carriage. Returning her attention to the inspector, and recalling what little she knew of him, she realized that he did not seem like one who would accept a bribe.

As though noticing her basket for the first time, Inspector Trent moved aside the corner of the linen cloth. Seeing the roses she had tucked inside, he lifted them out and met her gaze.

For some reason, the sight of those flowers clutched in the inspector's hand brought tears to Darcie's eyes. An eternity passed in a single moment, and then Trent's expression softened.

"Come with me," he said gruffly, tucking the flowers back into the basket. He glanced up, and Darcie felt a presence at her elbow. Turning her head, she found John standing by her side once more.

"Only her. You'll wait here," the inspector instructed.

Darcie silently willed John not to argue. He stared down at her, his eyes shadowed with concern, and gave a sharp nod.

"Right, then," he said, running one open palm nervously along his jaw, jerking his head toward the waiting throng. "I'll wait here with this lot."

Without preamble, Trent marched forward. Darcie hurried after him through the public rooms, up a flight of stairs at the back of the building, and then along a hallway to a closed door at the end. Trent nodded at the man stationed outside the door.

Darcie was nearly dizzy with relief. It seemed

that Damien had not been taken to a cell after all, and she was immensely grateful for that.

Pushing open the door, Inspector Trent fixed her with a stern eye. "You have fifteen minutes," he said brusquely.

Stepping across the threshold, Darcie entered a small bare room that contained two spindly chairs and an old, scarred wooden table. The door swung shut behind her, and she heard the click of the key turning in the lock. For a moment, she thought that Inspector Trent had lied to her and that she was alone.

"Darcie." The whisper came from behind her, tinged with wonder. "Why did you come here?"

Whirling, she found Damien standing in the corner of the room, one shoulder propped against the wall. He had shed his coat and stood before her in his vest and shirtsleeves. His golden hair hung in disarray, curling about his collar, and his beautiful gray eyes were heavily shadowed with fatigue. She took one joyful step toward him, and then stopped abruptly, uncertain.

For an endless moment, emotion wove through his features. Amazement, pleasure, concern. At last, he held out one arm, a silent invitation, and she rushed forward and collapsed against his firm chest, breathing in the scent of him, feeling the heat of his body, desperately aware of how very much she loved him. His arms closed around her, and she felt him rest his chin lightly against the crown of her head in a familiar gesture.

"I was so afraid," she blurted. "I thought they might have taken you to—" Her voice broke, the thought of Damien being taken to the strong room, to be beaten and forced to provide answers, was too overwhelming to voice aloud.

He tightened his embrace, and she felt the coiled tension in the arms that held her.

"Trent will only allow us fifteen minutes," she choked out, her voice muffled in the folds of his shirt.

Taking a step back, Damien held her at arm's length, but did not break contact, keeping the fingers of one hand curled loosely around her shoulder. He watched her intently, running the side of his thumb along her cheek.

"My God," he whispered brokenly, disbelief etched on his face, "you are truly here."

She turned her face into his hand, and pressed her lips to his palm, her eyes never leaving his.

"Of course I am." The words caught on a sob. She clung to him, her hands fisting the loose material of his shirt as she struggled for control. Leaning forward, she rested her weight against him, taking comfort from his solid form and sharing her own strength in return. "I came to tell Trent that he should concentrate his efforts elsewhere."

She felt his lips curve where they pressed against the top of her head. Drawing back enough to look upon his face, she found him smiling tiredly at her weak quip.

"I know who you are, Damien Cole. You are not a killer."

"You unman me," he rasped, his voice taut with barely suppressed emotion. "When Trent pulled the scalpel from his bag—" He paused, his expression pained. "Darcie, I am not the monster that Trent would paint me."

"Shhh." She pressed her fingers to his lips. "You need not defend yourself to me." Hot tears snaked a path along her cheeks.

Damien made a strangled sound, low in his throat. "Do not cry for me. I do not deserve your tears."

She shook her head from side to side. So many words tumbled to the fore, eager to be spoken, but she couldn't seem to wrap her tongue around a single one. Instead, all she could do was stand before him, silent sobs wracking her frame.

"I . . . *huh huh* . . . I—I came to reassure you." She released a shuddering breath as she struggled for control. "T-t-to offer comfort and support"—she lifted her arm, drawing his attention to the basket—"and fo-o-od."

The corner of his mouth curved in the hint of a smile. He took the basket from her and set it on the table, the fingers of one hand laced with hers, drawing her with him as though he was loathe to let her go. Turning, he stared down at her, his gray eyes fathomless. "I have let you down." A hiss of frustration escaped his lips. "My promises of protection are as worthless as lead coins, as worthless as those I made to Theresa. I cannot even protect myself from false accusations."

She flung herself against him, twining her fingers through his hair, tugging on the silky strands. At her silent urging, he lowered his lips to hers. Oh, the feeling of him against her. Warm, strong, alive. She would not lose him to this madness.

Darcie poured her love into him, opening to his caress, meeting the thrust of his tongue with a poignant and sharp urgency. His big hand stroked the length of her back, coming to rest on her buttock, pulling her closer. With a soft whimper she molded herself to his frame, trying to achieve a closeness that would sustain them until this nightmare ended. The dingy room faded from her awareness, and there was only Damien, solid and strong.

They stood still, silent, wrapped together as one, drawing strength from one another.

A series of sharp raps sliced through the silence as Inspector Trent, or perhaps the guard, sounded a warning on the door. How long did they have left? Five minutes? Three? Darcie choked back a strangled moan.

"Shhh." Damien pressed one last kiss to her lips, and then drew back. She watched the subtle shift in his expression, the slight tightening of the firm line of his mouth as he studied her face, taking in her pale cheeks, the purple shadows of fatigue beneath her eyes. She sighed.

"Darcie, listen to me. There is one protection I can offer." His tone was resolute. "If aught goes awry, there are funds—"

"No," she cried, turning her face aside so he would not see the renewed rush of tears that filled her eyes. "Nothing will happen to you. Nothing. This is all a terrible mistake. A miscarriage of justice. They will realize it. They will." She blinked against the beads of moisture on her lashes. "Trust me."

"Trust you." He whispered the words as though they held some secret meaning.

Reaching up, Darcie cupped his face with her palm, at a loss for words.

"You, who know the darker side of life and the nature of men, you still believe in the good." It was not a question, though his tone was incredulous.

Darcie leaned forward, resting her cheek against his warm chest, rubbing it back and forth. She thought of Steppy and his bitter betrayal of her, the memory of his terrible treachery like a yoke about her shoulders, and she thought of her own sister, Abigail, whose trust in a man had led to her devastation.

"How can you trust a man who is held on suspicion of murder?" Damien rasped, mistaking her silence. The question hovered, the stark reality of this terrible situation laid bare with a few simple words.

"I—" she began.

The door opened with a creak and Inspector Trent stepped into the small space. "Your time is up."

Darcie sent a single agonized glance at Damien, wishing there was one moment more to share the touch of a hand, the warmth of an embrace, the passion of a kiss. Oh, God, when would she see him again?

CHAPTER
FIFTEEN

Darcie felt a keen sense of loss as Damien took a small step away from her, the tension pulsing from him in waves. She glared at Inspector Trent and opened her mouth to protest, to beg for more time.

Trent beckoned to the guard she had seen earlier. "Johnson, take Dr. Cole to the other room. I'd like a word with Miss Finch." Returning his attention to Darcie, he continued, "I had intended to come and see you this morning. You have saved me the trip."

Stepping forward, Damien used his body to shield her from the inspector's view. "She has nothing to do with this," he said softly.

With his head tipped to one side and a sardonic expression on his face, Trent studied Damien for a protracted instant. "That may be the case, but I shall speak with her all the same."

Sensing some undercurrent passing between the two men, Darcie stepped between them. "Please," she said, resting one hand on Damien's arm. "I have nothing to hide, and if any information I may unwittingly provide helps bring the *real* murderer"— she shot a speaking glance at Inspector Trent—"to justice, then I am happy to comply."

The inspector's lips curved in a hard smile. "Your kitten has claws, Cole."

"I am no one's kitten," Darcie said firmly. "But I do have claws. And intelligence enough to recognize a man's innocence."

Trent inclined his head. "Your conviction and faith are admirable. For your sake, Miss Finch, I hope they are not misplaced."

Darcie sucked in a breath, angry at Trent's tone, for he seemed to imply that she had foolishly sided with a guilty man. Holding back an angry tirade, recognizing that Trent's intent was to befuddle and confuse her in order to extract information she might otherwise choose not to reveal, she turned to the guard, Johnson, and gestured toward the basket on the table. "Please, take that with you. Surely you have no intention of starving an innocent man?"

When the guard hesitated, she turned her head and looked over her shoulder at Inspector Trent. He nodded his agreement, and Johnson lifted the basket. Her heart wrenched as Damien moved past her, pausing to brush his thumb gently across her cheek. She longed to fling herself against him and sob out her terror and despair. It was so difficult to put on a brave face.

Damien's eyes met Trent's, and again something passed between the two men, a powerful current that pulsed with meaning. Damien's expression was not exactly threatening, but something about the way he looked at the inspector held a subtle warning. He was warning the inspector off, she realized with a start. Lord, the man was vexing. He was not in a position to try and protect her. She glanced nervously at Trent and found him regarding Damien with what appeared to be grudging respect.

Giving her hand a reassuring squeeze, Damien preceded the guard and left the room.

"He is very protective of you," Inspector Trent observed as he pulled one of the chairs away from the bare table and gestured for Darcie to sit. "I wonder, is his concern for you, or for what you might reveal?"

He was baiting her. She pressed her lips together, determined to speak only when she must, for though her instinct was to bombard the inspector with avowals of Damien's innocence, she realized that it would do little good. The man had a job to do, and he would do it in his own time, in his own way. Living on the streets had taught her patience—sometimes one had to wait for hours before the opportunity to pinch a potato from a stall presented itself—and at this moment she was heartily glad of those lessons.

"What exactly is the nature of your relationship with Dr. Cole, Miss Finch?" he asked, taking the seat opposite her, dangling his hands between his parted knees. There was an edge of sarcasm to his words, an unspoken implication that he knew quite a bit about the nature of her and Damien's relationship.

"I am his assistant." She met his gaze, keeping her answer as concise as possible.

The inspector leaned against the seat back. "How do you assist him?"

"I draw."

"What exactly do you draw?" There was a thread of impatience there now.

"Pictures." She kept her tone even, calm. In the alleys of Whitechapel she had faced more frightening threats than Inspector Trent.

After a moment's pause, Trent changed his tack. "You said that your sister was acquainted with Sally Booth. Did you know her?"

"Yes."

Trent waited a heartbeat, and seeing that she would not elaborate he continued, "When did you last see her?"

"I accompanied Dr. Cole to my sister's home where he treated a carbuncle on Sally's leg."

Resting his forearms on his thighs, the inspector leaned closer. Darcie swallowed and edged back in her seat, pressing her spine against the seat back.

"Sally worked for your sister?"

Darcie nodded.

"Did you work for your sister?"

Her gaze shot to his. "No."

Inspector Trent smiled tightly. "I meant no offence."

He *had* meant offence. Not maliciously, she thought, but rather as a means to an end. He meant to chip away at her until she revealed some secret that he could use against Damien. Clenching her hands in the folds of her skirt to still their quaking, Darcie bit back a reply. He was trying to unnerve her. She could sense it.

"How did Dr. Cole behave on the occasion you saw Miss Booth at your sister's home?"

Darcie stared at him. "He behaved like a doctor."

"Did he seem agitated? Angry?"

"No."

"Has he ever behaved oddly?" the inspector asked.

"I don't know what you mean by oddly." Darcie met his gaze unflinchingly.

Inspector Trent nodded. "Let me ask you this: Did you see Dr. Cole on the night Sally Booth was murdered?"

"Yes, I did."

"Did you notice anything out of the ordinary?"

Darcie was carried back to that night. She could see Damien's bloodied shirt, licked by flames as he tossed it in the fireplace. She had lost sleep over that bloodied shirt until Abigail explained the stains; it had been Mayna's blood, splashed on Damien as he struggled to save the girl's life. Had anything out of the ordinary happened that night? Nothing that should interest Inspector Trent.

"No, I noticed nothing out of the ordinary," she stated firmly. Watching him intently, Darcie leaned forward now. He did not retreat, and they sat, inches apart, caught in a silent contest of wills.

"Has anything happened that would cause you to say that you fear Dr. Cole? Any strange happenstance, however inconsequential you might think it?"

Darcie hesitated, thinking of the attack on Mary, and her bizarre conviction that the assault had some bearing on the Whitechapel murders. Unthinkingly, she put her hand in her pocket, her fingers closing around the scrap of cloth she had found in Damien's chamber. She thought about revealing her concerns to Trent, considered the possibility that he would follow the lead and search for the true perpetrator of the crimes.

Sensing the shift in her mood, Trent attacked with the speed of a striking cobra.

"Tell me." He shifted even closer. She could smell coffee on his breath. "*Tell me!* Do not protect that monster. Think of Sally Booth, her heart ripped from her breast. Think of Margaret Bailey, her body slit open like a gutted fish."

Darcie turned her face away, the horror of his words too vivid to be borne. Clenching her fist around the scrap of cloth in her pocket, she closed her eyes and concentrated on keeping her breakfast inside of her as it wriggled and turned in her belly, threatening to climb up her throat. Whatever she said now, he would twist it back on Damien. She swallowed and turned toward him once more, her gaze meeting and holding his.

"Inspector Trent, there is nothing I can tell you about these terrible crimes, save that Damien Cole is not capable of murder," she said in a clear, steady voice. "I would stake my life on it."

Something flickered in his expression at her words. "Stake your life on it?" he mused, leaning back in his chair. "You may very well be doing just that."

Clapping his palms down on his thighs, Inspector Trent bent forward at the waist, bringing his face close to hers. He opened his mouth to speak, eyes flashing his ire, when a knock at the door interrupted him. He made a sharp sound of impatience.

Darcie watched nervously as he rose and strode to the door. Fragments of his low voiced conversation drifted to her. She heard a name, Margaret Bailey, and another, Mrs. Zeona Brightly. The first was one of the murdered women. She furrowed her brow in concentration as she tried to recall why the second name sounded familiar.

Inspector Trent returned to her side. She could feel his presence, feel his eyes on her, though she shifted her gaze and held it fixed on her clasped hands. After a moment, he spoke.

"Please come with me."

Maintaining an outwardly calm demeanor even as her heart pounded in her breast, Darcie rose. She made a show of shaking out her skirt, buying herself time to rein her heightened emotions under control as she wondered where he was taking her. Trent gestured for her to precede him out the door.

In the hallway, she saw Johnson leaning negligently against the wall, and then, behind him, she saw Damien. Her heart skittered and stopped, only to resume pounding with an intensity that was almost painful. She stumbled to a halt as she took in the sight of him, his presence lighting the dim corridor. She had not expected this, had not thought to be able to see him again before she left.

Small details caught her notice. He had donned his coat and carried the basket over one arm. If not for the tension that bracketed his mouth, he would have looked like a gentleman ready to take a lady on a picnic.

Darcie almost laughed at the thought, feeling giddy and drunk at the sight of him. She longed to grab him and drag him from this dull and dingy place, to return him to the sunshine where he belonged. Yes, he belonged on a picnic in the park, not here at Bow Street, being questioned about gruesome crimes.

Ignoring the two men, Damien had eyes only for her.

"Are you well?" His voice was pitched low with concern.

"I am well." She managed the words, though her brain worked in a dizzying series of conjectures and supposition as she worried over Inspector Trent's intentions.

"You may leave." Darcie jerked back in surprise at the inspector's words, barely daring to hope that the offer included Damien as well. "Both of you," Trent clarified. "I've just had word. Constable Soames returned from the home of one Mrs. Zeona Brightly." He directed his comments to Damien. "Mrs. Brightly confirms your alibi. She insists that you did not leave her side the night that Margaret Bailey was murdered. She recalls you leaving at dawn."

The recollection came to Darcie then. Mrs. Brightly—the woman with the drunken husband and the gouty great toe. She was a patient that Damien had mentioned by name the night that Darcie had questioned him about his feelings for her. The night they had first made love.

"I see." His tone was cool. "Then I am no longer under suspicion?"

Inspector Trent smiled sardonically. "Let us just say that you are free to leave at the moment, but I would not like to see you go on an extended tour of the continent at this time."

Returning the inspector's tight smile with one of his own, Damien said, "I had no intention of doing so."

Darcie glanced back and forth between the two men. "An extended tour of the continent?" she asked in confusion.

His eyes fixed on Inspector Trent, Damien explained. "The inspector fears that I will flee the country, and his prime suspect will escape his grasp."

"No," Darcie gasped, whirling toward Trent, "you have heard from his patient that he could not have been responsible for the murder. He never left her side."

The inspector inclined his head. "So she states now. But people are fallible. She may find that she was mistaken after all." He made a dismissive gesture. "Johnson, see them out."

"Thank you, but we can find our own way." Damien took Darcie's arm and steered her along the corridor.

As they descended the stairs, she glanced behind them, making certain that they were alone.

"He is a vile man," she whispered.

"He is good at his job," Damien replied.

In her astonishment over his unexpected response, Darcie stumbled to a halt at the foot of the stairs.

"How can you say that, after what he has put us through?"

Damien smiled, and the lines of tension and fatigue faded. "Us?" he asked.

"Yes, us. I was worried sick." Not caring who saw, or what anyone thought of her forward behavior, Darcie threw her arms about him and hugged him tight.

"Come on. Let's go home." He rested his palm on the small of her back.

John's eyes widened in surprise as they crossed the public room and moved toward him. Grabbing Damien's hand, he pumped it with enormous enthusiasm. Damien suffered the attention with aplomb, allowing John his enjoyment of the moment before quietly suggesting that he would welcome a bath and his own bed. Within minutes they were safely ensconced in the carriage.

Cocooned within the privacy of the upholstered interior, Darcie felt suddenly shy. Ducking her head, she cast Damien a sidelong glance. With a low laugh, he slipped one arm beneath her bent knees and the other about her shoulders, and lifted her full onto his lap. He clasped her to him. She could feel the steady rhythm of his heart, its cadence soothing to her.

"You had visitors last night," she said. "Robbie and Jack."

Drawing back slightly, Damien caught her chin between his thumb and forefinger and gently tipped her head until he was looking into her eyes.

"They usually come near midnight. How did you know they were there?"

"I followed them."

His brows drew down in concern. "At midnight? Alone?"

"I thought they were resurrectionists." Darcie rested her palm against his chest as she felt him tense. "They were quite polite. Truly."

"Resurrectionists?" Damien set her back on the seat, twisting so he faced her in the gently rocking carriage. "And if they had been? What were you thinking to put yourself in harm's way?"

"I was thinking that they might have some connection to the murders . . ."

"So you followed them out, alone, in the middle of the night?" he exclaimed incredulously. "Where was Grammercy?"

"Sleeping. But they were perfectly polite, and after the initial fear at being grabbed by Robbie . . ."

Damien made a strangled sound, somewhere between amusement and exasperation.

"He didn't want me to fall," she explained. "But Damien, if *they* do not bring you bodies for dissection, where do you get them?"

"My bodies come from the gallows, or the hospital. All perfectly legal, I assure you."

The high wheels of the carriage dipped into a rut in the road, causing the vehicle to pitch sharply to one side. Darcie snuggled against Damien's side as he caught her, holding her steady.

"The first night I came here, there was a body in the carriage. Where did he come from?" she asked, tilting her head to look up at him.

He stared at her for a moment, his expression inscrutable, and then he leaned close to whisper against her ear. "Did you think I dug him up from a fresh pit? Or perhaps nabbed him from the under-taker's cart?"

"Tell me." She cuffed him lightly on the shoulder.

As though a dam had been opened, he threw back his head and laughed, and she could hear the tension and strain pouring from him, released by the wave of humor.

"Darcie, my precious." He pressed a quick kiss to her lips, and then shook his head in exasperation. "He came from the hospital. His heart failed him. I do not snatch people from the grave. I am a respected anatomist. I guest lecture at medical schools throughout Her Majesty's kingdom."

A well-respected anatomist. A guest lecturer at medical schools. Darcie opened her mouth to ask him about the stories Dr. Grammercy had told her about Edinburgh and about Damien's dismissal from the university here, but his expression was so earnest, so open, she had not the heart. It would keep, she thought.

Smiling up at him, she grabbed his hands, drawing them to her lips and pressing a kiss to each one.

Damien pulled her into his embrace once more.

"Do not ever put yourself in such danger again. I could not bear it if harm befell you, if I failed to keep you safe," he whispered against her hair. "Promise me, my Darcie."

His words made her heart soar on wings of joy. She closed her eyes, reveling in the feel of him against her, in his arms wrapped around her. The coach rocked and swayed, and soon Damien's grip relaxed, and his breathing became deep and even. Darcie felt him slump back against the seat.

Sitting upright, she gazed at his face, relaxed now in slumber, his sleepless night reflected in the dark crescents beneath his eyes. She touched her lips to his, a butterfly's soft caress.

Only when she knew he was asleep, that her words were for her ears alone, did she speak. "I promise to love you forever," she whispered, smoothing an errant lock from his forehead. "But as to keeping me safe . . ." She thought of Abigail, who had run away and left her with a dying mother and a stepfather who was rapidly losing his grasp on reality as he sank deeper into the drink. She thought of Mama, who died and left her an orphan, and of Steppy—who promised to keep her safe despite their terrible descent into poverty—but in the end had sold her for a bag of coins. Tears pricked her eyes. "As to keeping me safe, my darling Damien, in that I can trust only myself."

"I fell asleep in the carriage." Damien shook his head ruefully.

"You were exhausted. I cannot imagine you slept at all in that horrible little room." Darcie snuggled closer against his side, enjoying the feel of his warm body next to hers, hugging her happiness about her like a cloak.

They had returned from Bow Street that morning. In a flurry of activity the staff had assembled in a line in the front foyer, faces aglow, smiles barely held in check. Even Poole had looked inordinately

pleased, making Darcie feel that she wanted to
pinch herself to ensure that she wasn't imagining
the whole of it. She had seen the awed expression
that crossed Damien's features as he realized they
were showing support. For him. His surprise had
been a poignant reminder of how distanced he
had become from normal human relationships
and expectations.

Damien had taken a moment to greet each person before escorting Darcie up the stairs. Unwilling
to leave his side even for a solitary second, she had
attended his bath, and eventually ended up in the
cast-iron tub with him, her dress discarded in an
untidy heap on the floor.

Now, from her place beside him on the bed, she
glanced at the cooled tub, and smiled at the memory.

"Tomorrow, we shop," Damien said. "I never
wish to see you wear black again. Were I not such a
dunderhead, I would have seen to your wardrobe
weeks ago."

Frowning at him in mock anger as she re-
arranged herself to meet his gaze, Darcie thumped
him on the shoulder. "You insult the man I love,
sirrah, for he is no dunderhead."

At her words Damien's smile flickered, then
faded. He stared down at her, his eyes wary, revealing a depth of emotion that made her own nerves
quiver and jump. Those eyes seemed to plumb the
depths of her soul, and under such close scrutiny,
she realized the blatant meaning of the declaration that had popped so blithely from her mouth.
The man I love.

There was a moment of acknowledgment, where

each became aware of the transition her lightly voiced statement had caused, for though the words were spoken unthinkingly, the emotion behind them was pure. They both knew it.

She had said those words aloud before. She was certain of it. *Yes,* an insidious voice whispered at the back of her mind, *you declared your love while he slept, while there was no danger that he might disappoint.* For what would she do if he said nothing in return?

Darcie looked away, focusing her gaze on the glowing embers in the fireplace. She realized the magnitude of her blunder in voicing aloud that which should have remained in a secret corner of her heart. She had changed everything. A sharp pain twisted in her chest.

A lifetime she had trusted Steppy, and he had sold her for a few coins. She had thought it a lesson well learned, one she would never forget. And now, foolish girl that she was, she had given her love to a man.

No, he was not just a man. He was Damien. And she *had* learned those lessons, for in truth, she could not fully trust anyone.

Unable to bear the silence, Darcie shifted her legs over the side of the bed and rose, dragging one of the sheets with her.

"The fire, I'll just—" Her voice broke. She moved across the room on legs that felt rubbery and weak, wrapping the sheet about her as she went. Grabbing the poker, she broke up the coals so energetically that ash rose and blew in all directions. Startled she jumped back, directly into the solid wall of Damien's chest. He had come silently behind her.

His warm hands closed over her shoulders, turning her slowly to face him. Her throat felt tight, as though a choking band was closed around it. She was having trouble drawing breath. Panic swelled and crested within her. He would dissemble now, adroitly hedge his way around the issue, her Damien. Her cool, controlled, unemotional Damien.

Oh, what had she done?

"Darcie, look at me." Resting the pad of his index finger beneath her chin, he tipped her face up until her eyes met his.

Her tongue darted out, wetting her too dry lips. She felt caught, trapped in a noose of her own making.

"What do you fear?" he asked, his eyes glittering intensely.

She blinked, trying to assimilate his meaning, for he seemed to have made a leap of logic she could not follow. She shook her head. "I don't understand."

"I know what it means to be alone, Darcie, to live without love. My sister's death was my fault." He pressed a finger to her lips as she opened her mouth to protest. "Mine alone. And with her death, I closed myself off behind the wall of my own self-loathing and blame. Better to control every emotion, every thought, than to suffer the agony of loss. Better to hold the world at arm's length than to fail on such a catastrophic level. How much easier it was to let myself feel nothing and to let no one have expectations of me, expectations that I would only disappoint."

She felt as though she swam through a fog as she struggled to understand.

"How much easier . . ." she whispered woodenly. He did not love her, would not allow himself to love her. To open himself to love meant opening himself to pain. That she understood only too well.

Her hands fisted in the draped material of the sheet, crushing the cloth. She thought she might be sick. He had asked what she feared. There. She had her answer. She feared the pain of losing him, feared the blank wasteland her life would be without him.

Suddenly, he sank to his knees before her, laying his cheek on the thin layer of cloth that draped across her belly. She sucked in a startled breath, reaching one hand to the silken length of his hair, but stopped short of touching him, uncertain.

"I fear losing you." His softly voiced words were an echo of her own thoughts.

Her heart stuttered and stopped, then began to pound so hard that it was almost painful. She wove her fingers through his hair, holding him against her.

"But even more than your loss, I fear never having you at all."

A low moan escaped her, forced out by fierce and untamed hope.

"Darcie . . . I do love you." The words sounded stiff, rusty. Damien gave a shaky laugh, a short, hesitant sound that grew and swelled until it sprang free, unfettered. "My God, I love you. With everything I am. You are my soul, my breath, my life." The words flowed with ease now. "You once thought that I robbed graves, but in truth 'tis you who are the resurrectionist, you who have lifted me from my living tomb for you have resurrected me from a life devoid of feeling, a blank terrain of desolation and loneliness."

Her legs gave way then, collapsing out from under her, and she sank to the thick rug, supported by his strong hands. Damien caught her against his chest, and she could feel the pounding of his heart melding with the beat of her own. She had so needed him to say it aloud, but more than that, she realized now, the words had freed him from the past.

"I love you," he whispered, nipping at her lips, his tongue stroking the corner of her mouth. A wry smile curved his lips. "As you love me."

"I do love you," she murmured, her thoughts spinning with dizzying bliss.

Cupping her face, he dragged his thumb across her lower lip, and then claimed her with a wide, open-mouthed kiss that left her breathless.

Damien shifted, as though to roll her beneath him, but Darcie resisted. Placing her hands on his shoulders she pushed him back on the soft rug, pressing hot kisses to his jaw, his chest, the ridged plane of his abdomen. With her tongue, she traced the thin line of hair that arrowed below his navel, her hand grasping his hips as she moved her mouth lower still.

The heavy length of him jutted forward and she pressed heated kisses along his shaft. He rasped her name, tangling his hands in her hair, letting her do what she would, giving himself over to her tender ministrations. She reveled in the pleasure of pleasuring him.

With a hoarse groan he dragged her along the

length of his firm body, kissing her hungrily as he
scooped her up and deposited her on the bed. She
opened to him, welcoming him deep inside as
he surged into her with a fluid thrust.

"My Darcie," he rasped. "My love."

Arching her hips she rose to meet him, wilder
and faster, until together they crested, tumbling
over the edge in wicked delight.

Hours, or perhaps only moments later, Darcie
lay beneath Damien's welcome weight. Once, as a
very young girl, she had been permitted a taste of
champagne. The bubbles had effervesced through
her body, making her feel giddy and dizzy and un-
believably good. She felt that way now, as though
she floated on a cloud.

"Until you, I was alone, frozen in a hell of my
own making with only my demons for company,"
he said, his breath fanning the curve of her cheek.
"And I did not recognize it for the bitter and small
life that it was."

He raised himself on his forearms, taking the
bulk of his weight from her. "There was no one to
care if I lived or died. Some nights, not even I
cared. After my sister died, I drank to forget. Not
to forget her, but to bury my responsibility for
what happened. And then one night, I recalled
how Mrs. Feather had tried to save Theresa, and
suddenly, I knew there would never be a possibility
of forgetting, but perhaps I could do something
good in my sister's memory. It was then that I
opened my offices in Whitechapel, to care for those
in the most desperate need."

Darcie ran the back of her hand along his cheek,
wishing he had never had to suffer such loss.

"Sometimes, I pour myself a brandy and I watch its amber color shift in the light. I smell the promise of oblivion. And I remember what I become when I choose that path. Since that night, I have not had a drink." He paused, gazing down at her with eyes that spoke of both tragedy and possibility. "And I never will. I needed you to know."

"I believe in you," Darcie whispered, and she meant it, with almost all her heart. Yet, there in a dark corner lurked the seed of her unease, the inability to fully trust another living soul. Purposefully, she banished the realization, wanting nothing to destroy this precious moment.

CHAPTER SIXTEEN

Much later, Darcie woke to the sound of the clock. Only last night as she sat in the parlor worrying over Damien's fate, she had likened the chime of the clock to a death knell, but tonight, she lay next to her lover and thought the clock's music sweet indeed. She smiled in contentment as Damien shifted in his sleep, draping one arm over her shoulder. He roused no further than that.

Her stomach rumbled, and she realized she was hungry. While Damien had proceeded to demolish everything on the heaping plate sent up by Cook, Darcie had, for the first time in recent memory, been unable to swallow a morsel of food.

Carefully lifting Damien's arm and sliding out from under it, Darcie rolled from the bed and crossed to the fireplace. Damien had added fresh coals to the fire just before they had drifted off. Lifting the poker, Darcie prodded the embers and watched them glow with renewed life.

She drifted to the small table that held the leftovers from their meal and blinked in astonishment as she realized that Damien had eaten his food and hers as well. There was nothing left on the tray save empty dishes and crumbs.

Glancing over her shoulder at the bed, she pondered its inviting warmth, weighing the desire to climb back under the covers against her desire for something to eat. She would have both, she decided. Food first and then a hasty return to Damien's bed. Silently, so as not to disturb him, she slipped into her dress and tiptoed from the room.

In the kitchen she fixed a plate of cold meat and cheese and had just finished her meal when the rapid patter of someone hurrying along the hall caught her attention. Taking up her lamp, she walked into the narrow corridor, but found no one there. Puzzled, she was about to return to the kitchen, when again she heard a sound coming from the back of the house near the servants' staircase.

She followed the noise, turning right, then left, quickening her pace, then skidding to a halt as she reached the stairs, and there, above her, she saw the hem of a skirt and a pair of sturdy boots plodding up the steps. Mary's boots, she thought. About to call out, she hesitated as a second sound came from behind her.

Snuffing her lamp, Darcie melted into the shadows under the stairs and held herself still as the sound of footsteps, slow and measured, echoed in the silence. Darcie was shivering now, pressing herself as tightly to the wall as she possibly could, silently praying that the shadows would hide her from view. The footsteps drew closer and closer still.

A man's shadow, elongated and narrow, extended across the floor. Cast there by the moonlight that filtered through the house, it heralded the man's arrival. Darcie clamped her teeth together, focusing on the shape of that shadow. There was something about the way he walked, his height, the size of him . . .

Poole! Startled, Darcie bit back a gasp. The idea of Poole and Mary, meeting outside the house after midnight, and then creeping back inside was so unlikely, so inexplicable, that Darcie almost laughed. Then, realization dawned.

Poole had access to all Damien's things, including his surgical tools. Poole was a large man, a strong man. Could it have been Poole who attacked Mary? Darcie shook her head in confusion as a thousand questions tumbled through her mind. A man who could attack a woman might be a man who could do murder.

Darcie's legs buckled out from beneath her, and she sank bonelessly down the wall, watching as Poole hesitated at the bottom of the stairs then turned and strode away. Hugging her knees, she sat, oblivious to the cold floor beneath her buttocks. The Whitechapel murderer. Poole was as likely a candidate as any, especially given the fact that Poole could have taken Damien's scalpel at any time.

With a soft sound of confusion, Darcie shook her head. She disliked Poole, true. He had been unkind to her in the beginning, and then his unkindness had turned to strangeness. She frowned. Poole was aloof, and cold, and, yes, even nasty, but did nastiness make a man a murderer? What exactly had he been doing, following Mary through the dark hallway?

Thrusting her hand into her pocket, she pulled out the torn scrap of cloth that she had found in Damien's chamber. The sound of her own ragged breathing filled her ears, and it made her feel angry. She would not be afraid! She was no quivering dormouse, shivering at the slightest prospect of adversity.

She pushed herself upright and thrusting the scrap of cloth back into her pocket, she walked silently through the house, climbing one more story and another, finally making her way to the room that she had shared with Mary. The chamber was dark, but she could make out a lumpy form in one bed. Sitting on the pallet below the window, Darcie folded her legs up beneath her, running her palm over the familiar coverlet, an anchor in the unsteady sea of her uncertainty. At length, unsure of her words, but determined to seek out answers, she spoke.

"Mary, I know you are awake."

"Awake. Awake. I wish I was asleep. I wish I could sleep and never wake up."

"You don't mean that, Mary."

The other woman sighed, and sat up, keeping the covers clutched about her shoulders. Darcie squinted into the dimness.

"No, I don't mean it. I am blessed, or maybe cursed, with a strong appreciation for life. Or perhaps it is only a fear of death," Mary said matter-of-factly. "Here. I'll light the candle."

The light flared, and Darcie blinked, taking a second to adjust to the relative brightness.

"Mary, what were you doing wandering about like a ghost?"

Mary's head snapped up at the question, her face a stark mask of apprehension. Her gaze slid away.

"Please, Mary. I want to help you."

Looking down, Mary meticulously smoothed the creases from her blanket. "There's none what can help me. What's done is done."

Darcie stared at her friend's bowed head, wishing she could find a way to comfort her. She sensed there was more to Mary's turmoil than the attack on her person. There was an ongoing fear of something more.

"What are you afraid of Mary? Tell me, please. I'll talk to Dr. Cole—"

"He's not the one," Mary cried, cutting off Darcie's words.

At that cryptic statement, Darcie's heart lurched and she tamped down the urge to grab Mary's arms. Instead, she focused on choosing her words with care. "He's not the one, Mary? Not which one?"

"You know."

"You mean he isn't the Whitechapel murderer?" Darcie prodded carefully.

Mary shrugged and shot her a questioning glance. "How'm I to know that?"

"Then what did you mean?" She fought to keep her tone neutral.

"He's not the one who hurt me."

"I know," Darcie whispered, unsurprised by Mary's admission. "Who did hurt you, Mary? Was it Poole?"

Mary's eyes widened, showing white in the dimness. Looking away, she shook her head frantically. "Don't ask me about Poole. I can't say! Don't ask me to say."

Darcie blinked, wondering if it was the mention of Poole that had caused the other woman's dismay or simply the line of questioning.

"It's all right, Mary. You don't have to say anything if you don't want to."

Confused, she recalled the way that Mary and Poole had behaved that morning, the baffling, soft expression in Poole's eyes as he'd looked at the maid. Mary had not seemed afraid of him then. Struggling with the wave of frustration that crashed over her, Darcie tried to make sense of it all.

Suddenly, Mary rose from her bed, dragging the coverlet with her. She crossed to Darcie's bed, the blankets trailing across the floor. Sinking down, Mary laid her head on Darcie's shoulder, holding the blankets close about her throat.

"Do you ever wish you could be a little girl again? You know, young enough that you know nothing of hurt or fear?"

Darcie nodded. "Sometimes. But when I think of the girl I used to be, I feel glad that I am so much stronger than she was." Even as she said the words, she realized how very true they were. She was so much more resilient now than that innocent young girl had been, so much more able to confront the realities of life.

"I don't see myself as being very strong." Mary's

voice was wistful. "I'd like to be, but mostly I just feel afraid."

Her heart constricting at Mary's admission, Darcie nodded. She remembered a time, not long past, when she, too, had mostly felt afraid.

"Oh! I nearly forgot!" Mary jumped to her feet and kneeling next to her bed, pulled a small wooden box from beneath it. "I wanted you to read this to me. It came for me this morning." Smiling shyly she held a folded letter out toward Darcie. "I've never had a letter before."

Taking the note from Mary, Darcie moved the lamp closer and unfolded the parchment. The letter was written in a delicate, feminine hand.

Dearest Mary,

I wanted to write before this, but with the new baby I just could not find the time. Dr. Cole was kind enough to find Robbie a lovely post in the country, and we're married now. I have my own pretty house here in Shropshire, and Robbie has a fine position. My little girl is named Catherine Joy, for she is my joy. Never did I imagine that Dr. Cole would be so kind. That morning when he came to find me in the scullery and bid me pack my things together, I thought he would toss me out without a reference. Instead, he brought me here and made all my dreams come true. There was no time to say farewell. Mr. Farrell needed a steward right away, and there was no time to delay. Dr. Cole brought us forthwith, and Robbie took up his post. My warmest regards to Cook and Tandis.

Your friend,
Janie McBride

The missing maid, Janie. Not dead, Darcie realized, but safe and happy with her new husband in the country. All thanks to Damien.

"Oh, my goodness," Mary whispered as Darcie finished reading. "All these months, I thought she was dead. I thought Dr. Cole might have—" She broke off, looking slightly sheepish. "Well, not really. It was more of a good story to scare myself at night. I never truly imagined that Dr. Cole would . . . that he could have . . ." Her voice trailed away, and she rolled her eyes before continuing. "I'm very glad to hear that she is well and happy."

Darcie smiled, relieved that the mystery of the girl's disappearance had been explained. Janie had been pregnant, and Damien had helped her. She, too, felt happy for this unknown girl, happy that Damien had done her a good turn. Yet, a part of her could not let go of the suspicion that had prompted her to follow Mary to her chamber.

Mary had explained nothing, and the question of why Poole had been skulking at her heels in the night-darkened house gnawed at Darcie like a sore tooth.

Late the following afternoon, Darcie sat in Damien's study, frowning at the anatomy book she held open in her lap. The drawing of the ethmoid bone with its elaborately scrolled delicate conchae began to blur before her on the page. A rumble of thunder sounded in the distance distracting her. She glanced out the window to find the sky filled with ominous gray clouds. Deciding that there was only so much Latin nomenclature she could absorb at any one time, she closed the book with a soft thud.

Although the weather had turned foul, she refused to let it affect her mood. She crossed to the bookshelf and carefully returned the tome to its place. She wondered if Damien would return soon and could not suppress the smile that rose to her lips at the thought of him. He had told her that morning that there were several urgent errands he needed to attend to, a mysterious smile playing about his lips. Darcie suspected those errands had something to do with her.

Turning away from the shelves, she was about to leave the room when she heard the welcome sound of Damien's footfall on the stairs. Smiling, she went to the door of the study and watched him stride along the hallway toward her. His honeyed hair was combed and tamed into tidiness. The white linen of his shirt contrasted with the black cloth of his trousers and waistcoat, accentuating the hard muscled leanness of his long body.

"You are magnificent," she said.

"You are biased." He pressed a kiss to her lips, drew back for a second, and then returned for a longer, more thorough greeting. "I couldn't resist," he said with a grin, then stepped full into the room, drawing her against his side. "Come sit with me."

Darcie allowed him to escort her back to the chair she had sat in for some hours. As she sank down on the cushioned seat, she ran her hand along his forearm, twining her fingers with his for the span of a second before allowing his hand to slide free of her grasp. She could not seem to get enough of touching him.

He sat in the chair that was beside hers, angling it so he faced her.

"So what mischief have you been about today?"

"None today," she said. "But last night, I did come upon a puzzle." Thrusting her hand in the pocket of her dress, she closed her fingers around the scrap of cloth.

"Why the frown, Darcie? Your mood mirrors the weather, for it seems to have turned suddenly. What troubles you?" Damien asked, instantly alert.

Drawing the cloth from her pocket, Darcie smoothed it flat on the desktop. "Do you recognize this?"

Damien picked it up and turned it over in his hands, before laying it back on the desk. He met her gaze, his expression inscrutable.

"Where did you get this?" he asked.

"I found it on the floor of your chamber. Beneath the nightstand. Do you recognize it?"

He nodded. "I do. The shape of it is odd, like a map of Italy. I must have thrust it into my pocket."

"And then it fell beneath your nightstand." Darcie took a breath then continued in a rush. "Damien, I know where this came from. Mary was attacked, and her smock was torn—"

"What? When?" In his shock, Damien half rose from his chair before, realizing his actions, he sank down once more.

"The night we worked on Dr. Grammercy's heart . . ."

"The day we dissected the heart," Damien mused, staring absently toward the neat rows of books on the opposite wall. "I recall that I worked late that night. Long past midnight I had a brief visit from an old acquaintance." There was an odd inflection in his voice, leading Darcie to wonder if he had been pleased about that visit. It sounded as though he had not.

Darcie tipped her head, studying him. "The way you said that, I hardly think that you consider the gentleman a friend."

"He is not. I had not expected him, nor do I understand what he wanted here. It was an inane encounter, and it seemed his sole purpose was to remind me of the occasion of another time we had met. In Edinburgh, many years ago." He was silent for a moment, and then continued. "When I left the laboratory I found the cloth at the bottom of the stairs." His gaze shot to hers, anxious, troubled. "That was the night Mary was attacked? Are you certain?"

"Yes, I found her in her bed. She was distraught. Her smock was torn and there were marks on her neck." Closing her eyes, Darcie vividly recalled the horrific bruises on Mary's throat.

"Marks? What do you mean?" He leaned forward in his chair, his expression intent.

Darcie struggled to explain. "Finger marks. As though someone had put his hand about her throat and choked her." She shuddered at the memory. "It was horrible."

Damien looked ill. "Our Mary? Why was I not told? My God—" He lifted the cloth from the desk, turning it slowly in his hands, his expression distant, unsettled. "Finger marks? Around her throat?"

He seemed to wrestle with some unknown concern, and then raised his eyes to hers. "Who, Darcie? Did she tell you who?"

There was something in his eyes, some dark and desperate recognition that made her swallow against the nervousness that skittered through her belly. Feeling suddenly afraid, she shook her head.

"It was the same in Edinburgh. The girl in Edinburgh," he whispered, more to himself than to her.

Confused, she waited for him to explain. As the seconds ticked past she realized that she needed no explanation. He was referring to the girl who was killed in Edinburgh, the one Dr. Grammercy had told her about. Damien knew something about her death, and somehow it was linked to the attack on Mary.

Suddenly, Damien leaped to his feet. "I must speak with Mary. She's seen his face."

"Oh, my God," Darcie breathed. "She's not safe."

Shaking his head, Damien touched her cheek, his long bluntly squared fingers caressing her skin as her stared into her eyes. She saw the turmoil of emotions boiling within the tightly held bounds of his control.

"She is not safe. No one in this house is safe. I am taking her to Bow Street, to Trent." He turned and strode toward the door.

"Damien," she called after him.

His shoulders tensed, and he turned slowly to face her.

"You know who it is, don't you?"

"I have my suspicions. I won't know until I speak to Mary." His expression was bleak. "I thought it was coincidence. He was there in Edinburgh, even acting as my alibi, and again, at Mrs. Feather's House on the night that Sally was killed. Here, the night Mary was attacked . . . The acquaintance I told you about." His brow creased as he struggled with some memory. "He was in Whitechapel the night I first met you, at Mrs. Feather's House. If I am right . . . Darcie, let no one into this house while I am gone. No one. Do you understand?"

Mutely, she nodded.

Taking her hand, Damien gently pulled her from her seat into his warm embrace. "I shall not be gone long, and when I return, this will all be over."

The storm arrived with a vengeance. Darcie paced the confines of Damien's chamber, wondering what exactly was transpiring at Bow Street. Did Damien truly know the identity of the terrifying fiend, the murderer unburdened by guilt or remorse, who stalked the alleys of Whitechapel? The wind wailed and howled, rattling the window in its wooden frame. Rain pelted the glass, sluicing in thick rivulets from the gutters.

Darcie paced ten steps to the casement, then turned and counted ten steps back to the foot of the bed. She repeated the trip again and again. The household had retired long ago, though she suspected that the servants were equally unnerved by the fact that Damien and Mary had yet to return. Poole had acted nervous as a cat, stalking to the window of the front parlor and peering out into the street, twitching the curtain back in place, then repeating the whole thing over, again and again.

"She's safe with Dr. Cole," he had muttered, turning to Darcie as though for reassurance. "She'll come back to me safe and sound, won't she?"

In that moment, Darcie had realized that Poole's nocturnal wanderings had nothing to do with the sinister, and everything to do with love. He must have been meeting Mary in the moonlight, and Darcie had come upon them as they returned from a tryst. Despite the oddness of the pairing, Darcie was glad for her friend's good fortune, for it was clear that Poole's emotions were genuinely engaged.

Wrapping her arms about herself, Darcie sank down on the bed in Damien's chamber. Her agitated emotions allowed her no ease, and she rose once more and strode to the window. She allowed her thoughts to wander, and though she started out trying to recollect the names of the bones of the cranium, she ended up recalling her conversation with Damien.

He was there in Edinburgh, even acting as my alibi, and again, at Mrs. Feather's House on the night that Sally was killed. Damien's words played over and over in her mind. She gasped as a jagged bolt of lightning rent the dark night. Whirling from the window, she tried to think of something else, but again her concentration was dragged back to their earlier conversation. *Acting as my alibi.* Dr. Grammercy had tried to remember the man's name . . . Lord Ashton. Lord Alton. He could not recall.

Darcie chewed on the inner edge of her lip, lost

in reflection of the maddening certainty that there was some connection she was missing.

The night Sally was killed. Poor Sally.

But you were here before. Sally had recognized her as the bedraggled waif who had come to Mrs. Feather's House on a rain-soaked night. *I remember, 'cause it was the night Lord Albright . . .* Darcie froze as Sally's words slammed through her mind. An image formed in her mind, and she shivered. The man who had followed her to Hyde Park. She had glimpsed his dark hair and long black cloak from the carriage window.

Dark hair. There were many dark-haired men.

He was in Whitechapel the night I first met you.

That night, she had huddled in a shadowed doorway and breathed in the smell of death as she stared at the hem of a demon's long black cloak. That night she had met Lord Albright and known that he treasured the suffering of others.

Lord Albright.

Dr. Grammercy's voice came to mind, naming the man who had been in Edinburgh at the same time as Damien. Lord Ashton, he had said, or Lord Alton. But no, that was not right. Suddenly, with a chilling certainty, she knew the name of the man. *Lord Albright.* She remembered too well the first night she had gone to Abigail's, the way he had enjoyed her pain when she jumped away from his touch, banging her arm on the table in her sister's front hall.

A man without a conscience, without a heart, without a soul. She remembered the way he had looked at her, his eyes a window to the bottomless black pit that was the wasteland of his being. She knew who the killer was.

Oh God! Abigail.

Her sister was not safe. Damien had realized the likelihood that Albright was the murderer, had taken Mary to share her story with Inspector Trent. Was it not possible that Abigail might reach the same conclusion? And even if her sister did not realize the connection, she very well might be in mortal danger.

Snatching up her shawl and wrapping it about her shoulders, Darcie took her reticule and hurried from the room. She must warn Abigail. The thought tolled through her consciousness like a bell, obliterating caution and reason. Grabbing an umbrella from the stand in the front hallway, Darcie left the house. The wind caught her and nearly spun her about as she descended the front stairs of the house. Bending forward, she pushed on, her entire concentration focused on finding a hack to take her to Hadley Street.

The rain hammered her mercilessly, obscuring her vision, the pounding intensity of it, combined with the wretched viciousness of the wind, soaked her to the skin within minutes. The umbrella proved sorry protection against the storm.

She bent low against the buffeting strength of the wind, struggling every step of the way to Hyde Park. There she spotted a lone carriage for hire. Waving frantically, she summoned the attention of the driver and was quickly ensconced in the dry, if somewhat malodorous interior of the conveyance. She sat, shivering, praying that she was not too late. Her entire being was focused on a solitary goal. She must warn Abigail. She could not bear the thought of losing her sister once more, having only so recently found her.

She huddled against the squab, the damp and the cool evening air taking its toll. By the time she reached Hadley Street, she was shivering uncontrollably and her teeth were chattering so hard they clacked against each other. The driver took her coins, and when she bid him wait for her, he looked nervously about and shook his head, his words snatched by the storm, but his meaning clear. With sinking heart, Darcie stood in the drenching rain watching as the hack drove away.

She was alone then, on the streets of Whitechapel in the darkness of the night and the fury of the storm. Running through the narrow alley, she stumbled, pressing one hand against the cold slick wall to right herself, then stumbled to her sister's door. She banged with a closed fist on the portal, wondering why there were not more people about. This was night, the time that Mrs. Feather's House did its business. Why, oh why, did no one answer the door? With each strike of her hand against the wood, her desperation grew, her imagination conjuring horrific images of what might have already come to pass.

At last, the door opened, and she fell across the threshold into Abigail's arms. A relief so keen as to be almost painful shot through her at the sight of her sister, safe, alive. She would save her. She would not fail in this as she had failed with Mama and Steppy. Her sister had been lost to her once, but having found her, she would not lose her again.

"Darcie!" Abigail cried, half carrying her into

the house. She glanced out into the street, stagger-
ing under Darcie's leaden weight.

"L-l-lock the door," Darcie said, her teeth clat-
tering against each other with such force that even
that small sentence proved a challenge. Her energy depleted, her legs crumpled, and she sank to
the floor.

"My God, you're soaked through. I'll get you
something dry."

"The door!" Darcie cried, and Abigail turned
the key in the lock before she hurried up the
stairs, leaving Darcie sitting on the hallway floor.
She was back within moments, bringing with her a
simple day dress and clean underclothes. Together,
they managed to get Darcie out of her sopping
garments and into dry clothes. Abigail was taller
and fuller of figure, but the gown was warm and
dry, and Darcie was grateful.

Wrapping her arms around Darcie, Abigail held
her until her shivers subsided.

"Come to the kitchen. I shall make tea." Abigail
sent her a measured look. "When you have come
to yourself then you can tell me what possessed
you to come here on such a night."

"Where is everyone?" Darcie asked, looking
around at the dark and deserted house as they
walked toward the kitchen.

"Gone. All gone." Abigail shrugged. "I've closed
the house to business. Dismissed the maid. Sent
the girls away."

"Closed the house?" Darcie could hardly fathom
it. "But why?"

"I see myself differently now. Since Sally. I see

something different in my future." Abigail shrugged. "People change."

"What will you do? How will you survive?"

"Practical girl." Abigail gave a short bark of laughter. "Sit." She waved in the direction of one of the kitchen chairs.

Darcie sank down, rubbing her hands along the outsides of her arms. She was starting to feel a thaw in the bone-numbing chill that had penetrated her body.

"I always knew there would come a time when I would close Mrs. Feather's House. I've saved enough to live a quiet life, if I'm careful, and I counseled my girls to do the same. In the end, I am my father's daughter, and all those times he instilled his merchant's instincts have stood me in good stead." She smiled, a wistful, sad smile. "I thought I'd find somewhere in the country. Somewhere that no one has ever heard of Mrs. Feather." Taking out the tea things, she set them neatly in a row then paused and glanced at Darcie over her shoulder. "Somewhere where the widowed Mrs. Finch could find a place."

"Oh, Abigail." Darcie felt overwhelmed. The idea that her sister would leave London was certainly no cause for celebration. Having so recently been reunited, Darcie had no wish to be parted from her. But greater than her sadness was the unmitigated joy that coursed through her. Abigail would be safe. She would no longer be subjected to the desperate life she had led. Instead, she could find a place . . .

As though continuing Darcie's thoughts out loud,

Abigail laughed. "A garden," she said. "Can you imagine, a garden with flowers?" She winked at Darcie. "Maybe I'll even marry a vicar."

Strangely, Darcie didn't find the thought to be so very impossible. She looked at her sister in the dim light of the kitchen. Her face was devoid of makeup, her hair braided down her back in a single plait. Darcie thought she looked wonderful. Clean and fresh. It was symbolic of a new start.

Abigail prepared the tea, rinsing the pot first with hot water before adding a measure of tea leaves and pouring the boiling water over top. She set two cups and saucers on the table, along with sugar and milk, and then returned for the teapot.

Deftly, she filled a cup for Darcie, adding two lumps of sugar and topping it off with milk.

"Old habits," Darcie mused as she watched her sister's actions.

Abigail glanced at her quizzically.

Nodding toward the cup, Darcie clarified, "You added the milk last, just as Mama taught us."

"Ahhh, yes. I have come down a notch or two, but I have not forgotten that a lady never puts the milk in the cup first."

Their eyes caught and held as the shared understanding of how their world had changed passed between them. The two women sipped their tea in silence, tacitly agreeing not to open the subject of what might have been.

Darcie glanced at the flame of the candle. It flickered and danced, sending jittery silhouettes across the bare walls. Now that she was here, Darcie felt uncertain. If she was mistaken in her suspicions, then her mad flight was simply the outcome of an overactive imagination. Yet, the possibility that Abigail knew the Whitechapel murderer, was in fact well-acquainted with him, was too dangerous a prospect to ignore.

Dragging in a breath, Darcie stared into the depths her cup. "Abigail, tell me the name of the man who did this to you. The man who brought you"—she looked around the kitchen—"here."

She heard the sharp hiss of her sister's indrawn breath. "What does it matter?" Abigail asked dully. "It was so long ago. There is nothing I can do about it now."

"Not so long ago." Darcie raised her head and found herself staring into blue eyes dark with remembered pain. A part of her wanted to let it go, to save her sister further grief. There was no certainty in her suspicion. She could be wrong about Lord Albright. Pressing her lips together, Darcie chose her words with care. "Does he visit you still?"

Abigail started, jerking back as though she had been struck. Her gaze slid away from Darcie's, then returned. "I think the rain has stopped. I don't hear the rain."

"He hurt you. Please, Abigail, I think he might be the one who—" Her words froze in her throat as Abigail turned toward her, her face ravaged by an expression of soul-deep horror.

"Do not say it." She moaned. "If you do not say it then maybe it will not be true. Oh, Darcie, I cannot bear for it to be true."

Therein lay her answer. She *knew.* Darcie felt not a sliver of doubt. Abigail knew the name of the killer. Had lain with the killer. Had loved the killer. Lord Albright. "Abigail, you must stop protecting him. He is not worth your life."

Abigail faltered, her cup rattling loudly in the stillness as she set it on the saucer. She rose, striding away from Darcie to the shadowed corner of the kitchen, her shoulders set in a tense line, her rapid breathing loud in the silence.

"Well," she said with forced brightness. "These clothes will never dry if we don't hang them before the fire."

Suddenly, she became a whirlwind of activity, grabbing her chair and dragging it before the fire, then energetically shaking out Darcie's sodden dress from the bundle they had left it in when they carried it to the kitchen. Droplets of water sprayed in every direction.

"Abigail, more women will die."

As quickly as it began, the storm of Abigail's activity stopped, and she stood, frozen, her face a mask of desperation.

"How long have you known?" she whispered brokenly.

"I didn't know for certain. Not until this very moment. But you did, you must have."

Abigail shook her head, her hands dropping heavily to her sides, the dress falling unheeded to the floor. "Just now, really. When you asked me about him. The pieces fell into place." She sank bonelessly to the chair at her side, as though all her strength had been sucked out of her. "I did not know until just this instant. Perhaps I closed my eyes to it. I did not want to know." She buried her face in her hands.

Darcie felt sick, for a part of her had hoped she was mistaken.

Abigail dropped her hands, meeting Darcie's gaze. "He was here, in my house, in Whitechapel on the night of each murder. I never thought . . ."

The long, slow rasp of an unoiled hinge twisted through the stillness of the house. Darcie sucked in a startled gasp, her hands closing tightly around her teacup as her gaze darted to the shadowed corners of the kitchen. Perhaps she had imagined it. Perhaps—

There. It came again, followed by the sound of footfall, from within the house. They were no longer alone.

CHAPTER
SEVENTEEN

"What was that?" Abigail whispered, her eyes wide. She brought one hand up to swipe at the tendrils that had escaped her plait while pressing her other hand against her chest.

Darcie lifted her finger to her lips, motioning Abigail to keep silent. She shook her head frantically as her sister opened her mouth to speak once more.

Rising, she crossed the kitchen, her eyes drawn to the knives whose handles protruded from the wooden block on the countertop. No, they would not do. She had not the strength or the skill to wield such a weapon. Better to choose something she could swing like a club, something she could throw her entire body weight behind, something like . . . yes. Her hand snaked out and she closed her fingers around the heavy wooden rolling pin.

She felt her sister's presence at her side, and reaching back, she groped blindly for Abigail's hand. Their fingers connected, and Darcie held fast, deriving strength from the connection.

Seconds ticked past, then minutes, and no further sound was heard. The kitchen smelled of lye soap and mildew. Darcie wondered why she hadn't noticed that before.

Leaning close, Abigail whispered against Darcie's ear. "Perhaps we imagined it. Perhaps there is no one here."

Darcie wanted to believe that. Her heart clutched and stuttered as she strained to hear any sound, however faint. She shook her head. He was here. She could feel his presence as she had that night so long ago when she had huddled in a shadowed doorway, breathing in the scent of evil, staring at the hem of his long black cloak.

She understood now that he was stalking her. He had meant her for his victim that night, hunted her, lusted for her blood. And she had denied him. She shivered, every muscle in her body held tense and ready, for she sensed he was near.

All these months, the intuition that had whispered of danger had been true. But not from Damien. Oh God, never from Damien. Foolish girl that she had ever thought it so.

Darcie clenched her fingers around the handle of the rolling pin. Every nerve cried out against this imposed inactivity. *Flee*, her instincts demanded as terror built in her throat. But her mind bid her stay, for she knew not where he was, and taking chaotic flight could well lead her to death's embrace.

She could feel Abigail pressing against her back,

shivering in terror, her fingers grasping Darcie's tightly, to a point beyond pain.

He had killed Sally. He had hurt Mary. Because of her? Because he had come searching for her that night? The thought revolted her.

"We must run for the front door," Abigail whispered.

The front door. Darcie frowned, turning to look at Abigail. "I told you to lock the front door," she breathed. "Didn't you lock the door?"

Abigail pressed her lips together, her expression infinitely sad. "He has a key."

"The back door . . ." her voice trailed away as Abigail shook her head.

"I nailed it shut and blocked it with a cabinet after Sally was killed. I was afraid the murderer would sneak in and kill us in our beds."

The irony of it was not lost on Darcie.

"Up," she hissed. "We'll take the rear stairs. He won't expect that. Maybe we can climb out a window, or hide. Come on, Abigail. We cannot simply wait here for death to seek us out."

Not waiting for the other woman's agreement, Darcie dragged her toward the narrow staircase at the back of the house. They climbed to the second floor.

"Abigail." The sound of his voice drifted up the stairs, laced with the ghastly promise of his darkest longings. "Why do you run? Wait for me, Abigail."

Darcie shrank back against the wall, her heart pounding, numbing terror slowing her movements. She felt a sense of unreality as she was carried back to the night she had watched Steppy being stabbed.

She imagined the glint of the knife rising and falling again and again until he lay motionless on the dirty floor.

Hide in the shadows. Run, girl, run.

That night she had hesitated, had almost been too slow. She could hear his footsteps on the stairs, creeping steadily closer.

"Come on," Abigail yanked her arm hard.

Together, they ran along the hall to the room at the far end. Slamming the door behind them, they heaved and pushed, struggling to shove a large bureau in front of the door.

"It won't move!" Abigail's voice was high-pitched, thin and thready with unutterable fear.

"The window." Darcie yanked the sash up. "Go, go!"

She half pushed Abigail out into the rain-drenched night. Water struck her face, the wind whipping it like a thousand stinging pins. Standing next to the casement, Darcie turned her face toward the door. A jagged flash of lightning illuminated the room, casting its eerie glow on the face of her tormentor.

He smiled, lips pulling back from sharp, pointed teeth.

"You were to be mine that night. I could taste you, smell you. I paid for you, and you ran away."

He had *paid* for her. Oh, God. He was the man she was meant for that night, the night Steppy was killed.

"And then you ran right back to me. So pleased I was to see you here that night. It was you I followed in the street, wasn't it?"

Darcie stared in mute horror as he took a step

closer. "I was not sure, but I see that you *do* remember. . . . Did you think I would not find you?" He lifted a knife, leering at her. "Tonight, you will not escape."

Looking into his soulless eyes, she saw the promise of her death. Darcie clenched her fingers around the rolling pin that she had instinctively brought from the kitchen.

Damien. She whispered his name, or perhaps she yelled it aloud. Damien. He was her talisman, her amulet against this evil. His love for her, and hers for him, gave her strength. She would not die here this night, leaving him alone and hopeless once more.

Dragging her arm back, Darcie aimed for the terrifying face of the Whitechapel murderer, and hurling the wooden rolling pin at him with all her might, she clambered out the window into the cold embrace of the raging storm.

Her feet slid precariously as she balanced on the rain-slick ledge, the wind clawing at her skirt, the rain soaking her to the skin. She inched to her left, slowly, moving away from the open window. Above the sound of the storm, she heard her name. Plastering herself against the rough wall at her back, she glanced to her right. Abigail was standing on the roof of the next building, screaming and waving frantically—her voice was swallowed by the howling wind.

She could see Abigail's lips moving, but she was unable to make out her sister's frenzied cries. Darcie stared at Abigail, watching the movement of her arms, the direction of her gaze, and in that moment, she understood her precarious position. It did not matter that she heard not the words, for the message was clear. She had gone the wrong way.

An icy fist clenched around her heart as she looked to her left and saw the smooth face of another house. No ledge, no handhold, nowhere to hide. A low moan of despair escaped her as she looked back to her right and saw Lord Albright's head poke through the open window.

There was no possibility of backtracking, no chance to escape that way. Her breath came in rasping gasps. Her heart thumped a painful rhythm. Blinding panic assailed her as she realized there were no options left to her.

She looked down, trying to steady her frantic breathing, wondering how far to the street below. Too far. Such a leap would mean her certain death. She squinted against the heavy sheet of rain that pounded her with driving force. Her breath caught, hanging suspended in her throat. There on the street below, legs braced, head flung back as he searched the ledge, stood Damien. Her Damien, illuminated by the glow of the street lamp. She screamed his name, again and again.

His features were a taut stark mask of horror as his gaze shifted to her right. She knew what he saw there. Death, waiting to claim her.

Inching farther along the limited space, she glanced to the side, watching in dread as Lord Albright climbed the rest of the way out the window and rose to stand erect. He inched toward her, matching each step she took, stalking her, his lips drawing back in a feral snarl.

"You were meant for me, that first night, my tasty dish. Now you will be mine for eternity." His eyes burned with an unholy light, and his words froze Darcie's blood in her veins.

Instinctively, she shrank back. Her left foot slid, and she screamed, terror throbbing through her as she struggled to stop herself from plummeting to the ground so far below.

Her fingers clawed the rough surface of the wall at her back, scrabbling for purchase, while she urgently scanned the street, searching for Damien. Somewhere deep inside she thought that if she could only hold on to him, to the treasured sight of him, she would find the strength to survive this nightmare. Abigail was there now, her upturned face a pale oval against the dark backdrop of the street. Darcie felt a moment's relief at the knowledge that her sister was safe.

From the corner of her eye, she saw Lord Albright shift along the ledge, one step closer and another. He reached one hand toward her. Her skin crawled at the thought of his touch.

Inspector Trent was there on the street and several uniform-clad constables. But Damien, where was Damien?

She felt strangely detached, watching as a carriage rolled along the road, its spoked wheels splashing sheets of water in all directions. Her mind fixated on one thought.

Damien. Damien. Damien.

She so wanted to see him one last time. Tears stung her eyes, blinding her.

The carriage stopped directly beneath her. Damien clambered onto the roof, the wind catching his cloak, making it billow wildly about his tall frame. His face was a mask of concentration, focused on her. At the sight of him, her heart gave a tiny leap of joy that broke through the overwhelming tide of terror that swamped her. Her world seemed to contract until there was only Damien, looking up at her with such love and concern.

"Jump, Darcie," he called, his voice overcoming the storm, his eyes fixed on hers with steadfast intensity.

She shrank back against the wall. He was nearly there, Lord Albright, the knife in his hand glittering with fiendish promise. He would kill her, here, in front of all these people. He was mad.

Darcie returned her gaze to Damien. He stood on the top of the carriage in the same posture as he had taken on the street, his legs braced, his head thrown back, every fiber of his being focused on her. She loved him so much.

"Darcie," he screamed again. "Jump."

Oh, God! She didn't want him to watch her die, could not bear the thought that he would suffer for the loss of her as he had suffered at the death of his sister.

Jump. Jump. Jump. To the street that seemed miles away. She stared, transfixed at the cobbles below.

"Jump, Darcie." His voice was tight, urgent. "Trust me."

Trust me. Those two words shook her from her stupor. She heard the echo of the things he did not say. *Trust me to love you forever. Trust me to catch you when you fall.*

Her heart twisted, a sharp, hard clutch of terror. If she jumped, and he was wrong, she would shatter in pieces on the cobbled road. *Trust me.* Her head jerked up, and eyes locked on his, she knew that she did trust him, with all her heart and soul. He stood silent, his arms flung wide calling her to his embrace. *Trust me.*

Clutching her hands together to still their violent quaking, Darcie threw herself from the ledge.

So this was what it felt like to fly. Her skirt caught the wind, flapping about her like the wings of a huge bird. She tried to keep her eyes on Damien but the rain pounded down on her, drenching her face, obscuring her vision. She felt she was beyond time, hurtling through the dark night.

With a jarring force she slammed into him, felt his arms close around her, his solid weight fall back beneath hers as they both tumbled flat on the roof of the carriage that rocked and squeaked in protest. Together they slid across the slick surface and for an instant she thought they would fall. Then Damien reached out and caught the raised edge of the roof, the muscles of his chest and arms flexing as he held her tight and safe.

Disoriented, she lay atop him, her head against his chest, the sound of his heartbeat roaring in her ears.

After a moment, she realized that he was whispering her name, over and over, his arms wrapped so tightly around her that she could hardly breathe. Slowly, she became aware of other sounds. Abigail's hysterical cries. The sound of Inspector Trent's voice. The nicker of one of the horses.

She was alive. She was *alive.*

Damien's fingers tangled in her hair, pulling her head back as his mouth sought hers. His kiss was frantic, ungentle. He kissed her with a wild desperation, his lips grinding against hers, his tongue licking, tasting.

Inhaling the rain-soaked scent of him, Darcie ran her fingers over the wet cloth of his cloak. With a soft cry, she tore free two buttons of his shirt, thrusting her hand beneath the soft linen to rest it against the damp warmth of his living breathing skin. He had not abandoned her to her fate. He was here.

"You came for me." She drew back, taking in every beautifully sculpted line and curve of his beloved face.

His expression reflected wonder and absolute joy. "You jumped."

"I jumped." A wild laugh escaped her, half hysteria, half unmitigated euphoria.

She struggled to absorb the narrowness of her escape, the magnitude of her relief. They lay on the roof of the carriage, arms and legs entwined, not moving, not speaking as the rain abated, slowing to a drizzle, then stopping altogether. Vaguely aware of the sounds of Inspector Trent's voice and the men he had brought with him, she could not rouse herself enough to investigate the commotion.

"How did you know where I had gone?" she asked, her attention riveted on Damien, the feel of his skin beneath her hand, the welcome warmth of his embrace.

He kissed the top of her head. "Poole saw you leave. He struck out after you, but was too late to catch you. By the time he reached Hyde Park, you were climbing into the hack." He shot her a reproving glance. "You were nearly the death of me

Darcie. When I saw you there, on that ledge, my brain ceased all logical function."

Her own emotions were stripped bare by the pain she heard in his voice.

"Not all logical function. Your intellect saved me."

A harsh bark of laughter escaped him. "No, Darcie. Not intellect. Desperation." He cupped her cheek. "And trust. You trusted me."

"Yes." The simple word held an abundance of meaning. "But even though Poole witnessed my departure, that does not tell me how you knew where I had gone."

"That, my love, was blind luck. Upon my return from Bow Street, Poole greeted me at the door with the news of your precipitous exit. Having no other place to begin my search, I traced your footsteps to the park. As luck would have it, the hack returned there after dropping you here. I was able to question the driver."

Darcie stared at him, stunned. "I asked the man to wait, but he disliked the look of the neighborhood and refused."

"Blessed luck that he left you, for if he had not . . ." His voice trailed away.

She frowned. "I would not have thought you believed in luck, Damien."

"I did not. Until tonight."

Their gazes met, full of unspoken understanding.

"Lord Albright, stay where you are." Inspector Trent's voice boomed from the street, making Darcie aware of her surroundings, reminding her that the murderer was yet to be apprehended.

Shifting to a sitting position, she turned to look

at the surreal tableau that unfolded before her. Lord Albright balanced on the ledge, his knife clasped in one hand. His head whipped frantically back and forth, as though he searched for some means of escape.

"Come no closer," he bellowed.

A large, burly constable applied his shoulder to the front door of Abigail's house. The sound of splintering wood was followed by a loud thud as what remained of the door swung back and slammed into the wall. Two constables rushed through the opening.

"Stay back." Albright's voice had risen a notch. "I am a peer of the realm. You have no right . . ." Lord Albright shook his head from side to side as though trying to clear it. "Where is my valet? My coat is wet. I need my valet."

He looked toward Darcie, then away, searching out Abigail who stood alone on the street below.

"Abigail, my pet," he said plaintively. "I cannot find my valet." His face seemed to collapse on itself, leaving him standing, cold and wet on a precarious ledge, a man lost in his own mind. Head cocked to one side, he looked at Trent before glancing back at the open window, his expression one of pained bafflement.

And then he flung himself from the ledge.

Darcie screamed, watching in frozen shock, unable to look away as Lord Albright fell from the sky, landing with a sickening thud on the cobbled road, limp, like a sac of soiled linens.

With a gasp of horror, she averted her face, turning it into Damien's shoulder. She could not help but think that but for Damien's ingenuity, that would have been her fate. He cradled her against his chest, infinitely gentle.

After some time, Damien climbed down from the top of the carriage, reaching up to lift Darcie down as well. Shrugging out of his cloak, he wrapped it around her shoulders. He kissed her lips, her cheeks, her eyes, then drew back, gazing down at her with great tenderness.

"Come, it is time to go home."

At the sound of footsteps they turned and found Inspector Trent approaching them. "I'll need to ask some questions—"

Damien slashed the air with his hand in a curt gesture of denial. "Tomorrow will be soon enough. You may call upon me in the evening," he said, his tone polite but firm.

Without waiting for a reply, he beckoned to Abigail and led the two women to the waiting carriage. Abigail hesitated, her gaze sliding to John, who stood to one side holding the open door, and then returning to Damien.

"You have always been kind to me, and it is for that reason that I cannot come to your home. Think of the scandal," Abigail whispered, her voice thick with unshed tears, her shoulders bowed with the strain of the past hours.

Damien laughed shortly, his brows rising skeptically. "You speak to me of scandal?"

Darcie bit her lip against the urge to laugh at the incredulous tone of his voice, for so raw were her emotions that she feared she would lose control entirely.

"You are my wife-to-be's sister. You belong in my wife's home." His words fell into the night air.

"Wife?" Darcie gasped, her head jerking up in surprise as the enormity of his words penetrated her mind. "I—I—"

Smiling at her, Damien smoothed a wet tendril of hair from her brow. "I never did get to tell you about my day. I acquired a special license." His grin broadened. "I trust tomorrow morning will not be too soon?"

Dragging in a shivering breath, Darcie tried to assimilate his meaning. Wife. He wanted her to be his wife.

"I have no words," she whispered.

"You only need one," he responded dryly. "The word is yes."

Her pulse hammered in her ears. "Yes, yes, a thousand times yes."

She threw herself into his open arms, crying, laughing, her lips seeking his.

"I was so afraid I had lost you, so afraid you would fall . . ." His eyes were the windows to his innermost sentiments, his love, and his passion glowing there for her to see. "So afraid I would be too late."

Her heart expanded near to bursting. "You were there to catch me when I fell."

"So I was." He smiled. "And I always will be."

The light of the street lamp shone over his wet, golden hair, making it gleam, almost as though a halo of light surrounded him. Darcie was reminded of the very first time she had seen him, when she had lain in the roadway, and at the sight of him had thought an angel had come to lead her home.

She sucked in a breath, letting the rain-washed air fill her lungs, fresh and clean and new. A smile curved her lips as Damien's hand sought hers, his fingers twining together with her own. Their eyes met, and then their lips, as a silent communication passed between them, one of strength and love and trust.

Darcie let herself fall into the wonder of his kiss, thinking that she had not been so very wrong that long-ago night. Damien was her angel, and in his love she had found her home.

ABOUT THE AUTHOR

Eve Silver read her first romance novel when she was in her teens. She fell in love with these tales of love, honor, strength and perseverance, these stories that transported her and helped carry her through the rough patches of life.

Eve holds two post-secondary degrees. She teaches microbiology and human anatomy at a local college. After school she returns to romance, having found her own happily-ever-after with her husband and two sons. She is currently working on her next historical romance, which will be published in November 2006.

She loves to hear from readers. You can contact her through her website at www.evesilver.net